THE BEST
OF
EVERYTHING

THE BEST OF EVERYTHING

KIT DE WAAL

TINDER
PRESS

Copyright © 2025 Kit de Waal

The right of Kit de Waal to be identified as the Author of
the Work has been asserted by her in accordance with the
Copyright, Designs and Patents Act 1988.

First published in Great Britain in 2025 by Tinder Press
An imprint of HEADLINE PUBLISHING GROUP

1

Cataloguing in Publication Data is available from the British Library.

Hardback ISBN 978 1 0354 0479 7
Trade paperback ISBN 978 1 0354 0480 3

Designed and typeset by EM&EN
Printed and bound in Great Britain by Clays Ltd, Elcograf S.p.A.

Headline's policy is to use papers that are natural, renewable and recyclable
products and made from wood grown in well-managed forests and other
controlled sources. The logging and manufacturing processes are expected
to conform to the environmental regulations of the country of origin.

FSC
www.fsc.org

MIX
Paper | Supporting
responsible forestry
FSC® C104740

HEADLINE PUBLISHING GROUP
An Hachette UK Company
Carmelite House
50 Victoria Embankment
London EC4Y 0DZ

The authorised representative in the EEA is Hachette Ireland, 8 Castlecourt
Centre, Dublin 15, D15 XTP3, Ireland (email: info@hbgi.ie)

www.tinderpress.co.uk
www.headline.co.uk
www.hachette.co.uk

For all the people that have shown me kindness

'Try to be a little kinder than is necessary'

J M Barrie, *Peter Pan*

1

1972

Midnight.

Paulette is still awake. A thin, freezing wind slips through an inch of open window and makes the curtains dance. When the room is cool, Denton sleeps heavy and won't feel the weight of her head on his chest or the leg she drapes over his, running the sole of her foot from his knee to his ankle.

She pulls one of his arms around her shoulders like a fur stole and nestles in. Skin on skin. The smell of Denton is pure man – sweat, soap and sex.

Bonfire Night come Saturday. Paulette's going to ask Denton if they can go to the big display in town and watch the rockets and Catherine wheels making patterns in the sky. They could eat candyfloss and toffee apples and mingle with the crowd. He could wear the good leather driving gloves she got him last week. The thing is, Denton never likes to make plans too far in advance, says he doesn't know his shifts and he doesn't like to let her down at the last minute. There again, Saturday is only three days away, so Paulette is hoping.

She feels a warm slick of sweat run off her breast and, suddenly, she's too hot. She doesn't sleep so good when Denton stays over because the man takes up more than his own half of the bed, and anyway, she likes to make the most of their time together.

She slips from under the blankets and shucks on her dressing gown, the one he bought her for her birthday, the one he didn't even get a chance to wrap so she saw the price tag. Paulette had to pretend she didn't notice because the thing wasn't that expensive, but she had to remember they were saving, saving, saving. A house one day. Semi-detached, car on the drive, flowers in the front garden on a nice quiet road, grass on the verge and street lights that worked. That's the plan. They're a year and a half into it with a couple more to go. Before long, she'll have everything she wants. Patience, Paulette.

She stands at the window to catch a little cool breeze and parts the curtains for a splash of moonlight on Denton's face. How can a man have beautiful eyes even when they're closed? High forehead, close-cut hair and skin oiled so slick it shines. Yes, Paulette looks the man over like she's searching for disease but all she finds is things that makes her love him more.

She's pulled back to the window by a noise in the garden next door. New neighbour putting her rubbish in the bins. It's late to be up when you've got children. White woman, about Paulette's age. Red hair in plaits on top of her head. Irish or something. Not a smiling kind of person but then she's got one baby and one toddler and no man as far as Paulette can tell. Some people might get funny about the amount of noise coming out of that house day and night but there's something about the cry of a baby that twists at Paulette's twenty-nine-year-old womb.

When the alarm goes at eight, Denton's side of the bed is empty. He went straight into the shower at six. Full fifteen minutes he was in there, humming and washing himself. He got dressed, kissed her and was gone. Paulette went back to sleep even though she'd told Denton she could make him a breakfast and pack him a lunch, but Denton isn't a man that likes a fuss, and anyway, he has to pick up the fool Garfield on his way to work so he can't be late. Why Denton doesn't just move in with her she does not know. Denton doesn't like going out, doesn't like noise and doesn't like too many questions either, so how things are is how things are.

When Paulette starts to tell him how easy it would be if they lived together, cheaper too, that they could save more and get to their goal quicker, he kisses her and says, 'Is today all right, Paulette?' And she always says yes. And then he says, 'Well, today is all anybody has got,' and she can't argue with the truth.

Paulette gets dressed in the uniform they give her for work, a dark brown colour that is so close to Paulette's own skin that she seems to fade into it. Not that Paulette cares. Nursing auxiliary is a good job with maternity benefits when the time comes and until then it's nice going home at night knowing you've helped people.

Take the old man who came in last week. For seven days, he didn't get a single visitor. Not one. So, Paulette spent a bit

longer tidying up his bed and bringing his food. Mr Siskins
he was called, and he came from Yorkshire near the sea and
talked with a nice accent. Said he used to make shoes and
had his own shop. He sat up and showed her how he used to
use a little hammer to knock tacks into the leather, his hands
shaking, his voice weak and rasping. Told her about glue and
stitching and polishing like Paulette didn't have eighteen beds
to fix and eighteen other patients to tend to. But still, the man
hadn't had anyone to talk to for a long time so while he told
her about his two children living overseas, Paulette sat him in
his chair while she changed the sheets.

'Really?' she kept saying. 'Oh, that's nice.'

But when he said he had a wife who died before she could
retire, Paulette could hear the sorrow in his voice and, quick,
quick, before he could dwell on the past, she asked him about
his hobbies. Mr Siskins said he liked his garden and sometimes he played the piano in a little band with his friends. By
the time she moved on, he was smiling and chatting with the
man in the next bed.

Paulette likes them kind of stories from old people, it's
like reaching a hand into the future and imagining someone
saying to her when she's an old lady, 'Where did you used
to live, Paulette?' and she will say, 'Me? Oh, I lived on the
Belmonte Estate, a little two-bedroomed house, 14 Rosam-
und Grove. But that was before I met my husband and got
married. Then, when the kids came, we moved out to the
countryside. Yes, me and Denton. I used to love cooking
and I used to work at the Princess Alexandria Hospital as an

auxiliary nurse. But now that we're older and have time on our hands, me and Denton go travelling as much as we can to see the world.'

She's quick downstairs, her feet drumming on the steps, into the kitchen to put some meat to season for later. She opens the fridge. Everything is ordered, one shelf for dairy, eggs and cheese, another for cold meat and cold food, and then fresh meat or fish on the bottom. Really, she needs one of them big larder fridges and a chest freezer for when she overcooks, but for a long time it was just Paulette on her own and the little under-counter fridge was fine. Now, with Denton and with children on the horizon, she needs a fridge fit for family. She might get a catalogue and see how much they cost. Pay weekly.

She takes out the mutton and scalds it with hot water, squeezes lemon juice on as it cools. She chops up an onion and garlic, adds thyme and salt, black pepper and a sprinkle of brown sugar in her spice mix. Not too much. She keeps her eye on the clock because she must leave at nine on the dot. She kneads the flesh hard to break up the tough fibres. To and fro with the heel of her hand until she feels it give, just slightly, and then she covers it over and puts it back on the bottom shelf where the goodness will seep in and do its job while she's at work keeping the wolf from the door.

Time for a quick cup of coffee and a piece of toast. Her uniform is just a little tight these days and she's been thinking about asking for a size up, maybe get a size 14 this time. But no, no, no. Paulette's seen the women who let themselves go soon as they get a man and she's not one of them. She throws the second half of her toast in the bin and smooths her hand over her stomach. No lunch today. And no chocolates from the sideboard in the staffroom. She checks the fridge. One piece of chicken left over that Denton couldn't manage last night. That will be her dinner. One chicken leg, nothing else.

Quilted coat with a zip, loose hat on her greased-back hair, nice and neat, and a warm scarf, double-wrapped. Simple gold earrings and her crucifix. A check in the mirror. Her face always shines when she's seen Denton. A sparkle in her brown eyes and the corners of her lips turned upwards. Everyone is pretty when they're in love.

2

Paulette has to get two buses to work, the 61 into town, then a walk across Cathedral Green to catch the number 18 going north. Right near the bus stop, there's a new children's shop with pushchairs and cots in the window. She checks her watch. Ten minutes before the bus comes. She walks up to the front door and pushes it open.

It smells fresh, clean and new. There's a choice of three different prams and a white highchair with a row of coloured balls on a loop that fixes on to the front, and then, when you want to feed the baby, it moves aside. Not too expensive neither. At the back of the shop there's a little pretend baby's bedroom with an ABC rug and a rocking chair with a footstool for nursing the baby. And in the centre of the room there's a cot that becomes a little bed when you pull the levers on the side. Paulette's never seen anything like it. A cot for a baby and bed for your boy or girl all in one. Bright yellow gingham baby quilt on top with a white-and-yellow tiger pillow. Just beautiful. Smooth wood, not made in some factory on the other side of the world. No, this is made by a proper carpenter with half-moon glasses and a little chisel in his hand.

A girl comes and stands next to Paulette. 'Adele' says the badge on her chest.

'Lovely, isn't it?' she says.

'Beautiful,' says Paulette. 'How much is it?'

'Depends on whether you want the natural wood or the white wood. Or we do a limed oak. We've also got an opening offer, the whole package with the bed, the covers and the linen.'

Paulette likes the idea of a package where you get everything one time and you don't have to wait.

'And we do finance,' says the girl quickly. 'Is it for yourself? Or . . .'

'Yes,' says Paulette and without thinking, without no plan, Paulette's hand moves over her stomach and stays there. The girl does the same and whispers, 'I'm three months gone. Not really showing yet.'

'Nor me,' says Paulette and because she's started and she wants to know what it's like to say it out loud, because she wants the feeling that it could be true, because it might as well be, she just carries on. 'I'm three months as well.'

'Oh, congratulations!' says the girl. 'What's your due date?'

But Paulette doesn't have a calendar at the tip of her tongue so she just says, 'Summertime.'

The two of them stare at the cot that becomes a bed until Paulette says, 'I want the baby's room ready early. How much did you say it was?'

When the bus comes, Paulette sits up at the front on her own. She faces the window but she sees nothing. Not the weaving, stuttering cars, not the headscarved women shopping for vegetables, nor the tears of rain chasing one another against the glass, nor the dark, dark sky meaning more rain, meaning Paulette getting soaked before she even starts her shift. No, Paulette is all the way back home, standing at the door of her second bedroom, seeing the carpet that she will rip up and change to mint green. And them purple curtains so thin you can see the morning sun right through them? Change them for pale green velvet with little silver moons and stars sprinkled all over so the baby has something to look at while it's going to sleep. She sees the cot that becomes a bed and wonders if she should go ahead and put a down payment on it. But maybe that would be inviting bad luck. No, better to wait until she's actually pregnant. Whenever it is, Paulette's baby will have the best of everything and won't be waking up too early because the mattress is uncomfortable or she didn't invest in good blackout curtains, no. But then again, a baby will do whatever it wants and it's the mother that works around it. So Paulette's heard.

Paulette was lucky. She slept in the same bed as her grandmother until she was six years old. A small house at the bottom of the hill in Basseterre with a verandah wrapped right round the front and two steps down to the trickle of river that would dry up every summer. The smell of the Caribbean sea, the night rain beating down on the corrugated iron roof, soft as a lullaby, fierce as a fight. Granny slept hot like a furnace, same as Denton, and little Paulette would slide to the far corner of the bed to keep clear and get some sleep.

Sometimes when she woke up in the morning, Granny would be looking at her and smiling, calling 'My Sweet Pea' in her sing-song voice. Then breakfast of scrambled egg with chopped onion and pimento, Johnny Cakes and tea in Paulette's special enamel cup, three sugars and condensed milk. Paulette sat on the floor between Granny's legs to get her hair oiled and plaited.

'What time is, Paulette?' her grandmother would ask and Paulette would have to recite the Lord's Prayer before she went off to school.

'You hear that? Lead us not into temptation. That's the most important one, Sweet Pea. And then love. And forgiveness,' her grandmother would say. 'Remember, now.'

Okay, so Paulette told the girl in the shop a white lie but really it was only telling the truth in advance. Sooner or later, she will have a baby. She doesn't nag Denton about it because he likes to take one step at a time, but she knows he wants children, he told her so enough times, just not yet.

When Paulette's baby is born, she'll have it christened in the cathedral in town where all the upstanding people gather, where good families walk slowly up the path, arm in arm, in suits and hats and handbags. That's where Paulette will thank the Lord and baptize her child into the Christian faith and have a little party afterwards. With her own hands, she'll bake an iced-white fruitcake with pink edible roses round the edge. She will probably be married by then, but if she's not, then their own child can be bridesmaid or pageboy, throwing petals on the floor.

The Best of Everything

Honeymoon is obvious. Jamaica for Denton and St Kitts for Paulette. There's a few old aunties and a couple of cousins there. Not really people she keeps in touch with but if she had to call on family they're the only ones left out there. So, a good couple of weeks in the sun while someone looks after the baby. But stop! There is no one on this earth Paulette would ever trust with her child, not one single person, so the baby will come too. Maybe by that time there would be two children. Maybe there would be three, who knows? But anyway, they will all go away together and make it a family holiday as well as a honeymoon. Sweet Pea, Denton and their little tribe.

Princess Alexandria Hospital, Men's Ward, day shift. Every auxiliary nurse comes to the job with their own ways. For example, Paulette doesn't mind feeding people, bed-making and cleaning, but she can do without bedpans and washing. If she's on with Marcia and Tanya, they have a good system, swapping jobs and helping each other out until the shift runs sweet and quick and it's done before you know it. Sister McKenzie always says that when the three of them are on shift, the world is a better place, but then Sister McKenzie knows how to get the best out of her staff.

Marcia just got married last month. Paulette was invited and Marcia said she could bring someone but Denton was on a job in Amsterdam so she went on her own and told Denton all about it while he was eating his dinner. Stew-down chicken, yam, green banana, sweet potatoes and coleslaw on the side.

Paulette likes to eat quick and then bustle about in the kitchen, chatting to Denton while he cleans his plate.

'Who is Maria again?' he says.

'Marcia, Denton. She works with me. The one whose boyfriend bought the BMW. Well, it's her husband now.'

'The Three Series?'

'I don't know. It's green.'

She fills his glass, wipes up a few grains of rice from her plastic tablecloth.

'She looked lovely, Denton. They must have spent some serious money, that's all I can say. White Rolls-Royce and six bridesmaids with little silver shoes and ribbons in their hair. And one pageboy at the front. Flowers everywhere. Shame you couldn't come. Food, as much as you could eat, and a DJ all night. I got you a piece of the wedding cake for later. There was a really good sound system so I even had a little dance but some of the guys were getting too fresh. You know what they're like when there's a lot of drinking. Anyway, I didn't get in too late but it was a really good night. Wish you could have come, Denton.'

'Three Series is a good car but the Six or the Eight Series is better. Me and Garfield saw a nice one up Baldwins Lane last week. Garfield couldn't stop talking about it. It was nice, man. Good shape.'

He reaches out and slides his hand around the top of her leg.

'Talking of good shape . . .'

He tugs her away from the sink and on to his lap. 'You'd look good in the passenger seat of a Six Series with a fold-down top, Paulette.'

She digs his fork into the last piece of yam on his plate and holds it to his lips, but he rears back.

'No, P, I beg you.'

Paulette picks up his plate and slides the debris into the bin. 'Marcia's dress was what they call "blush" with pretty embroidery all up the edge of the veil. Tight, fitted here round the chest. She had her hair straightened as well. And a tiara.'

'Yeah?'

'Yeah.' She looks at him loosening his belt. 'But you know what, Denton? Like you say, I could think of better uses for that kind of money.'

He takes the last sip of Appleton's rum that she's diluted with a little bit of water. He sits back in his chair. 'My God, Paulette, don't give me so much next time. My belly is hurting.'

'You don't have to eat it all, you know.'

'I can't say no to anything, Paulette, you know that,' he says, grabbing her again, drawing her down. 'I always want more.'

Marcia, who is thirty, and Tanya, who is thirty-four, are both married and Paulette is not. Then again, both of them had the good sense to choose a man who doesn't work in European construction and can come home every night.

Not a man who still keeps a room in his best friend's flat, especially when that same best friend, Garfield, happens to be a fool with scutter-level morals. And Paulette has never seen this room, never been in it once. Denton says he'd be embarrassed to bring her there, because Garfield has different women every night, low-grade women he wouldn't like Paulette to meet, and anyway, the place isn't kept nice. Denton's own bedroom is full of his records and his hi-fi and not much else, stuff that would mess up Paulette's tidy house. And it's cheap. Garfield doesn't charge him much and it's useful to have somewhere to lay his head for them rare, rare times him and Garfield go out late and come in making a whole heap of noise. Garfield is like that, a drinker and a playboy, and Denton is good to keep him around. Anyway, all in all, Denton will keep his little room until they're ready to make the move to their new house together.

If you want the truth, Paulette's getting impatient. Can't help it. Tanya has a little boy, eight years old, and Marcia will take exactly five minutes to get pregnant because she's like that, very ambitious and a bit superior. Paulette will be last. And they're always saying that Paulette should put her foot down and make Denton show her that he's serious. Both of them asking why she doesn't bring him round to their houses and let everyone meet him. Or at the very least, make some kind of date for moving in. Nothing she hasn't thought herself, but at the end of the day, Denton is different to other men. Denton is better looking, funnier, a big thinker with big plans and a big heart. And that's all that matters.

3

A cherry-red Toyota Celica. 1600 GT. Leather seats and corner lights. Fastback. How many weeks was he talking about the car, telling her how good it looks and how everyone on the street stares when it drives past?

And she said, 'Denton, that's a car for popping style, not a car for a family. A car for racing, not for going to the supermarket.'

That's what she said. And she said it more than once. And if it wasn't for that car, which she begged him not to buy, there wouldn't have been no accident, and if there hadn't been no accident, Denton would be coming home to her tonight, kissing her at the front door and eating his dinner while they chatted about their day.

But no. Mould, grease, filth, dust, stains, dirt, creases, smells, marks. They will have to take his place. Cleaning and bleaching helps. Weeks she's been at it. Paulette can rise in the morning and spend the whole day in the kitchen, moving Pyrex dishes out of cupboards, taking out her once-a-year saucepans to scour and put right back where they came from, putting the dining chairs up on the table so she can scald the floor with boiling water and good strong disinfectant.

The tops of the kitchen cupboards, which she is pretty sure she's never tackled before, are scrubbed hard with the rough side of the sponge and then wiped, yellow grease staining the dishcloths. And when the kitchen is done and her eyes sting from the mixture of cheap chemicals and salt tears, Paulette starts on the bathroom.

She has six hours before her shift and that's a long time to fill. But if you keep your hands busy and focus, focus, focus on the mould between them bathroom tiles then, before you know it, you're not thinking of living without Denton. Because if you do think of him, gone for good, there's nothing left but some survival instinct God created in you from the beginning of time. But she's not sure about survival right at this moment because the will to carry on is not even skin deep, it's lighter than that.

She stops suddenly, bent over the bath, scourer in hand, and closes her eyes. She's trying to trace back to the moment before she knew. It was May. It was Sunday. It was evening when she found out but what was she doing when the accident actually happened? Ten o'clock in the morning. Twelve minutes past ten exactly. Was she stirring soup? Was she plucking her eyebrows? Muhammad Ali won the boxing and it was all over the newspapers. Is that what she was doing, reading about left hooks and uppercuts so she could join in with Denton when he told her all about it? Or was she sitting with a cup of coffee and a magazine, waiting for him to call, the low-level hum of desire as much a part of her as the breath and blood in her veins?

It won't come. Everything before she knew has turned to mush, flipped and twisted. Days and weeks have blurred into a single moment. The knock on the door. Garfield there telling her to let him in, pushing past her with his renk self even though Denton wasn't at home. He never came without Denton being there.

'Paulette,' he says, standing right inside her house, his eyes roving all over the room except at her.

'What you looking for? What's wrong?'

'Denton.'

'What about him?'

What she thinks right then, this she remembers good, is that the skinny, shifty Garfield, constant and dark as a shadow, is trying to tell her that him and Denton had been out and got involved in a fight, that Denton was arrested and is sitting in a cell up at Queens Road police station with a busted mouth. That would be Denton all over. Temper.

'What's he done?' she says, folding her arms.

'Paulette, I'm sorry. He's dead.'

She kisses her teeth long and loud. Garfield is wrong, simple as that. Wrong in every way, wrong-looking, wrong sly fox intelligence and wrong morals, so Paulette isn't even worried. Not one bit.

'What you talking about, Garfield?'

'He's dead, Paulette. He's gone. Car accident.'

'Garfield, speak properly, man. You're not making sense. Where? When?'

'Today. Listen to me, Paulette. I'm telling you the truth. He was in an accident. He's dead.'

Paulette sits down on the arm of the sofa and considers what Garfield is saying. She puts it to him like a judge.

'What time?'

'This morning, I don't know what time. Morning.'

'Where?'

'Between Laycock Street and George Road. That crossroads. The blind spot there where people just bust out into the traffic without looking.'

'Just up there? I didn't hear nothing. I didn't hear no police cars. Ambulance would have come right along the bypass. I've been in all day and I didn't hear nothing.'

'I don't know, Paulette, I don't know. I just come to tell you.'

'How come you know? Who told you?'

'I don't know.'

'You don't know who told you, Garfield? Someone must have told you. Were you with him?'

'Everyone's talking about it. A man drove into him. There was a girl in the car as well. The man's alive. Denton is dead, Paulette. Honest.'

It's the one word that does it. Never heard Garfield use it before. Makes her know it's true. Or at least Garfield thinks it's true. But that don't necessarily make it a fact.

She picks up her handbag and goes to the front door. She takes her coat off the hook and puts it on.

'Where is he?'

He comes up close, grabs her arm so hard she draws back. 'You can't go,' he says softly.

She looks at him good because she's getting frightened now. If Denton's in hospital injured and this fool is trying to stop her, or worse still, knowing Garfield's reputation, trying to make a move on her, she would have to drop him where he stood. Bam!

'Garfield, come out of my way before me and you have to fight.' She reaches for the lock. 'Run me up to the hospital. It must be Heathlands. Or the Accident and Emergency in town. Or even the Princess Alexandria itself. Come.'

But he presses himself against the door. 'His wife is there. His kids. You can't go.'

'Wife?'

'His wife is at the hospital. His mother. His kids. Everybody. They're all messed up. You can't go. You must stay here. His wife is there, Paulette. Honest.'

And just like that, Paulette knows it is true. All of it. Wife. Kids. Death. Everything.

4

Denton's wife could hardly stand at the graveside. So Paulette heard. Three kids, he had, ten, seven and five. All bawling.

Denton's wife had to be helped up off the floor when she got the news. Had to be sedated and then, when it wore off, she had to go and identify the body. So Paulette was told. And Denton's wife had two brothers and the two brothers were getting stories about Denton having a woman on the outskirts of town, or the next town, or somewhere, stashed away nice and quiet, fucking her between shifts and coming home to his wife unclean. That's the word that got back to Paulette and the brothers were looking for Paulette to tell her what they thought of her.

And all of Denton's wife's friends had made a pact to never tell her Paulette even existed because Paulette was a home-wrecking bitch and if wasn't for her he wouldn't even have been on that road on his way to her bed, being pulled right into the line of fire. No, the wife must never know. The wife, she must be spared. So Paulette understood.

And now Denton's wife is getting flowers and dinners left for her and her children, getting bottles of brandy and beer in the fridge for the visitors who are still coming round, months after Denton is cold in the ground. Denton's wife will get his life insurance. Denton's wife is Denton's Widow and Widow had a capital letter and the Widow has everything on her side in her grief. Grief without shame is the pure kind, makes people rub your back when you walk past, touch your hand, give it a little squeeze to make sure you know they care.

All Paulette got was a week off work with the flu, so she told people. She got the flu and she got a false smile. And then after a little while Paulette discovered a routine. She wakes up and starts crying like a tap until she walks through the staff entrance to the hospital. She does her work, cleaning and serving, tidying up, changing beds and wiping private parts, and then soon as she's off the bus and puts the key in her front door, she lets out all her tears until she goes to bed. She prays that one day it will stop.

Only Marcia and Tanya know the truth and they start off nice, taking her to the pub and telling her about all the useless men and two-timing players they've known in the past, but after a while, she begins to notice a little something different with them. They're sitting in her front room with a bottle of cherry brandy in front of them. Paulette has put some nuts in a bowl, but the thought of food is making her feel sick. All the weight she wanted to lose has gone and she can't even enjoy it. Marcia can't drink because of the baby. She's only two months gone and already she's talking about backache and sore breasts. She puts a cushion behind her and sits with one hand on her flat, flat belly and the other round a glass of Ribena.

'How long altogether was it you knew him, Paulette?'

'Nearly two years.'

'All that time, you didn't guess?'

Paulette shakes her head.

Then Tanya, older, wiser, harder: 'Where did you think he was when he wasn't with you?'

'Tanya, I told you already. I didn't think nothing. He worked abroad.'

'You mean *he said* he worked abroad. Now you know the truth, the crook was working shifts at Hagley Hall Hotel on security, telling his wife he was working nights when he was with you. The man was clever.'

Back to Marcia with her superior ways: 'Tell us again what he said.'

Paulette's told them and told them and told them already. Contract construction worker is what he said, twelve or fourteen hours at a stretch, and slept on the job. Sometimes the work took him clean to the other side of the country, even overseas, industrial and commercial contracts he said, living with ten other men in a mobile home, building supermarkets and factories. Sometimes he couldn't ring her for days, he was pouring concrete, or he couldn't ring because he was taking important instructions from the boss, or he couldn't ring her because he was up a ladder.

Did she want him to crawl down fifty feet to make a phone call? What if he slipped off the roof and crashed into a solid marble floor? Sometimes he was so tired after working all day and half the night, he just fell into his cot and passed out. And other times, the guys went out for a few drinks and it was bad manners not to go along. She didn't want him to ring when he was pissed, did she?

And when Christmas comes he tells her he can get triple time working in Amsterdam or on the rigs. And yeah, yeah, he could pop out to the phone box but the boss didn't like them to be off the job when he was paying triple time. With triple time they could save for a future. How many times did he say to be patient and think of their future together? *Don't cause no fuss, Paulette.*

Denton was like a magician. He would appear out of the blue, flowers and wine, and stay overnight. Of course, he could take her out to the best restaurants, to bars and clubs and the cinema if that's what she wanted. But if it was up to him after weeks on the job, missing her and pining for her, he would prefer it just the two of them, lying on the sofa, lying on the bed, a quiet dinner together, the good home cooking he longed for, her yielding body at the end of the evening.

All Denton's whispers were about the future, about time to come, when the long days apart and the long weeks away would be in the past. All his family was still in the Caribbean, he said, so Paulette was more important than ever.

Tanya kisses her teeth sharp. 'Denton played you, man. He played you good. No man could pull the wool over my eyes with that kind of nonsense. You should have followed him, Paulette. You should have found out where he really lived and rung the doorbell. Shamed him. Anyhow my Howard pops up with any foolishness, I just give him one look. You should have asked more questions, Paulette. Didn't you ever ask him any questions about the places he said he was? Where was it again, Amsterdam and Brussels?'

Marcia actually laughs. 'European construction!'

Tanya says again, 'You didn't see him for six days straight and you never suspected anything?'

Them with their side-eye. Them with their cleverness. The rough questions with the smooth sympathy, the mocking voice and the sisterly advice, lacing their interrogation with wine and sweet drink. How they would never fall for it because they know better and how they wouldn't be blinded by some pretty-boy sweet talk and how two and two always makes four but Paulette can't count.

Weeks it goes on until Paulette eases back, starts missing their calls, stays in her house, says she's not well, says she's busy. She tells Sister McKenzie at work that she wants to volunteer for weekend night shifts that nobody likes so she doesn't have to share the ward with the two of them. And Sister McKenzie is only too pleased to have a volunteer. She notices Paulette works right through her break times and says that if Paulette carries on like that, she will put another nurse out of a job. Work is the only place where Paulette can forget, where no one asks any questions, where she finds a little balm to put on her burning shame. Soon enough, the gap between meeting up with Marcia and Tanya gets so long they feel like strangers when she bumps into them in the car park or at the bus stop and she doesn't have to swallow the acid pity they pour on her soul.

Then, when she's not on shift, she cleans her house from top to bottom, working all the overtime she can get because when Paulette is working, she's not thinking about nothing.

Nights are the worst. She aches for him and can only get to sleep with the help of Mr Appleton. Mr Appleton is light brown, liquid, smooth and deadly. Enough Appleton Estate Signature Rum and Paulette ends up talking to Denton's wife and telling her everything, chapter, verse, chorus, back to the verse and hallelujah. Bam! Her and her good clothes and buttoned-up self. So proper and composed. What's to stop Paulette telling Denton's kids about their daddy and his fucking promises and the names Paulette picked out for their baby and how he would have loved that baby more than he ever loved them? Fact. What's to stop Paulette making his wife weep good when she hears how Denton took her breast in his mouth and whispered hot words in her ear until she yelled his name over and over and over? But Paulette never actually gets around to ringing the number because she doesn't know it. And in her fractured heart she still has the good Christian manners her grandmother put in from the day she was born. So, Paulette asks forgiveness and good old, reliable Mr Appleton rocks her to sleep.

One day, she opens the back door to hang out the washing. It might rain, it might not, she doesn't care. Next door, she hears Maggie doing the same but singing along to the radio in her kitchen. Paulette stands and listens.

'*Guess I'll spend my whole life throoouuugghhh, loving you!*'

For the first time in months, Paulette smiles. She listens

for a little while because, actually, Maggie has a good voice even though she has to cough between verses because of the cigarettes and you can still hear her Irish accent on every word.

When the song finishes, Maggie calls over. 'Morning, Paulette.'

There's a panel missing in the wooden fence right up by their back door; they both walk to it and look through.

'You could have been a pop star, Maggie,' Paulette says.

Maggie is quiet for a moment. 'You all right, missus?'

Words won't come. If she talks in that moment, she will break down, so Paulette just stands there with her lips together. Her nostrils flare with the effort.

Maggie puts her washing basket down and, turning to the side, she forces herself through the gap in the fence, pushing her heavy chest against her ribcage with the flat of her hand. She's halfway through when she screams.

'Ah, Christ,' she says, 'I've got a splinter in my nipple!'

And what tears Paulette was holding in come out with laughter and screams, the two of them, hauling Maggie one way then the other, snagging her jeans on a nail, pulling the fence to and fro until Maggie is released.

'Jesus, I only wanted to do this.' She puts her arms around Paulette and gives her a hug. 'And now I'm cut to ribbons.'

In Paulette's kitchen, Maggie dabs pink ointment on her scratches as Paulette tells her story. Maggie barely speaks until the end, by when she's finished a cup of tea and is on her second cigarette from the ruined packet in her back pocket. She leans her elbow on the kitchen table and squints against the smoke.

'Well,' she says when Paulette has finished, 'that's him down there for his sins.' She points to hell below her feet. 'And I'm not one for judgement, not with my family.'

'Don't say that, Maggie,' says Paulette. Some nights, Paulette doesn't even get to sleep from imagining what actually happened to Denton in that crash, how he must have hurt and bled, his body mashed up so bad it just couldn't function. If that isn't hell, she doesn't know what is.

'Ah, no, no, Paulette. Pay no attention to me. There's no heaven and there's no hell, and if there's a God, I've yet to see the evidence. And I'm no better than any other sinner. The father of my girls was a vicious bully and yet I stayed, didn't I? He was all right until he was in the drink, made me promises upon promises. "Oh, this is my last bottle, I swear, Maggie. And I'll never lay another finger on you as long as I live. Cross my heart." And I believed him every time. Then one day, it was like a light went on inside of me. Whoosh! And I realized just like that: this man will never change. Still took me a year to find the courage and the cash to get over here, though. I knew that if I moved anywhere in Wexford, anywhere in Ireland, sooner or later he'd find me. And what is worse, I'd have him back because I loved him. Still love him, if you want the truth. That's the kind of halfwit you've got living next door.'

'Sorry,' says Paulette.

Maggie smokes slow and quiet, and then, right before her cigarette goes out, she lights another and draws in deep.

'Ah, no!' she says on the outbreath. 'You're not to be sorry. Listen, between the jigs and reels, that man did me a favour. Have you seen my Kathleen? She's the face of an angel and Gemma is barely walking but has the run of the house. And me? I have my freedom. I go out where I want, with who I want, and I'm out of debt despite the price of bread and Irish butter. I am the master of my own destiny for good or for bad and that's what everyone deserves, isn't it? And anyway, I hear on the jungle drums that he's reduced his intake to just five pints a day, God bless him, and has found a female drinking buddy with an enormous arse and matching savings account. On Sundays, I say a rosary for the poor woman.'

'I didn't know you went to church, Maggie,' Paulette says.

Maggie strokes her chest and winks. 'It's in here I say it, Paulette. Silently.'

Paulette laughs as Maggie gets up and smooths her T-shirt over her belly.

'Well,' she says, 'you better come and help me get back through the fence unless you know some speedy diets.'

They're better at it this time and push the fence instead of pulling and Maggie steps through with ease.

'And listen,' she says when she's on the other side, 'you won't see it now, but that Denton has done you a favour too.'

Paulette feels the tears close again. 'I can't see it, Maggie. I just can't.'

'Imagine if it had gone on longer, eh? Imagine how many years he could have strung you along. Think about that. You're free now. You can start again.' Then she points her finger at Paulette and says, 'And I've seen what drink can do to a face, so don't start using rum as face cream. It doesn't work.'

Garfield starts coming round regularly. Says he's checking on her, says Denton would want him to make sure she was all right. She tries to run him, hits him once or twice, screams at him and tells him to get out. He knew! He knew Denton was married! He knew Denton was cheating her! He knew and said nothing.

But Garfield always comes back, a bottle of Mr Appleton under his arm, hunched over like a stalking cat, watching her like they're playing cards and he's got the ace. She's not the only one hurting, he tells her. Denton conned them both. Denton told everyone it was Garfield with the women and the slack ways, and all the while Denton was the one doing wrong. And yet, says Garfield, Denton was his friend and he misses him. Why can't the two of them mourn him together, pass the bottle like a baton, running down the lanes of their memories? What else is she doing with her time?

Soon enough it's Garfield that rocks her to sleep at night, Garfield that wants to hold her hand on the street and buy furniture. And it's Garfield that gives her a baby.

5

All through her pregnancy, Garfield steps up like a man. When the sun is blazing and people are talking about drought and sunburn, he visits every evening after work, turns on the fan and puts ice water on her swollen feet. He tells her she looks beautiful when the mirror tells her different.

He takes her to get her hair pressed, books her a pedicure at a nice salon in town. Bits and pieces for the baby come every week. Toys and romper suits and even food his mother said is good for pregnant women. Yam, breadfruit, bell peppers. Everything she wanted from Denton is delivered twice over by Garfield.

On the day she goes into labour, Garfield in his car coat and picky hair paces up and down the hospital like he's training for a race. She can hear him every time the birthing room door opens, asking for her and asking for news.

Then finally, when the midwife puts Paulette's baby on her chest, when she feels the warm wetness of him, when the nurse says everything is fine, fingers and toes and limbs, when she realizes the baby is truly and righteously out of her belly and alive in the world, drawing the same breath as every living being, she gives thanks to God and weeps for her grandmother and for the end of yearning, but she's smiling with it. A boy! She thought she knew love and fulfilment with

Denton but this is a different thing altogether, it's the purpose of life itself.

She doesn't think about Garfield, she doesn't give thanks for him and she knows she should.

When she comes home with the baby, without her knowing, Garfield has been clear into town and bought the cot that turns into the bed, the white one with the yellow check cover. He said she told him about it and he stored it up in his heart until he could afford it.

And it's Garfield that springs up in the night before the baby has even broken into a proper cry, before she can even move. He cradles the child in the crook of his arm and moves across the carpet like a ballet dancer, silent, changing nappies, giving him his bottle, talking to him, words she can't hear through her tiredness.

The baby is placid and calm as a mountain lake. He doesn't keep her awake until all hours like the children next door and sometimes because he's not making a noise Paulette will rise up in the night to check on him, to look at him in his white cot under his yellow quilt, his two little fists thrown back against the mattress.

She's stopped watching telly because she has her son for entertainment. When he puts his two arms around her neck, she knows there is no better feeling in this world or the next. She dresses him in nothing but the best. He is washed and creamed, his hair is oiled, his skin as soft as new suede. He is the type of baby that sleeps when it is time for sleep, laughs when you pick him up, and the only time you know the boy is hungry is a little mew he makes. No one has a baby like hers. Gentle as a leaf on water, sweet and pretty as a bird.

Stitch by stitch, Garfield moves himself in. He paints the kitchen and the front door, retiles the bathroom and pays for carpet top to bottom.

'Bird's crawling now,' he says. 'We have to make sure the floor is clean and safe.'

He puts some grey slabs down in the backyard and puts in a sandpit for Bird even though any woman could tell him sand and black hair don't mix. Still, he says hello to Maggie next door, puts the bins out early and takes the leaves out of the drain. If Paulette needs scouring cream or window cleaner or bleach, she only has to say it once and, when she opens the cupboard under the sink, there it is. In such a short piece of time, he's done everything a man could do when he loves someone.

And fatherhood was made for the man. All right, so she has to bite her tongue when he tells Bird off, but even she can see if she's not careful she will spoil the boy. She buys him too many toys, he says, and too many clothes. Garfield has a way of getting it right with Bird, the tender hand or the strong arm, where Paulette can only smother her son with pure love. Not that love ever hurt anyone.

Not for one single solitary moment can Paulette say she loves Garfield but she has to give him his due. He loves her, he loves Bird and he tries. He brings Bird pure educational toys, nothing plastic, and sits with his son on his lap and points at all the colours and animals, spelling each one out so Bird can get ahead when he goes to school. He gives her money for the bills even when she doesn't need it and says nice things to her.

'You were born to be a mother, Paulette.'

'You done your hair different, Paulette?'

'Red is your colour, Paulette.'

If he disappeared, she would miss him, miss his noise in the house and the childcare and the regular shekels, but most of all, God forgive her, what she would miss the most is the way, now and again, the smell and the feel of him and his turn of phrase will remind her of Denton even still.

'Come, Paulette,' he says, 'come sit next to me,' or 'I'm full as a barrel from your cooking,' or 'You look good, Paulette.' Sometimes, in the night, when he reaches for her, she just closes her eyes and remembers.

It's late summer. Paulette is out at the park with Garfield and Bird in his pram, navy blue and white with chrome wheels. Paulette's bought the matching rain cover and the parasol. If there is a Silver Cross accessory, Paulette owns it.

The weather's turning. She can feel the autumn in the air, winter even, like far-off music: you only hear one note but the rest is coming. The park is full of blood-red flowers, coughing their petals on the path like a bridal aisle. Her and Garfield have taken Bird to the park to get a little fresh air in the brown coat with the wooden buttons that Paulette knitted with her own two hands. It took her so long, it looked

like Bird would be drawing his pension by the time she finished, but she persisted and persisted and, in the end, it looks
beautiful and it's warm, which is the main thing.

Garfield's pushing the pram, stopping now and again to
adjust Bird's blanket or wipe a little dribble from his face.

'Maybe we could take a holiday,' he says. 'Autumn holiday,
go to Spain or somewhere like that. You want to go up to the
travel agent and see if they have bargains?'

'Yes,' she says. 'It won't be too hot then. But I'll have to ask
Sister McKenzie because you have to give plenty of notice.'

'You know what? Maybe we get a swing for the back
garden,' he says and carries on about what he might do and
how much they need to spend time together as a family and
his plans for their future, when he suddenly stops and looks
off into the distance at a man walking through the park with
two bags of shopping.

'What?' she says.

'That's him,' Garfield says, his voice quiet and slow.
'That's the man.'

'What man?'

'The man from the car crash. The one that killed Denton.'

'Him?'

'Him. I saw him at the court case, we all saw him. Same
man.'

Paulette doesn't really know what she's doing, that's all
she can say to the police later. She doesn't ask Garfield if he's
sure or how he can tell from such a distance because inside
her there's so much anger for Denton and for his wife and

for being kept away from the funeral and for the shame of making secret visits to the grave and for wondering if the brothers would find her and for knowing in her heart someone as handsome as Denton had to be married but sleeping with him anyway and missing him every day of her life while Garfield snored in her bed and draped his lazy arm across her belly. She just drops her bag, runs across the grass and stands in front of the man.

'You!' she says and points right in his face. 'It's you, isn't it?'

The man is shivering. He don't look right at all. He looks at her but not at her at the same time and Paulette has to shout to get his attention.

'You! You killed Denton! You did it!'

He puts his head on one side and closes his eyes. Stays like that while time stands still. Then nods and says, 'Yes.'

Paulette pushes him. Both hands, palms up, flat against his chest, just pushes him and pushes him again and down the man goes. Crumples down to the ground. His shopping spills out. A miniature bottle of vodka, a loaf of bread, shaving foam, apples. She didn't even push him hard but still, he's on the ground and the man won't get up, looks like he's fainted or something.

'You killed him!' she says. Then, before she knows it, there are people everywhere. A white man and a white woman are shouting, 'Hey! Leave him alone!' and an old white lady with a dog is shouting, 'I saw that!' And although five minutes ago the park was half empty, all of a sudden there's a crowd, white people everywhere, surrounding them.

KIT DE WAAL

Garfield runs across the grass, tries to put the handle of the pram in Paulette's clenched fist, saying, 'Paulette! Come on!'

But she stands over the man who's rocking now on the ground, half trying to get up, half trying to lie down like he's drunk or lost his mind. One little push and he's carrying on dramatic. Someone in an overcoat is trying to help him while people cluster around, saying 'She hit him . . .' and 'She attacked him . . .' and 'Assault!' and then Paulette comes to and sees the scene loud and clear like she's floating above herself. She knows how it looks.

'Get out of here, Garfield,' she whispers.

But he pulls her arm. 'Come, Paulette. We got to go.'

She stops and looks at him because she hears the police car coming.

'Go,' she whispers hard. 'Take the baby.'

The look she gives him says everything a black woman can say to a black man in England in 1976. It says, when the police come they will know who to blame. They will hear how the angry black woman assaulted an innocent white man in broad daylight. And everyone knows what an angry black woman is capable of.

And if there's a black man there, the story will get worse. It will be the violent black man and the angry black woman assaulting a decent Englishman going about his lawful business in a public park with flowers planted by the council and now the poor man can't get up off the floor.

And never mind if the dangerous black people have a baby, you need to lock them up, officer! And put that black baby in foster care on the other side of the country with people who will tell the child all sorts of rubbish and lies about you. And it might be you never persuade the social workers and the courts you need your baby like life itself and, in the end, you never get your baby back and he grows up never knowing a single thing about you. And every black woman knows the ending of the story and has known it from time. You never recover and you die without your children.

And lastly, what Paulette's look says to Garfield is don't let them put their hands on you. Because if you start fighting, that's another story altogether, and it ends in a police station at best and a prison at worst and sometimes it ends in a mortuary. Just go, Garfield. Take Bird. Walk away and go.

But Garfield hangs back with the pram, stays on the other side of the park, watching. She sees him moving from foot to foot, itching to come over, but she shakes her head and waves him away. And, sure as the day follows night, the police come quick, two women. They drive right through the big iron gates to the park with their lights on, making enough noise to wake the dead.

Paulette tells them everything, tells them who she is, name, address and date of birth, and she tells them she has a baby, she's a mother and with a good, permanent, full-time job working at the Princess Alexandria Hospital as an Auxiliary Nurse and she puts capital letters on her job so they know she's an upright person. She tells them who the white man is and what he did, that he killed someone in broad daylight, a good man called Denton who was minding his own business, but the man wasn't paying attention to his driving and he killed an innocent man and ruined Paulette's life.

The crowd is listening. They go quiet so she says it again, loud. She brings herself up tall because she has things to say and she speaks the truth. He killed an innocent man! She doesn't care. Let them lock her up for a hundred years, she would still confront the man, push him again, yes. Bam! He deserves it.

The man is standing up by now, people crowding round. Nobody looks at Paulette no more. No. They're looking hard at the man with his shirt hanging out of the back of his trousers and his untidy self, not as proper and righteous as he first looked when he was lying on the grass. And someone whispers, a loud, loud whisper, 'I think he's drunk.'

It's true the man's got something wrong with him, can't even brush the leaves off his trousers without stumbling.

But the police aren't looking at the white man, they're too busy telling Paulette it doesn't matter what he did, she can't go round taking the law into her own hands, attacking people. If she thinks a crime has been committed, she can report it to the police, and if she thinks she has a case against him, there's the civil courts for that and she can sue him. But, right now, she has committed a crime under the Offences Against the Person Act from 18-something and they carry on talking about different types of assault and how people like Paulette can end up in prison, job or no job, child or no child.

But just then, the man holds his hands up and pushes himself between the police officers and Paulette.

'No, no. No,' he says in his posh voice, every word clear and slow. 'She is quite correct, officers. She is perfectly within her rights. I'm afraid everything she says is true. She's upset and very understandably, under the circumstances.'

In the end, because the white man keeps talking, the police let her go with a warning. Even they could see he wasn't right in his head. The crowd wanders away and the police help the man pick up his shopping and guide him to their car. Paulette follows a few paces behind.

'We'll give you a lift home, sir. Where do you live?' they ask him and when Paulette hears what he says she stores it up in her heart.

6

The man lives in her area, which is strange. You don't get many white men like him living out on the Belmonte Estate, beyond the forgotten edge of town, where they built tower blocks and maisonettes and quick, quick houses to hide the forgotten people, the people with no choice, them who make trouble and them who can't trouble anyone any more. All the houses look the same, the groves look the same, the flats look the same, squares and rectangles and no trees for mile after mile.

She waits a couple of weeks and gets off the bus early from work and walks past the end of the road. Garfield's taken Bird to see his mother and his sisters so she can take her time to come home. Do a little investigating. This man's side of the estate is rough so she knows what to expect but, even so, the street doesn't look good, not like where she lives, where the neighbours put flowers in pots and paint their front doors and buy proper net curtains for the windows. She walks up the street and then back down like she has somewhere to go, not dilly-dallying or looking lost so if the man comes out and sees her, she can say she has a friend living round the corner. Then again, if the man comes out, she might not be able to answer for her actions.

Then she goes home. She waits a few more weeks and does it again. And again, until it becomes a habit with her. The anger and the grief bubble upside her and, when she can stand it no more, she gets off the bus early, takes a little detour. Two houses on the man's street are boarded up and under a big tarpaulin is half a car with no wheels on it. She walks past the house; she thinks about the man inside and then she goes home.

Then one time, just as she's passing, he opens the door. She looks him good in the eye. He killed Denton. And Garfield told her the man's own daughter was in the car and she was mashed up bad. The man even went to prison so Paulette doesn't have to look away like she's the guilty one. But then the man walks slowly to his gate where she stands with her bag on her shoulder wearing her nurse's shoes and he holds his hand out.

'Francis Bowen,' he says.

He looks the same, watery eyes, quivering all over, but this time he's wearing a shirt and tie that make him look like a teacher – though as sure as Paulette has worked in Princess Alexandria Hospital as a senior nursing auxiliary for seven years, the man is on some heavy kind of drug.

Paulette kisses her teeth good and hard and cuts her eye so sharp she wonders the man doesn't bleed out where he's stood.

Take the man's hand? What? He thinks an English handshake makes things normal, makes people rise up out of their coffin and the world turn right? *Francis Bowen*, he says, like she hasn't read about him in the newspapers, like she doesn't know the name of the man who killed her dreams. She turns her back on him and walks home.

Garfield is out with Bird and the house is silent. In a different life, Paulette would have five or six children round her feet and noise in every room. Garfield likes things quiet and ordered but she would like a bit of chaos now and again, the washing machine spinning and three pots bubbling on the stove. Maybe someone upstairs singing in the bath and a baby programme on the telly.

Take Maggie's house. It's the same council house like hers and the same size but in every other way it's different. You couldn't call it tidy, not to Paulette's standards anyway, and too much furniture and the wallpaper is too loud, but there's something about seeing toys everywhere and damp washing on the airer and the woman herself with her baggy clothes and the telly always on. Maggie lives outside of herself. She's not standing up by the sink thinking of what could have been and how things might be different. Too busy being here and now to be there and then.

It starts when she's chopping onions. Paulette stops suddenly. If she closes her eyes, she is nearly back there at the foot of the hill in St Kitts. The light through the shutters and the smell of fresh herbs and pepper, the spice of warm resin and dry leaves. Weathered wood, smooth and polished underfoot. Her grandmother sitting at the table with her long, long apron and an enamel bowl on her lap, her grandmother's beautiful, elegant hands, splitting bean pods. Those hands did the most mundane things, like putting a knife through a carrot or plaiting hair, and they turned that nothing into something. Granny used to tell Paulette stories about the mother she never knew and showed her the few photographs she had of a smiling woman with smiling eyes who died just after Paulette was born. You don't get good medical care when you're poor but even so it was diabetes that she couldn't control, and according to Granny she passed quick. Paulette barely feels the loss because she has not one single memory of her mother and can't imagine being loved any better than Granny loved her.

Paulette rinses her hands under the tap and goes to the top of the fridge for a little barley wine. She sits down at the kitchen table to do it properly, really go back there and feel it. The barley wine will see to that.

The loss of Granny, now that cut deep. And then there was the funeral she couldn't afford to attend. Paulette got the news in a telegram. It was sudden, she didn't suffer. Heart attack. It was six hundred pounds and thousands of miles away and Paulette was pregnant with Bird and couldn't travel. She sent money for the best coffin she could afford and flowers and a good wake with food and wine afterwards. Fifteen days later, a big envelope arrived by registered post. Paulette took it from Garfield and went upstairs to her bedroom. There was the coffin propped up for Paulette to see and Granny inside. Strangers standing around it, barely anyone she recognized. Granny was gone. Paulette raises her glass towards the west, wherever that is, and toasts her grand-mother. The power and the glory, forever and ever. Amen.

And from the loss of her grandmother, Paulette goes to the gift of Bird, nearly three years old and a prettier baby you could not imagine. But the barley wine smile doesn't last long because straight from the gift of Bird, Paulette slips downhill to poor Garfield, who she can never love, who has no secret wife on the other side of town, who has never lied to her as far as she knows and who tries in every way to please her. And then from Garfield, it's inevitable.

Denton.

Denton is another barley wine and a tot of rum. Nor-mally, she would spend some time with Denton, thinking about him like some people think about a good party or a summer holiday. Thinking about him like he didn't ruin her life and make a fool out of her. Yes, normally she would spend a good long while with Denton and his sweet loving and kisses but today out of nowhere, trampling on her nice memories, comes the man with the shirt and tie that she pushed in the chest.

She thinks about the way he didn't stand up for himself in the park. She thinks about his reasonableness which to Pau-lette's thinking is pure guilt. The man with the shirt and tie who sees her walk past his house and introduces himself like he's selling her a car and offers her his hand, the same fucking hand that couldn't steer his fucking car out of the way of an innocent driver. All right, so he didn't bad-mouth her to the police women. Of course he didn't! What could he say? *I am a murderer*, that's what he could say. *I killed Denton in cold blood.* Damaged his own child too. It's a wonder Mr Francis Bowen don't just lay down and expire.

Before she knows it, Paulette has her arms in her coat, she's through the front door and on the street. She's still wearing house slippers and, yes, she's drunk and she don't care one bit. It's dark anyway, February dark that starts at three o'clock in the afternoon. She rounds the corner of the man's road, just to see if he's there, just to see if the light is on, just to see if she can hear the television and him inside watching a game show, having a good time. Maybe he's having a little drink-up with his old white friends, running English jokes, watching a documentary about the Second World War, living his good life while Denton is lying cold in his grave.

She's out of breath by the time she gets there, her coat undone, flapping in the wind, with the fire of fury keeping her warm. She stops at the gate. The next-door house is dark, no one at home. She creeps slowly up the path. The light is on. The curtains aren't drawn properly, there's a three-inch gap. She steps off the path and goes, foot by foot, to the window. Still no one on the street. No one to see her and, in this area, maybe no one would care.

She stands on her tiptoes, peers through the gap. There he is, sitting on a big old sofa wearing his shirt and tie, both hands over his face like he's crying. Paulette looks further in. She looks at the room. No telly and no documentary, no friends and no drinking. No laughter. No lampshade. No cushions and one dry picture on the wall. Just shirt and tie and a cot, and in that cot there's a little boy. He's a bit older than Bird, at least three years old, a little boy who's too old for a cot in the first place, a boy who should be playing or taking a nap in his own bedroom on a little blue bed with a blue quilt with fire engines on it and thick curtains to keep out the cold. But this cot is in a front room that looks like the man moved in yesterday. And instead of picking up the little boy that's holding on to the side of the cot and crying, shirt-and-tie man is sitting there with his hands over his eyes.

Paulette wants to scream, wants to shout at him all over again, but there are too many things to say and not enough words to say them, and anyway, words can't explain what's in her heart. She grips the window ledge and watches the glass mist up with her breath.

Then suddenly the boy stops crying. He sees her and stares with his mouth open and the man looks up. He looks at the child and then looks at Paulette. Now they're both looking at her and she looks back and there are ten clear seconds of silence between them until Paulette takes her hand off the window ledge and slowly walks away.

7

When Paulette finishes work, she picks Bird up from nursery and takes him straight home. The boy is three and a half going on ten. Clever? You should see how he knows his colours and numbers and ABC. You should hear the questions even Garfield can't answer, like 'Why is the sky blue, Daddy?' And 'Why is my hair curly?' Oh, the boy is going to be somebody when he grows up.

Soon as they get in, she puts on the telly for Bird's programmes and starts cooking. Fresh food, every day. Yam and green banana and sweet potato and callaloo. Mutton and chicken and beef and ribs. Nothing too spicy because Bird's still a child but seasoned well and full of goodness. Then Bird straight into the bath, dried with a soft towel, creamed all over and put into some nice clean clothes that don't have the smell of nursery all over them. Then the best part of the day when it's just her and Bird before Garfield comes home. She sits with him and teaches him his shapes or his letters. Or they play with Lego and building blocks or colouring in and she tells him about his great-grandmother and about St Kitts and the history of his people and about the future he will have. She tells him how much she loves him and stops just short of telling him about Denton because that's one bit of history he doesn't need to know and she has to remind herself of that every single day.

One day she comes in from shopping and sees Garfield quickly putting down the phone. Then twice she catches him smelling of woman. She has to be careful because Garfield is sneaky, and he might just spray himself with bargain-basement perfume before he comes home to make out someone else is interested in him, so Paulette says nothing. And then Garfield decides to call her bluff by staying out for a whole weekend just to make a point. And the point is sex, his lack and her not giving a fuck. Literally.

Now, Garfield is sly but not actually clever and doesn't know you never bluff unless you got at least one good card. Or you really don't care about the outcome. And Garfield cares. And what is more, Garfield loves Bird which, when all is said and done, means this is a game he can't win because that baby belongs to Paulette.

Sunday night, he returns after being missing in action for forty-eight hours. Walks in the kitchen, takes off his jacket and asks about dinner like everything is normal. Paulette folds her arms and leans against the sink.

'Garfield, we have to talk.'

He puts his yellow eyes on her and she comes straight to it.

'You can't stay here no more.'

Garfield sits down, calm and slow. 'I thought I was living here, Paulette. Living isn't staying.'

'And staying out for two nights isn't living here either,

Garfield. And anyway, it was never right between us. This is my place, Garfield, and we have to call it a day.'

Instead of speaking straight away, he lays his hands flat on the table like they're having a seance and he's feeling the spirit. He is mad all right.

'Who said it was never right?' he says. 'You like to tell me what I think, don't you, Paulette? Like to tell me when to look after Bird and when to touch you and when you need your space and where to sit and what needs doing in the house. Now you say it was never right for us? It was right for me.'

Paulette studies Garfield hard. She tries to put herself in his shoes, tries to let a little softness and kindness into her eyes.

'I'm sorry, Garfield. That's all I can say.'

'You're not sorry enough to try, though? We could make a go of it if you wanted to.'

She hears the pleading in his voice. 'I have tried, Garfield. Honestly. I have tried and I've done my best from the bottom of my heart. And I'm not saying it's anything you've done. I'm really sorry. It's just not working.'

'For you.'

'Yes, for me. And this is my house. I'm sorry.'

The room rattles with his hurt and if she was a different woman with a different story, she could go over to him even now, put her arms around him and say, yes they could give it another try. If she could make it better, she would.

'Maybe if . . .'

'If what? Say it,' he snaps.

'If I could get over Denton.'

It was a cruel laugh he let out. Cruel and superior with no fakery in it whatsoever.

'Denton? How many years is it now? I hope that's just an excuse, Paulette, because if it's the real reason you are more of an idiot than I thought. Denton?'

More laughter, holding his belly even though the noise came clean out of his poisonous heart. 'Say it again, Paulette. Denton?'

'Shut up, Garfield. It's over. That's it. We done. You must take your things and leave.'

'Oh, I'm leaving.' He gets up. 'And let me tell you something, Paulette. One of us is a fool and it ain't me.'

He stands up by the kitchen door and slowly, slowly, slowly puts his jacket on, one sleeve at a time, zipping it inch by inch, looking at her and smiling and talking and giving free rein to all he wanted to say from day one.

'Listen good. You weren't Denton's only woman. He had a nice redskin piece called Charmaine. Yeah, Charmaine. I've met her plenty of times. Good-looking, man, tall and nice. Working as a secretary, dresses in suits and high heels. And you know that sound system you bought him for his car? He took it straight across town to give to her. He told you it got stolen, yeah? Well, Charmaine runs that in her little Metro. She's nice. She knew about you and she knew about his wife but she was easy, you know, cool. Her and Denton understood each other. She wasn't talking about weddings every five minutes, trying to tie him down, asking him questions all the time. Oh yeah, he told me all about you and your ways. To be honest, I wondered what he was doing here. You're a good-looking woman, Paulette, no one can deny that, but you're uptight, man. So, he kept you as his fallback position. When he was too tired to go out or when Charmaine was busy or when he just wanted a nice dinner and a warm bed and someone to wait on him hand and foot, Denton called you. He had a name for you as well. What was it now?'

He looks up at the ceiling.

'Oh yes, Pum-Pum. Said that was the only good thing about you.' He looks down at Paulette's crotch.

Paulette covers herself with her hands. Can't help it.

Garfield smiles. 'But then again, Denton was wrong about a lot of things. Your pum-pum not that sweet.'

He saunters out of the kitchen and walks upstairs. She stands still as a tree. She can hear him making a mess, rattling the doors of the wardrobe, ripping open the chest of drawers. He's back down in ten minutes and Paulette makes sure her eyes are dry. She holds her hand out for the key and makes sure it doesn't shake one tiny bit.

Garfield opens the front door and looks at her from head to toe with his lip curled and his nostrils wide. He leans in so close she can smell his breath.

'Upstairs, it is my son asleep, Paulette. My son, not Denton's. He is sleeping in the bed I bought him, you remember? It's me he calls Daddy. Me.' He jabs his chest with his thumb. 'Bird is mine, Paulette. Mine. Remember that. I'm leaving but I will be back to see him. Regular. And if you ever try and separate me from my son, you will be sorry.'

He throws the key on the floor and walks out.

Why she bothers to go to bed, she couldn't say. She doesn't even close her eyes because she knows every word is true and now there is nothing left for her to hold on to. When she'd been thinking of weddings, Denton was fixing a speaker into another woman's car or he was sitting watching telly with his wife, one of his children on his lap. When she'd been waiting at home with the pot full of meat, he'd been planning what lies to tell her, and every lie he said, she believed. Charmaine. The woman even had a pretty name. Paulette can see her, red-skinned, bright, slim and sparkling. The two of them laughing about the nagging third wheel on the wrong side of town. She sees him lying in Charmaine's bed opening his arms for her and, even now, even after all that, when she remembers his smile her stomach lurches for the want of him.

She gets up. It's three o'clock in the morning. She goes into Bird's room, eases him out of his bed and cradles him. He draws his chubby arms around her neck and she leans in, smells his skin, soap and baby and warm, pure, innocent life. Years and years and years before her boy grows up. Years and years before he leaves home and gets married and brings her grandchildren to care for the way Granny cared for her. Now the house can go back to how it was before Garfield moved himself in. Just her and Bird.

The Best of Everything

She carries him into her bed and looks at his beautiful face, places her hand on the soft curve of his skull. While she still has him, he will have all of her love, every scrap, every kiss, every touch, it will all be for him.

8

For two years, life falls into a routine. Every single Sunday morning, Garfield knocks the door at nine o'clock, not a time he would normally have one eye open let alone two. He never misses. Paulette tells him he can come in and wait by the fire on cold days but he just shakes his head and asks for his boy.

But there's no need. As soon as Bird hears his father's voice he comes running downstairs and jumps into Garfield's arms from the third step and Garfield catches him like he's the most precious thing in the world, because he is. If Bird is watching the telly, he turns and runs to the door so Garfield can scoop him up and love him.

'You got everything, Bird?' he says, meaning hat and gloves and scarf, meaning Bird's favourite toy or his bike if they need it, meaning any little Lego model Bird has made for his father during the week.

Bird always races around and collects his things, eager to be gone, and Paulette makes sure the boy looks perfect from his head to his toes and everything in between. Garfield's family will see she's a good mother whatever else they think of her.

And Garfield never says a bad word to Paulette, never again. He puts cash in her hand as soon as she opens the front door and even brings her a birthday card on the right day. It just said 'from Garfield' inside. No kiss, nothing. What else can she expect?

He's cut his hair close and shaved his scraggy beard. He's wearing his glasses full-time now so he's lost that side-eye look. When his job tells him he has to work weekends, he hands in his notice and gets another one. Says nothing can interfere with his time with Bird. It's hard to admit but Paulette underestimated the man. She has been as wrong about Garfield as she was about Denton. He's been there in the background, a witness to all the big events in her life. Denton's death and her depression, Bird's birth and all his milestones, crawling, walking, teething, speaking. And then there's their shared love of the boy. Sometimes, she finds herself crying about it, the same tears she would cry if her heart was broken, but it is not.

It's nearly Christmas, the tree is up and there's tinsel around the front door. Garfield comes and Paulette waits up by the front door with him while Bird runs upstairs to get something. Paulette smiles maybe the first loving smile she has ever given him.

'You sure you don't want to come in? It's cold and wet out here.'

'I'm all right,' he says.

'He's got a Christmas present for you, Garfield. You have to pretend not to see it.'

'Okay.'

'It's a pair of gloves. It was his idea and he chose them himself from the catalogue. They'll be good for work.'

'Okay.'

She watches Garfield, impatient to see Bird, eager to hold him and love him and show him off.

'You're an example to him, Garfield, how a father should be.'

He nods. 'I'd like to keep him overnight next week. New Year's Eve. It's a family thing.'

'New Year's Eve?'

'I'll bring him back by six o'clock the next day.'

Bird runs downstairs with a package he's trying to hide behind him.

'Found it, Daddy!'

Garfield buttons Bird into his coat and makes him put his mittens on and picks him up, kisses him on the cheek.

'He'll be back by six?' Paulette asks.

'That's what I said. It's a family day at my mother's. Bank holiday. Everyone will be there. I want to keep him overnight.'

Bird jumps up and down. 'Can I, Mommy?'

'One night?'

'Yes, Monday, Paulette.'

She nods. She swallows and puts on a good smile as she waves goodbye.

The Sunday house is never right without Bird and usually Paulette goes out, sometimes catches the bus up to the reservoir where there's a café selling nice West Indian bun, sometimes meets one of her friends, but they all have kids of their own and a man so they never stay long and some of them even go to church and call it a 'family day' which means Paulette isn't included. But when Marcia asked her to come round for a little Christmas drink, she decided to put down the grudge she'd had against her and turn up with a card and a bottle.

There were enough people there so it felt like a proper party with music and drinking. The food was plentiful. Marcia had gone to a lot of effort. There was a nice man there she recognized from her past when she used to go out dancing who sat next to her and made her laugh. He talked to her most of the evening and let her know he was interested but she told him she was busy with her child and her job and didn't have time for a man in her life. She took the bus home and got off early.

Wherever she goes, it always includes a walk by the shirt-and-tie man's house. There's nothing to see except the curtains are open. The curtains are shut. The lights are on. The lights are off.

Monday. New Year's Eve. She can't blame Garfield. It wasn't unreasonable for him to take Bird overnight, but he didn't factor in Paulette on her own on the same evening when the whole world is in celebration, turning from 1979 to 1980. Paulette doesn't love Garfield, she doesn't want Garfield. And the man is doing the right thing bringing his son to his family and making a place for him. But still.

So. Paulette takes stock. There must be better to come.

England has got a woman prime minister for the first time ever which is progress however you look at it. Times are changing and she must change with them. Look to the future.

Paulette is thirty-six years old. Still got a good shape but wider on the hip these days and her chest is pulling on the seams of her uniform. Still walking at a good stride and not out of breath if she has to run for the bus. Hair and face in reasonable condition considering she doesn't spend much time on either of them. One son, God bless his soul. No daughter and no more children on the horizon. A job she's good at that pays the rent. Little bit left over. Only a few friends but none of them deep in her heart because it's still full of Denton. Lord God. She hears Garfield like he's sitting next to her. *Denton, Paulette? You really bringing Denton into this after so long? What kind of woman holds a place for a man who never loved her?* Paulette, that's who.

To see in the brand-new decade Paulette has bought a brand-new bottle of rum. She likes to have a little nip some nights when it's dark outside and Bird is at Garfield's or fast asleep upstairs. It sits on the coffee table in front of her, seal intact. A nice heavy tumbler next to it. She's bought a crisp, new notepad and took a biro from the ward. She puts a cushion on her lap to use for a desk because this is serious now. She's going to make a list of all the things that are going to change in the next ten years. All right, start with one year and work her way up.

First. No more chocolates and sweets from the staffroom. Anytime someone comes to collect their father or brother or husband they put a box of chocolates on the side and every time Paulette walks past her hand moves into the box without her even thinking. That has to stop. She writes *No more automatic eating.*

Next is saving. If her boy wants to go to university then why shouldn't he? Not one single person in her family or even any of her friends have been to university but Bird is different. The boy is bright, everyone says it, and he could even end up a doctor or a lawyer for all she knows. The idea that the boy could have unfulfilled dreams is a horror to Paulette. Yes, she must be saving each and every week. A little bit here and there, and if Garfield puts in a share, between the two of them the boy can go as far as he likes. She writes *New bank account for Bird.*

On the telly, there's a singalong with two comedians. Paulette hums under her breath. She picks up the bottle of rum. It's Appleton's Special 8 Year Reserve, expensive. When they first got together, she and Garfield grew more than a little fond of Mr Appleton, but as soon as their son was born, they only used to drink on special occasions. If she doesn't break the seal, she could keep the new bottle for a present or even for her birthday in the autumn. But if she opens it tonight, feeling like she does, then she's likely to drink a good clean half.

She puts it back on the table. What about a cup of coffee? It's too late for caffeine but she's not going to sleep anyway so what's the difference? Bird will be in a strange bed and maybe he will miss his mother, and if Garfield has to bring him home in the middle of the night, he'll find her wide awake and waiting.

No late-night drinking.

Big Ben sounds the end of the year. Both hands of the clock pointing straight up and Paulette knows she must start again. She puts her hands together in the same way as the clock and promises herself, here and now, before the bells finish, she must make a new life for herself, free of the memory of Denton, and look to Bird's future. And maybe even her own. It's not too late.

She picks up the pad and writes *Find love*.

She unscrews the bottle of rum and pours barely a quarter-inch into the tumbler. She holds it up to the telly just as the last bell sounds.

'To me and you, Bird,' she says quietly and throws the rum straight down.

She claps her hands together. 'Happy New Year.'

But that night in her bed, with a third of the bottle gone and a little tot in a pretty little wine glass next to the bed, Paulette loosens the lid on her memories and slips easily, willingly down the road to Denton.

1971 is good and hot. For the first time in her life, England feels like St Kitts, dry earth everywhere you look, cracked and dusty. She's just off her shift, still in her brown uniform, stinking of disinfectant, wearing shoes so sensible they could pass A-level maths. She's squinting to see if the bus on the horizon is hers because she's in a rush. Straight home, quick shower and then out with Benjie. Benjie is new, only two or three months they've been seeing each other, but he's nice and kind, got his own car, works as a mechanic in a good garage. Nice-looking. Bit short.

The car that pulls up by the bus stop has the music so loud she can barely hear what the driver is shouting to her. Must want directions.

She leans down and shouts, 'Sorry, what?' She keeps one eye on the bus and one eye on the extremely good-looking, high-quality man in the extremely good-looking, high-quality car.

'I said, I can give you a lift if you like.'

'Why?'

'Because it's hot and so are you.' The smile shows all of the man's thirty-two perfect teeth. She can't help but smile back.

'Boy, you must have better lines than that,' Paulette says and when she looks up she sees the bus is the 101 circular and not the 18.

'Come on,' he says, turning down the music which is a sweet lovers rock number she could listen to all night. 'You could be in town in ten minutes. Longer if you like.'

'I've got a boyfriend and I've just finished work,' she says.

'Two reasons to get home quicker.'

He turns the music off altogether and leans his arm on the open window. 'I've seen you here loads of times, you know. I beeped the horn once or twice and you never turn. I like that. You don't think anyone's noticing you, do you? But I see you, darlin'.'

'And all for nothing,' she says, but she's smiling.

'Tell me something,' he says, 'how come your boyfriend isn't collecting you from work? You think I would run the risk of a beautiful black queen getting away from me?'

He coaxes her in with his cheesy lines and blatant flirting. He talks all the way to town, charm dripping off his lips like coconut oil, says his name is Denton but she could call him 'sweetheart', says he's a man who's no good on his own, needs a woman in his life, it could be her. Every time she tells him to stop, he makes her laugh despite herself, drops her off right in front of the cathedral and drives away. The next night, same time, he's waiting with the engine running. Says he's been thinking about her, says they could go for a little spin, nurse's uniform or not. He coaxes her in. Kisses her. Tells her he works away and has only a couple of days off every month. And again, another night, he takes her all the way home and, as he drives, he tells her about his dreams. Tells her she could be part of them. Then he's gone.

Benjie lasted another few weeks but then Denton was back and soon enough he was in her bed and in her heart, coaxed and kissed and caught.

9

Bird must have managed to sleep right through at Garfield's so Paulette has the whole of the next day before he comes home. She can't do any more housework without going over what she's already done so she stays in bed late reading a magazine and then gets up and starts the dinner. She was going to braise some oxtail but oxtail needs twenty-four hours of rest to be at its sweetest. She should have started it the day before. So, she takes out the chicken legs seasoning in the fridge. Brown chicken and white rice is one of Bird's favourites.

One hour later, the Dutch pot is in the oven on low and the kitchen is pristine. It's much too early to lay the table so she puts on her coat. The Indian shop across from the park will be open, bank holiday or not. She can get some ice cream for Bird to have with a little bit of coconut cake. She's got all the ingredients for the cake which she can put in the oven soon as the chicken is done. The day is fine.

The park is full of families and couples. There are old people with young people and children and pushchairs, everyone all together for the holidays wrapped up good with Christmas-present scarves and bobble hats. The devil's wind is blowing but no rain and some bits of the sky are still blue. People have travelled up from the country to spend Christmas with the in-laws, with their married sister or brother, for the cousins to get to know each other. A woman smiles at Paulette as she walks past. No reason, just a smile, but Paulette can hardly smile back because the hard truth is she is jealous of the woman and the two children that hold her hands and the man that walks behind with the mother-in-law.

Right now, Bird is running around screaming and laughing with cousins Paulette doesn't know because she never got invited to meet them. And why? Because Paulette didn't want to. And why? Because her and Garfield were only ever temporary. He knew it. She knew it. His family knew it. And Paulette gets back what Paulette put in, which was precisely nothing.

But come on, Paulette! You just made a New Year's Resolution about the future being better. Fix up! Smile at people and put your face up to the sky where the sun shines bright every day of the week.

'Morning!' she says to the woman behind the counter, who smiles. 'Happy New Year.'

This is the kind of shop Paulette likes, tight aisles full of tins of food she's never seen before, strange vegetables and a whole row of spices that tickle your nose when you walk past. There's stainless-steel mixing bowls and mops and plastic toys, plugs for the sink and plugs for your kettle and, best of all, magazines.

Paulette takes her time. First of all, she looks at the Sunday paper headlines. Serial killers, war and strife, lots of pictures of the royal family because Prince Charles got himself a girlfriend, and a big earthquake that killed off a whole village on the other side of the world. God bless them all. Then on to the magazines, one by one. These days, magazines for women are expensive, the good ones anyway, but they know how to pull you in.

'Starting Your Best Decade – Your Thirties and Beyond.' Paulette flicks through the pages to find the article. According to *Woman's Realm*, Paulette can expect bodily changes and facial hair; her bones will weaken and her eyes are going to lose their brightness. But, on the flip side, Paulette can also expect a little more confidence and assertiveness. This is the time for making better life choices and choosing her friends more wisely. What a good article. She holds the magazine to her chest while she looks for another one. *Good Housekeeping* says that with very little money you can learn how to dress better for your age and make small changes to bring a bit of sparkle into your eyes. There's a recipe for sticky ribs and upside-down cake with tinned pineapple. And stuck on the front is a free gift of moisturizer and quiz book. Good. Paulette will treat herself to both. Why not?

She buys Neapolitan ice cream and a squeezy bottle of raspberry sauce. She buys a packet of plain biscuits, no chocolate and no cream filling, no sprinkled sugar on top and no jam in the middle. She will have exactly two with a cup of coffee when she gets back then seal up the packet and put it in the cupboard like normal people. Switch the gas fire on, sit on the sofa and try to relax for the rest of the day.

By the time she comes out of the shop, the blue sky has gone, people are rushing out of the park. The rain has come.

She carries the cheap plastic bag close to her chest to guard the magazines she should never have bought because she's supposed to be saving. If they get wet, they'll be ruined and it will all be a waste. She dashes through the park, hurrying now against the rain and the chicken in the oven that needs to be checked and uncooked coconut cake for Bird and also why didn't she bring an umbrella because when her hair gets wet it's another two hours to set it back how it should be.

She's just by the gate to the road, five minutes from home, when she sees him. Shirt-and-tie man. He's wearing a jumper and a jacket, and trousers that need ironing. He's walking slow, too slow for the weather. And beside him is the same little boy, bigger now but that's the only good thing she can say about the child. Skinny? The child looks like he never had a good meal in his young life. He's wearing a wool jumper right next to his young skin, a wet jumper two sizes too big. And the boy is wearing a hat that looks like it came clear from the First World War, green canvas with flaps on his ears and a tie under his chin. And some skimpy-looking canvas shoes. Short trousers. His legs and feet are soaking wet.

Shirt & Tie sees her. He stops like he's been shot and raises his hand, points at her.

And Paulette stops too. She feels the same old rage beating the hammer of her heart. 'What?' she says. 'What?'

Paulette knows the face of someone who's been too long crying or not sleeping or both. Shirt & Tie moves forward, both arms raised now like he's going to grab her up or, God have mercy, embrace her. Man has clean lost his mind, that's what is happening here. Paulette steps backwards and the man moves in closer. She can smell his unwashed self.

'What do you think you're doing? You fucking mad?' she says. And the minute the words are out of her mouth she remembers the boy. Paulette looks down at the child. His nose is running, pale green on his see-through white skin.

'You've got a boy,' says the man. 'I've seen you. You've got a boy like him.'

'And what?' she says.

'I can't do it. I can't do it any more,' he whispers, and he pushes the boy forward, nudging him towards her. 'Please,' he says. 'Take him.'

When she glances down, the boy gives Paulette a look that nearly splits her in two. He puts his hand out for her to shake and, without thinking, she takes it as if he's a big grown-up somebody.

'Good afternoon,' he says like he's sixty-five. 'My name is Cornelius.'

The name suits his outfit. And his little hand is cold as butter. Paulette can see the chest of the child heaving like his heart is breaking and he's trying to keep his pain in check. He drags his sleeve across his face.

She looks from the boy to the man and then walks around them. She would break into a run, but her legs are like straw. She turns at the gate and sees Shirt & Tie looking after her. She dashes onwards and looks back over her shoulder, sees the man walking away and the boy a pace behind him with his little head down on his chest.

Paulette opens her front door and throws the carrier bag on the sofa. She paces her living room, round and round, then looks out of the window. She has a drink of water. She goes upstairs and looks in the bathroom mirror. She opens the door to Bird's room. The bed's made and the toys are put away. She comes back down and puts the melting ice cream in the freezer and hopes it's still okay. She puts the biscuits in the cupboard. She sits on the sofa and puts the expensive magazines on her lap.

Straight away, she gets up again and looks out of the window. She draws the curtains and opens them again. That man has a fucking cheek. What was he saying? That Paulette should take the child? Was he offering her a child? Really? What was he doing? Who does he think she is? You can't just give away a child like it's a puppy you got for Christmas. The man is not right in his head.

She goes to the front door and opens it. Maybe he's left the boy in the park. Maybe he gave the boy to someone else. Any mad person could take a child. She puts her coat back on and runs to the gate of the park and looks up and down just to make sure the crazy bastard hasn't left the boy on a bench with a sign tied round his neck. By rights, she should ring social services and get the child put somewhere safe.

His little white face. His big, dark, dark eyes. The hand-shake. That stupid hat. The prickly wool of the jumper on his delicate skin. The water in the boy's eyes like he was holding in a month of tears. And the handshake. The handshake.

She dashes back home and remembers the chicken and throws open the oven door. Finished. She washes the rice for dinner, puts it in a saucepan with butter and salt. Won't take long. While the oven is still hot she can make her coconut cake. She leaves the butter out of the fridge for it to soften. She's got some cabbage to steam. She rinses it under the tap and stands gripping the edge of the sink. Who does he think he is? All right, so she's walked past his house a few times, but that doesn't give him the right to talk to her, put his arms out like the two of them are friends.

She can't rest. She has to think because sometimes Paulette gets things out of proportion. Stop and take it step by step. Was he really giving away the child? 'Please,' he said and pushed the child right up to Paulette's legs. 'Take him.' Did he really say that, maybe she didn't hear it right? The man talks posh so he could have said something else completely. Who would offer a living, breathing human child to a complete stranger? No. She must have it wrong. Did it actually happen like she remembered it?

Yes. Yes, it did. She looks at her hands and remembers the feel of the ice-cold little fingers in hers. She imagines Shirt & Tie telling him what to do, coaching him, rehearsing the scene. 'When you meet people, put your hand out and introduce yourself.' Just the same thing she says to Bird.

She'll do the cabbage later. She can't think. And she's not making no cake in this state neither.

She goes back to the living room and puts on the telly. Football. The magazines. Yes, let the magazines tell her how to make her life better and lose half a stone in a week. There's a knitting pattern on the back two pages for a child's jumper. A picture of a little boy with pink cheeks in a Fair Isle polo neck, his golden hair parted on the side, a glint of light in his blue eyes. Every child should have a jumper like that for the winter. She closes it quick and turns the telly over. Yes, good. A black-and-white afternoon film, England 1955, one of them family dramas with a good story and good acting where you can lose track of your troubles. She settles back on the sofa to watch it.

A lingering shot of a back-to-back terraced house in a dark industrial city. A young pregnant girl and her poor boyfriend walking the wet streets trying to work out what to do. The girl says she'd be better off dead but the young man takes her hand. 'We'll find a way,' he says.

Paulette doesn't even wait to see what happens. She runs upstairs, flings open some drawers in Bird's room and comes back down with a half-full bag of clothes. She goes into the kitchen and takes out her second-best Tupperware. She loads it with half the chicken and the barely cooked rice and puts it in another carrier bag with the biscuits on top. As a last thought she throws in a carton of orange juice.

They could be anywhere. What happens to the last puppy you can't find a home for? No, no, don't think like that, Paulette, always imagining the worst. But he could have walked the child to the park and left him there. Maybe she should have taken him after all. He was offering her a boy just like Bird, and she wasn't paying attention. She could see things weren't right in Shirt & Tie's house and she did nothing. Maybe she's missed the chance to save the boy. There's a quiver in her heart as she drags her coat on and doesn't even button it up. She runs to the park first and scans across the lawns. Nothing.

She runs back, round the corner and over to the other side of the estate. She raps his door hard with the edge of her knuckles and, as soon as Shirt & Tie comes to the door, Paulette hands him the bag with the dinner.

'It's hot. Eat it now.'

She puts the bag of Bird's old clothes just inside the door and raises her finger in the man's face.

'Listen, no matter what is wrong, you better fix up. Don't ever let me see that boy out in the cold again. And feed him properly. And dress him warm. And if you don't, I'll call the police. I'll call social services.'

She walks halfway down the path and then walks back to him. 'And if I hear you've hurt him or given him away or touched one single hair on his head, it's me you'll answer to and that's worse than any policeman. You get me?'

She's shaking when she gets home. Where was the boy? She didn't hear any noises from inside the house but then she didn't give Shirt & Tie any time to answer. All she can do is hope. She rides the spirals of worry until Garfield knocks the door at five to six. It's all she can do not to grab her child and kiss him from head to toe. She opens her mouth to tell Garfield about the white man giving away his boy, but Garfield gets in first.

'Next week, I want to take Bird to see my girlfriend.'

Paulette says yes before she can really take it in. Must be serious. Maybe she is—

'She's pregnant.'

'Oh,' is all she can manage to say.

'Bird will have a brother or a sister in a few months' time. I don't want it to be a surprise for him. I want them to know each other.'

'Yes,' she says and bends down to unzip Bird out of his jacket. She fusses over him until she can find her tongue.

'I'm pleased for you, Garfield. Who is she?'

'No one you know. Her name's Angela. He won't want to eat when he gets back. It's a party. My mother and sisters will be there with their kids. Everyone's coming. So, if I'm a bit late—'

'That's all right,' she says. 'He'll be ready. See you next week.'

She closes the door behind him.

Everyone's coming is it? Garfield's mother who never really liked her because she knew about Denton and suspected Garfield was the consolation prize. And Garfield's sisters, church-going, good girls with pressed hair that wear light brown tights on their dark brown legs. They'll all be there greeting Garfield's new woman with hugs and kisses. And she imagines Bird at the centre of things as usual, telling his little stories from school, talking about his rockets and spaceships and his favourite programmes, saying Nana and Auntie and Uncle.

Everyone's coming. Paulette has no Nana for Bird. No aunties because the two of them are in America now, thirty or forty years older than her, a generation and a thousand miles away. And she's got a half-brother still in St Kitts, but they never did see eye to eye on account of Paulette's womanizing father. There's no 'everyone' on Paulette's side.

She puts Bird straight in the bath so she can play with him and make sure he's all right, fit and healthy from the top of his head down to his little toenails. Skin still soft, plump arms and sturdy legs. She soaps him and oils him and runs her palms over his smooth back and shoulders. She pulls the plug and wraps Bird in a warm towel, sits him on her lap and wonders about the thin white boy with the cold fingers. Cornelius. What kind of name is that for a young boy? She closes her eyes and holds Bird close until he starts to wriggle.

'Can I stay up with you, Mommy?' he says.

She puts Bird in brand-new Mickey Mouse pyjamas and brings him downstairs so he can eat his bedtime snack in front of a video. That night, she gets up to watch him sleep.

10

Maggie comes round to ask her to keep her eye on the house while she takes the kids to Wexford for a wedding.

'Here's the keys in case you need them.' She's in the kitchen tapping her finger on a cigarette as the ash tips into a little glass dish Paulette bought specially.

'Listen to this,' says Paulette and just as she's about to tell her about the little boy in the park and the madman who was with him, Bird comes running into the kitchen.

'I'm going to have a baby brother or a sister,' he says and he shows Maggie a picture he's drawn, a sort of stick man and woman and two little figures below them with the sun shining on a blue sky.

'Ah, that's grand, Bird.' Maggie raises her eyes to Paulette. 'And that's a lovely picture as well. You're good at your drawings, aren't you?'

Bird takes the picture back. 'And it's up to me what the name is. Daddy told me.'

'You're a lucky boy, all right,' says Maggie as Bird runs back to the telly. 'And Mammy seems to be taking it well too.'

Paulette kicks the door closed and whispers. 'He's excited and he's looking forward to it. Garfield told me a couple of weeks ago and, so long as Bird doesn't get jealous, it's all right.'

'And you're not bothered about it?'

Paulette shrugs her shoulders and puts the kettle on. 'You got time for a cup of coffee and a piece of fruit cake?' she says.

'I wish I did,' Maggie says, opening the back door, 'but I've left the girls on their own and we're booked on the three-fifteen coach to Holyhead. We can't miss it.'

'Wait!' Paulette says. She wraps the remainder of the cake in foil and puts it in a carrier bag. 'Take this for the journey.'

'I thought you were my friend?' Maggie says, frowning. 'There's a four-inch deficit in the size of my old party dress. If I sneeze, it will split the seams. And that's without a bloody wedge of fruit cake. You know the girls won't eat it, so it's just me that will die of diabetes.'

Paulette laughs.

Maggie is halfway out of the door when she says, 'What were you going to tell me, Paulette? Was it about the baby?'

'Yes, yes,' says Paulette. 'Go on. You'll be late.'

But it's not about the baby. Paulette can accept that because she knew it would happen sooner or later. She's not saying it doesn't sting, but it's the way of the world and Paulette can't change that. No, what Paulette wants to tell someone is about the little boy in the park. The whole episode makes Paulette look as mad as Shirt & Tie, taking food round and clothes and talking to the man at all after what he had done. She wanted to tell Maggie she's been thinking about the child at least twice a day, wondering if Shirt & Tie is looking after Cornelius properly and wondering who collects him from school and wondering if he's happy. He's not at Bird's school which means either he's too young, which doesn't seem likely, or the man has sent him to Brookhurst School, which is a bad move. None of her business but still a bad move.

The man is old, sixty, maybe even more, and the child is young, which means the mother was younger than him. Must be she left him with the baby and the man had a breakdown or something. The car crash was nearly seven years ago, though, and that boy can't be more than five years old even if he talks like he draws his pension. *Pleased to meet you.*

Paulette collects Bird from school on Friday. Even right at the beginning of his school career the boy has taken to learning like a duck to water. He flies out of the classroom door with his coat trailing behind him and takes the little bag of sweets Paulette always brings to start the weekend with a treat.

'You had a good time at school, Bird?'

'Yes, Mommy,' he says.

'What did you do today?'

'We did numbers and reading and I got two gold stars.'

'I'm proud of you,' she says and squeezes his little hand, feels his fingers warm and soft in hers. She doesn't really plan it, but they walk a different way home, fifteen minutes out of their way, right to the end of Shirt & Tie Avenue. She sees the lights on. She has more sweets in her bag. She has her son by the hand. The handshake.

She turns the corner before she knows what she's doing. She knocks on the door and the child opens it. He's wearing a mash-down uniform, top too small, bottoms too big. He has a little white shirt under his jumper and he's had a haircut. The man is making an effort at least. Paulette feels relief wash over her.

'Hello,' she says. 'Cornelius?'

The boy stares at Bird. Bird hands him a sweet with no rehearsal and no coaching.

'Thank you,' he says, but before he can take it, Shirt & Tie appears behind him.

'I came for my Tupperware,' Paulette says. It comes out too stark and too gruff, but she can't take it back.

'Of course, of course,' he says and goes back inside. Paulette doesn't wait to be asked and steps right into his hallway. Bare walls and a thin runner carpet underfoot. There's better carpet on the stairs and the whole place looks like it needs paint and wallpaper but she can smell food cooking. She walks into the sitting room. Gas fire on low so there's heat in the house and with a woman's touch the room could be cosy. There's a train track in the middle of the room, one red-and-black engine and a few yards of metal track. It's old but shiny.

'Wow!' says Bird. He runs over to it with the boy, who quickly picks up the little engine and holds it out to Bird.

'It's mine,' he says. 'But you can touch it.'

Then Shirt & Tie comes in with the Tupperware in a plastic bag. 'I should have returned this weeks ago,' he says. 'But I don't know where you live. My apologies.'

Paulette watches the two boys on the floor pushing the train around the track, their heads together, Bird still in his coat, his furry hood over his head. It will be too small for him soon, the right size for Cornelius.

The man takes a step towards her. 'And may I also just say that—'

'You can bring him round tomorrow,' she interrupts. 'About two o'clock. Fourteen Rosamund Grove. Other side of the park near the community centre. Second house by the corner.'

She takes Bird by the hand and walks to the front door. 'You have to come back for him, though. Two hours. Bring him at two and come back at four. I'll feed him. Fourteen Rosamund Grove.'

'Thank you,' says the old man. 'That's very kind of you.'

Before she leaves, Paulette bends down to the child and gives him a little bag of sweets from her pocket. 'Nice to see you again, Cornelius,' she says.

He takes the sweets with one hand and the other he puts out to be shaken again. 'You're welcome.'

11

The boy starts to come regularly once a week after school or on a Saturday. Shirt & Tie drops him off always a bit too early and collects him a bit too late, but soon the boy and Bird are tight like brothers. And under Paulette's hand, Cornelius is filling out, nearly as big as Bird. He's got a little colour in his cheeks and, as soon as he comes through the door, whatever the boy is wearing comes straight off, goes in the washing machine on a short wash. She dips the two of them in the bath with blue bubbles and plastic toys and puts them both in pyjamas, lets them play on Bird's bed. Sometimes, the boy's clothes are still damp so she lets him wear something Bird's growing out of. And, on top of that, she always manages to make sure he has a nice bag of food for later he can share with Shirt & Tie if necessary.

For October half-term she has him for one whole day and one of the weekend days. She cleans his clothes, feeds him till his belly's tight and ships him home. And she notices, as the weeks go by, that Shirt & Tie has tidied himself up – not much but he looks like he has both feet on planet earth now and again.

Slowly, over the weeks and months, Cornelius lets a few things out about Shirt & Tie and Paulette manages to make some sense of it. First of all, Shirt & Tie, Francis Bowen, goes by the name of Frank, and Frank is Cornelius's grand-father not his father. So probably this is the child of Shirt & Tie's son or maybe the daughter from the accident. Garfield said the girl got injured bad but young people bounce back. Maybe she's a wild girl now. Maybe she's in prison, maybe in an institution, maybe just run off and left him with the baby. Who knows how many children the man has. She has more respect for him now she knows he's taken on responsibility for the child even though he finds it hard.

Secondly, the man used to have money, used to live in Earlswood or somewhere up them ways where there are no cheap houses whatsoever. And he used to work in an office, an accountant or something.

Lastly, he takes tablets but that's not news to Paulette. Sometimes they work, sometimes they don't. And when they don't, Cornelius can't make noise and has to go to bed early. His grandfather can't be disturbed. When his head is function-ing, Shirt & Tie reads books to Cornelius and tells him about the olden days and he does some kind of bookkeeping on piecework but there's not enough money in it and he always tells Cornelius they have to be careful because money doesn't grow on trees. Cornelius said he knew that bit already.

What Paulette doesn't know is why he's living in a council house on a bad estate and how come he fell so far. But again, none of her business.

Maggie comes up with far-fetched stories that don't make sense. 'He could be a gambler. Maybe he gambled his big house away and his daughter went on the game to make ends meet.'

Paulette is sitting in Maggie's untidy kitchen. Dishes in the sink and food left out on the side, a mop bucket of cold water left in one corner of the room and an enormous basket of ironing that Maggie is trying to whittle down between cigarettes. Paulette is folding the things that don't need to be pressed.

'The man's carrying some heavy load, Maggie. But the specific details I don't know.'

'Well, if you ask me, it's the kind that all men have. They need a woman to do the hard yards and without one they stumble from one crisis to another. And you've rescued him with your cooking and childcare. He should be grateful.'

'It's for the child, Maggie. Him and Bird are best friends now.'

Maggie raises her eyes as she tests the heat of the iron. 'You need a medal if you ask me. Or a bit of payment. Or a sainthood. Or all three.'

That night, Paulette lies in bed thinking about what Maggie says. Because she's right.

Whatever ails Shirt & Tie ails him and there's nothing she can do about it. She's not a doctor and she's not a psychiatrist. Sometimes when he comes to collect Cornelius, he looks like he hasn't slept in days, big black rings round his eyes. Other times he looks like he woke up five minutes before, puffy-faced and pale. The most important thing as far as Paulette is concerned is Cornelius. At least the boy seems to be happy and has even stopped the handshake business. Now, he gives Paulette a kiss on the cheek.

He started calling her 'Auntie Paulette' but one day out of the blue when Shirt & Tie has gone and Paulette thought he was upstairs playing with Bird, she turns round and there he is, on his own.

'Are you my aunt like my Aunt Clare?'

She shakes her head. 'No. It's just what children say to be polite.'

'But it's not true.'

'No, it isn't.'

'I don't want to say it any more, then.'

Paulette smiles. The boy has too much personality for his own good. 'So what do you want to call me?'

'Mum.'

Paulette looks at him, hard. His face is fresh and clean, pink in the cheek; his thick hair with flicks of white and gold is getting long again, needs a good cut; his eyes are sharp like two needles.

'That's only for Bird, Cornelius. You have your own mother.'

'No,' he says. 'No, I haven't.'

'Well, she might not be here right now, Cornelius, but everyone's got a mother.'

'No, she's dead.' He says this looking right into Paulette's face, plain and straight.

'Well,' says Paulette, 'you've got a father, haven't you?'

'No,' he says. 'No, I haven't because no one knows who it is.'

Paulette looks at him, too much information and too much understanding of things he should never have to know.

'You've got Frank,' she says, smiling, but the boy's eyes darken.

She puts her hand on Cornelius's cheek and he bends his head to it, closes his eyes like he could fall asleep then and there. She kisses him and holds him close.

'You can call me Pea,' she whispers. 'Sweet Pea.'

She goes into the kitchen and he follows, winding around her legs like a hungry cat.

'You want a snack, Nellie?'

'Yes, please, Pea.'

Paulette smiles. The name sounds sweet from the boy and it's many years since she heard it. 'Crisps or a biscuit?' she says.

He takes both from her hands and, with the biscuit half in his mouth, he says, 'Thank you, Sweet Pea.'

'Upstairs now, Nellie.'

For some reason the boy makes her happy. Talking with him is different to talking to Bird. Nellie is a man already, just needs the extra height. When he's with Bird he's just a normal little boy, but with Paulette, it's like the two of them know each other from some other time, like they have found each other again.

He will do something big with his life, Mr Cornelius Bowen. Or he will be so much trouble she will wish she had never known him. One or the other.

Then Christmas comes and what can she do? You think Paulette can just cook a big six-person turkey with macaroni cheese, roast potatoes, sprouts, carrots mashed in butter, mini sausages, gravy made with the sautéed giblets spiked with sherry and black pepper, handmade stuffing and all the different bits and pieces, and then sit down with Bird to tuck in knowing twenty minutes down the road the underweight Shirt & Tie is having beans on toast with little Cornelius? Paulette has been sighing over it since autumn time and, the closer Christmas gets, the less she has a choice. The 20th is a Saturday. Shirt & Tie brings Cornelius to the door.

'Nellie!' Bird pulls him upstairs. 'I've got a new car and . . .'

Shirt & Tie hovers by the door and then says the usual.

'I'm very grateful. He really enjoys it here. Thank you.'

Before he can turn to go, Paulette clears her throat and hopes it doesn't come out too reluctantly.

'What are you doing for Christmas, Frank?'

'Christmas? Well, I hadn't thought. It's a little while away yet, I think.'

'Days, Frank. Five days.'

He looks down. 'I see.'

'Christmas dinner?'

'Well, of course. He'd be very happy to come.'

Paulette raises her eyebrows. 'Both of you, Frank. You can come as well.'

She sees a little light in his eyes, no more than a flicker. 'Ah! That's extremely . . . thank you. If you're sure . . . thank you.'

'I'm sure,' she says.

But Paulette is not sure at all. On Boxing Day, Bird will be at Garfield's house for a whole twenty-four hours and she could have Christmas Day for just the two of them on their own. She's got an invitation from her second cousin in Manchester who she hardly ever sees on account of the woman being too holy for her own good but she could take Bird up there on Christmas Eve and stay the night. And Marcia keeps an open house, anyone can pop in and get a dinner and a drink, maybe Bird would like to be surrounded by noise and other children, but instead Paulette will be sitting down to a long, long meal with a strange old white man and a boy who by rights should be living with someone else, in a family with his own mother to tuck him in come night-time. But in her heart of hearts, she knows this is the right thing to do. Thy will be done.

Three o'clock she said and for once in his life Shirt & Tie is late. Five past three, ten past, quarter past. Finally, the door knocks.

You couldn't call them twins, of course, more like the three stages of man with the middle one missing. Two shirts, two ties, two jumpers and two anoraks. He's bought the boy new shoes. His own have been polished. Nellie has mittens and the old man is wearing oven gloves. He holds out a round cake in a tin then withdraws it immediately.

'Rather too hot at the moment,' he says. 'We had to wait for it to be cooked. We timed it but may have been somewhat over-optimistic.'

'Come in,' says Paulette, vowing to eat a good piece of that pale cake no matter what it tastes like. It has cherries on top which she hates, burnt cherries clustered together in the sunken middle. Yes, yes, she will eat it covered in ice cream and chocolate sauce if she has to.

Paulette has dragged the kitchen table into the living room for the occasion. The fire burns low and the television is on showing people singing hymns.

Shirt & Tie is mesmerized by it. 'Ely Cathedral,' he mutters. 'The Massacre of the Innocents.'

He puts his hands together and for a minute Paulette thinks he might ask her to pray, but he washes them over one another, and then looks at her.

'We went to the cemetery this morning, of course.'

Paulette doesn't know anything about the 'of course' bit of the conversation because he's never directly told her anything and today is not the day for confessions and sad stories, so she says nothing. He murmurs along with the Christmas carols, little notes and words escaping from time to time, while Nellie and Bird play on the floor.

Nellie is so handsome now. His strong face, his heavy eyelashes, but eyes so serious he could be reading the six o'clock news. The boy will have to be careful he doesn't get lines in his forehead before he's a teenager. He's watching Bird demonstrate the flight path of his new rocket and then she remembers.

'Bird! Bird!' She points upstairs. Bird jumps up straight away, runs to his bedroom and comes down with a gift bag.

'It's for you!' he says to Nellie and puts the bag in front of him. 'Open it!' he shouts.

Nellie looks at the old man before he touches it. The man gives the nod, grave and reserved, and Paulette wants to nudge him and say, 'Come on! It's Christmas. Be excited for the boy.' But the handwashing is in progress and the man just stands like a lamp post in front of the gas fire, blocking out the heat.

The boy unwraps the silver car that turns into a robot and, as he transforms it, slowly and carefully, he begins to cry. Ah, Nellie. Paulette wants to bundle up the child and hold him tight and tell him that good things can happen, Nellie, that people love him and there is sweetness and laughter in the world. But he keeps his face down and Paulette doesn't want to embarrass the child. Bird sees his friend's tears and looks up at his mother. Paulette shakes her head. Say nothing.

'Come, Bird,' she whispers. 'Help me with the food.'

In the end, it's all right. Better than all right. The two boys make enough noise so the adults don't have to say too much. Paulette hears the music coming from Maggie's house and she's glad she has a little party of her own with laughter on the telly and children running around.

Shirt & Tie eats his food with perfect manners, resting his cutlery down between each mouthful, drinking his wine white-man style in the new glasses she bought and using the green paper napkin like it was made of silk. Whenever he speaks to Nellie, it's to say something about 'use the napkin, Cornelius' or 'slowly' when he's gobbling and 'sit up straight'. Soft voice but the words don't match and if Nellie is in any doubt about what to do, like when he's offered chocolate sauce on his ice cream, he just looks at Frank and, when the nod comes, the boy looks at Paulette. 'Yes, please, if I may,' he says.

And the man can eat. Lord God! The more Paulette offers him, the more he devours because it's clear he's never had good West Indian cooking in his life and his tastebuds are dancing.

'Maybe I will have one more,' he says every time. 'Thank you.'

And then, slow but sure, the food disappears down the man's throat. He eats Christmas dinner with every kind of side dish you could imagine, trifle with brandy and cream and a grating of dark chocolate on top, hard cheese and bun, crackers, crisps, nuts, sherry, the lot. And then it can no longer be avoided.

Shirt & Tie is sitting in the armchair reading the free newspaper. Paulette is clearing the table. She's been topping up Shirt & Tie with sherry every half-hour and topping up her own glass in the kitchen, wine then rum, but she's sober enough to remember the last course of the meal.

'Hope you've got room for some of your cherry cake, Frank,' she says.

He smiles like a man that hasn't used those muscles in a long time.

'Well, don't cut it on my account,' he says but Paulette reckons if she has to eat it, so does he.

'No, no,' she says. 'I'm sure you've got room for a little piece with a cup of coffee.'

She bustles around in the kitchen, clearing up as best she can so it's not too much for later. Fat snowflakes tap the windowpane like some Christmas from a film, the boys watching a cartoon on the television, giggling together on the carpet, the lid of the kettle rattling against the steam, and for all the world it looks like a family Christmas, like Paulette has an 'everyone' to call her own.

The cake is cut. It's dense but cooked and it smells all right. She carries the tray into the living room and puts it down on the table. She hands Shirt & Tie his piece and takes hers. They bite down together and lock eyes.

'Surprisingly acceptable,' he says.

Paulette can't help but laugh. 'I was thinking the same thing.'

12

High summer, 1981. Weston-super-Mare. The sea is grey and flat but the boys don't care. Paulette's made a picnic, cooking all evening, making sure she has everything. Curry patties she made by hand, not too much pepper for the boys and a couple of spicy ones for the adults. She put coleslaw in a wide-mouthed flask so it can't spoil and some boiled eggs in their shells because the boys like to peel them. She puts in a couple of white-man sandwiches – ham and cucumber – just in case, and a selection of little cakes made by Mr Kipling that Paulette thinks are a waste of sugar and butter, but again, some people like them, so.

For drinks, she's bought squash and cola and a little half-bottle of rum because you can get away with a midday drink if you're on holiday and this is the only holiday she will get for the year. And there's something about a drink out of doors in the sun, makes you forget your troubles and makes the world feel right.

The trip is organized by the church near the hospital. Every year they put on a coach for the community to go to the seaside – anyone can come, subsidized and everything. The way the church looks at it, you have a nice time at the seaside at their expense and then you might think about going to church on a Sunday to give Jesus the praise due to him. And also, sharing is the Christian thing to do, casting your bread upon the waters. So, here's herself and Frank in the canvas deckchairs you hire by the hour. Paulette sits in the sun, Frank in the shade.

The coach took two full hours and once or twice she noticed Shirt & Tie looking uneasy, like he wanted to get off. The two boys sat together and she sat next to Frank, hoping nobody thought she and him were an item. But then again, there are some strange combinations of family these days and people can think what they want. Every so often, she watched Frank feed tablets into his mouth when he thought she wasn't looking and swallow them down without water. She wanted to tell him it was all right and there was no need to be ashamed, but sometimes people need to be left alone.

When she told him about the trip, he assumed he was invited, like Christmastime, but really Paulette intended to take both of the boys on her own.

'Oh, that would delightful,' he said and she didn't have the heart to disappoint him.

So, they're side by side on stripy chairs, watching the boys splashing at the edge of the water, noisy, screaming, laughing. Sometimes a little fight breaks out. One of them will do something or one of them will cry and come running to her.

'Mommy! Cornelius hit me!'

Or 'Paulette, Bird won't share.'

Frank says nothing but looks at Paulette like she has the answers to the universe.

'Okay,' she says. 'You want to go home? Good, come on, we'll go back to the coach and—'

'No!' they cry and run off.

'They are good friends, aren't they?' says Frank. The man hasn't opened his mouth since they arrived on the beach, sitting in his cream jumper like he's watching cricket. 'I didn't have many friends when I was his age. But then I did have my sister, who always stuck up for me. That was enough.'

'Nellie! Bird! Here!' Paulette brings out the little shovels and plastic things she's been saving for when the boys get bored.

'Build a sandcastle there,' she says. 'In the shade. Look, right there where there's a nice flat bit.'

The boys take the buckets and spades and little animal moulds out of her basket and, before you know it, the two of them are squatting down chatting their childish nonsense.

Once they've settled, Paulette takes a bottle of carrot punch from the cool bag. Nice and chilled. She pours some into two cups. Then she brings out the half-bottle of Appleton's. Tips a good slug in each.

'Here, Frank,' she says. 'Try some of this.'

He sniffs his plastic beaker and smiles. 'What is it?' he asks.

'Liquid summer,' she says. 'Drink it.'

He puts it to his nose and takes a few seconds to have a little sip. Then he smiles wide. 'It's very welcome,' he says. 'Thank you.'

Hard to imagine Shirt & Tie as a boy on the beach. Hard to imagine him playing and running wild along the sand with his shirt off and wet sand clinging to his trunks. Hard to imagine him any other way than how he is. As for a sister, how come she don't visit and help him with the child?

She offers him a Mr Kipling French Fancy to round off lunch. Frank is a man who can't say no and since he's half Kipling himself she tells him to take two.

'Where is your sister now?' Paulette asks when she's had a good bit of the rum.

'Cornwall,' he says and then the man gets into his stride and there's no stopping him, talking slow, like he's reading from a book.

'We will visit her next week. Clare, that's her name, and Clive is her husband. And she'll take Cornelius until school recommences. He will have a lovely time. They live quite close to the sea. Not as close as this, obviously, but just a little way from a delightful beach where there are rock pools and so forth. We used to holiday there as children. My father was a man of habits who liked to return to the same place again and again and I suppose that's why she chose it when she got married. In fact, I was best man at their wedding. Clive was my best friend, you see. In all honesty, he is my only friend now. You see, since the accident, I tend not to see many people because, well . . .'

He breaks off and drinks the rum punch for a little while. Paulette says nothing because she can see he's not finished.

'And in Cornwall, being free of my responsibilities, well, being free of Cornelius so to speak, that allows me to go walking. It's the only opportunity I have all year to think, to really think. I don't seem to have enough time to consider things deeply these days. And it's only by thinking that one can organize one's life and put things into context. To make or at least to attempt to make sense of where one finds oneself. There are steps, of course, that bring one to the present but determining exactly what those steps are, well, that's quite a task and one which, which I . . . sorry, where was I?'

He glances away, a look in his eyes like he's concentrating on something he can hardly see, and then suddenly looks at Paulette and says, 'Yes, Cornelius will be with Clare and I will go walking along the cliffs. Polperro, I think, this year.'

'Good,' says Paulette and she settles back in her chair to let the rays and the rum massage her soul. She's just about to close her eyes when she notices a man and woman ambling past, hand in hand. Not young either, forties at least. The woman is wearing sunglasses and red lipstick with an off-the-shoulder sundress and their hands are swinging like they just met last week. Maybe they did. Maybe she's been swept off her feet the same way it was for her and Denton.

But the more she looks, the more she sees it's an old kind of love, comfortable and long-standing. Footsteps in time, easy slow walking, nothing to say because they can read each other's mind, because the love they have doesn't need words and chitter-chatter. That's what Paulette wants. Someone at your side, making sure you don't trip, or helping you up when you do. Denton is dead and Garfield couldn't fill his shoes, but maybe one day Paulette could be in a yellow polka-dot dress with a man at her side. Not too late, is it?

'Penny for your thoughts?' says Frank. And when she comes back to earth she sees the two boys digging a little canal to take seawater to their castle, the sun low in the pink sky and sand whipping a white froth on the gentle waves. She shakes her head to empty it properly.

'Nothing,' she says, but it's too sharp and too blunt and Frank looks down at his drink, quietened by her. A penny won't cover it, Frank. The man hasn't got enough money in the whole world to pay for what she has lost, what he took from her. Sometimes, she feels so vex with him she could rip into him and tell him some home truths and it's only his brokenness that stops her. 'Here,' she says. 'Have another drink.'

By the time they get back on the bus at seven o'clock, the two of them have drunk every drop of everything in Paulette's cool bag. She is nice and relaxed, Bird sleeping, his head on her lap, beads of sweat shining on the bridge of his nose. Across the aisle, Cornelius leans his head on the coach window, nodding forward every five minutes, and Shirt & Tie is trying to sit up straight, his head weaving and bobbing with tiredness. The man's been on a long trip, all the way back to his childhood before he lost his way. And he's polished off the rum and punch and all the cakes. He will sleep tonight, she thinks. Tablets or no tablets.

13

Garfield's mother dies. Sudden. Went into hospital for a little operation and never came out.

First Paulette hears of it is when Garfield rings and says he can't come for Bird on the Sunday. And the man never, ever misses a Sunday. For a split-second she thought this was the beginning of Garfield taking his eye off Bird now that he has a new baby girl. Maybe his new wife doesn't like Bird taking up Garfield's attention when there's a child of her own to consider. True to his word, he let Bird name her, Bird choosing Rebecca from the three names he was offered. Now every Sunday Bird comes home with stories about Becca this and Becca that and Paulette has to smile and look interested.

'Everything all right?' she asks Garfield, though she's already planning her extra day with Bird and can't say she's disappointed to have her son for a whole weekend.

'My mother,' he says. 'She passed yesterday.' He tells her the whole story with a wobble in his voice, a little boy again. 'It was supposed to be simple. Just her varicose veins, you know. They said it would be one day and then she'd be out but as soon as they gave her the anaesthetic, something went wrong, and she never came round. A reaction or something.'

'Garfield, I am so sorry,' Paulette says and she means it. 'If there's anything I can do, let me know. When is the funeral?'

'I don't know. My sisters are arranging everything. Couple of weeks, I suppose. Bird will be upset. I'll have to tell him.'

'You want me to do it?'

'No, no. I'll come round tomorrow after church and tell him myself. They're having a service for her. The house is full of people already and more to come.'

Garfield's eyes are red and swollen when he turns up the next day. Face like stone. Paulette, out of her good heart, puts her arms out and holds him as soon as he walks through the door, long and hard.

'Garfield,' she says. He crumbles into her, heavy, and holds her close.

The familiar feel and the familiar smell and the familiar way they fit. It's a shock to Paulette. They stand there in the little hallway tight together for a few minutes until Bird comes downstairs. He stops halfway and shouts.

'I'm telling on you, Daddy!'

They pull away quickly and Garfield beckons Bird down to him.

'You have to listen, Bird. Something important has happened. Come sit down and listen to me.'

Paulette sits next to him on the sofa and grips Bird's hand for comfort.

'What is it?' he says.

'It's Nana. She passed away. She went to hospital because she was sick but now she's gone.'

'Is she dead?' says Bird.

Garfield winces. 'Yes, she's dead. Gone to heaven.'

'Why are you sad, then?'

Paulette puts her arms around Bird and whispers, 'Because Daddy loved her and he would like her to be here with him.'

Bird smiles. 'If she's in heaven, it's better,' he says. 'Can I take my Transformer with me, Mom?'

Garfield takes a deep breath. 'I can't take you with me today. I've got running around to do and lots of people at the house and—'

'I want to come with you!' Bird shouts. He stands up and stamps his right foot down on the carpet, his hands rigid by his sides. 'I want to see Becca!'

Garfield gathers him up and holds him, strokes his head. 'Ssssshhhh,' he says while Bird tries to wriggle away. 'Hush now, Bird. Hush up,' and Bird groaning and trying to fight his father.

Paulette watches the temper subside against Garfield's love and certainty. She sees Bird go limp and lean against Garfield's chest, trying and failing to keep the crying inside. 'But I haven't seen her for ages!'

'Sssshhh, sssshhh, sssshhh,' he says. 'Just wait until next Sunday, Bird. You know who else will be there?'

'No?'

'Rupie and Joshua and Bobby and his sister, remember his sister? The one that made you laugh? Remember? They'll all be there and June and Colin. And Uncle Terence, with the tricks. Remember the tricks with the sweets?'

Bird wipes his nose and starts to giggle and she sees Garfield shove down his grief for the child's sake and bring him back to himself, the good-mannered, sensible boy he is. Garfield puts Bird on his knee and plays with him for a little while, tells him what they will do next time they're all together, until Bird is happy again.

When Garfield gets up to leave, Paulette holds his arm and tells him again, she's ready if he needs her help.

'What do you mean, help?'

'I could make some food, maybe a fruit cake or some punch for the visitors. You'll have a lot of people to—'

He shakes his head. 'Angela and my sisters got it covered. Everything is planned already. And Auntie June will be there too and Terence is a good cook. We're all right.'

'Good,' she answers. 'The offer is there.'

'We're fine,' he repeats. 'See you next Sunday. I'll come a bit early and I'll let you know about the funeral because Bird is coming.'

'Garfield, he's not even nine years old. It's a bit young to—'

'Paulette, Bird is coming. He'll need a black suit and a shirt and tie. New black shoes. If you want to help, you can buy them and I'll bring you the money when I come.'

It's a Saturday morning, three weeks later. She watches Bird walking away down the path in his black suit and new black shoes. Growing up. She can see the man in him starting to take shape.

'Bye,' says Paulette but only Garfield turns round.

'Not sure what time he'll be back. I'll ring you.'

Bird is carrying a card for his aunties and a little posy of roses for the church and is under strict instructions to say 'passed' and not 'dead' because, as Paulette knows, dead is a harsh word when you're not ready for it.

She closes the door and ten minutes later there's a knock. She half expected it to tell the truth. On a day like today when everybody's emotions are high, high, high, what could be more natural than for Bird, who is a sensitive child, to get upset and need his mother? To be honest, she saw it coming, and she's already got a black dress pressed and ready upstairs. She's got nice black shoes and a handbag to match, which she took out of the wardrobe ready. She didn't want to push herself forward, and it's true no one invited her, but when all is said and done, Bird is still a young boy. And don't forget, Garfield has another child to look after and Bird might be jealous no matter how well he's taking it. Or Bird might not get the attention he needs and, if that's the case, Paulette can come and sit at the back, keep out of the way and then take Bird home afterwards.

But Shirt & Tie and Nellie stand at the door and, as soon as it opens, Nellie dashes past her and up the stairs before she can speak.

'Bird! Bird!' he shouts.

Paulette looks at Frank and shakes her head. 'I told you, today is the funeral, Frank. Bird's not here.'

'Ah, did you?' he says. 'Did you? I'm afraid, I – I . . .'

Nellie runs downstairs and jumps the last two steps. He dashes past Paulette and into the living room. Dashes back. 'Where is he?' he asks.

'Nellie, he's not here.'

'Oh,' he says. 'I'll have to play with you, then.' He holds up the toy he's brought. Some kind of metal truck with big wheels. 'Look at this, Paulette!'

She takes the car but looks at the boy. Eyes black like coal, every feature strong and proud, nose, chin, lips, everything. Like pure, sweet, concentrated man, just add water to make him grow. And the way he looks at her, there's no words for it, but if she had to choose one it would be something like love. She takes his hand.

'Come, Nellie.'

Shirt & Tie seems relieved and turns to leave and she calls to him, 'I'll drop him off later, Frank,' and she closes the door.

She leads Nellie to the kitchen and drags a chair to the sink.

'We're cooking,' she says. 'Paulette isn't good at playing cars.'

He puts the toy on the work surface and folds his arms. 'Cooking isn't a game,' he says.

'No, you like to eat, don't you? You like fried dumpling, don't you, Nellie? You like saltfish? You like chicken legs? You like corn porridge?' She says it all while she's taking ingredients out of the cupboard. When she turns round, he's smiling like a cat.

'Can I cut things?'

'Children don't use knives, Nellie.'

'But I'm going to be a soldier when I grow up, then I can have a gun and a knife. And I'm going to be in charge.'

'Well, for now you're going to be in charge of rolling dumplings. But first we have to measure out the ingredients. You can count?'

'Yes.'

'So, wash your hands and dry them.'

As he's washing his hands, he talks to her. Things he did at school and what is the best toy and what is the best programme and who he likes in his class and what he wants for his birthday.

'January tenth,' says Paulette. 'Nine years old. Big boy now, Nellie. And you're a clever boy as well.'

'I'm clever like my mother. Her name was Evie. She's dead.'

'She passed, Nellie. That's what you say. Not dead. Bird's grandmother has passed. Your mother has passed.'

'My granddad cries sometimes,' he says, watching the scales as the dial turns.

'What about?'

'Because he killed her.'

'Nellie, what are you talking about?'

'Eight ounces!' he shouts. 'Stop!'

Paulette looks at him. 'Your mom got hurt in the crash, Nellie. He didn't kill her. It was an accident,' she says.

She cuts in the cold butter and sugar and salt. 'Keep stirring,' she says, dripping the water in bit by bit. The dough starts to come together and she takes the wooden spoon off Nellie and brings it to a sticky ball. She dumps it on to the floured sideboard and shows Nellie how to make the right shape.

'Is this it?' he says, showing her a small round mess, half of it between his fingers.

'Perfect,' she says, 'perfect,' and kisses him on the cheek.

She has to keep the boy away from the hot fat when she's frying the dumplings. He talks almost all the time, to himself, to the telly, to his car, to Paulette. When he's sitting at the table in front of her, dipping the warm dumpling crust into the corned-beef hash, she asks him about his mother.

'How much do you know about what happened, Nellie?'

His eyes don't leave his plate. 'She's dead,' he says simply. 'When I was three, she died. I went to see her in the hospital and she died afterwards.'

'Is that what Frank told you?'

He looks up eventually and puts the last of his food into his mouth, balling it into his cheek.

'My grandfather said she died after I saw her in the special home, straight afterwards on the same day. I got scared because I thought it was my fault but he said the two things aren't related. He said just because two things happen next to each other doesn't mean anything. That's what he said. They aren't related. So it wasn't my fault she died. He said it couldn't be my fault anyway because it was his. Can I have some more, please?' he says.

She takes his plate and goes back to the stove. Frank is giving that little boy too much big-people information. If

Cornelius was hers, she would soften some of them details and let the boy have as much childhood as possible. Then again, Cornelius isn't like other children. As she's loading up his plate, she says, 'I hope your eyes aren't bigger than your belly, Cornelius, because sometimes food takes time to drop. You must eat slow,' but when she turns around she sees his chest heaving like he's running a race.

'What is it, Nellie?'

'Nothing.'

'You can tell me,' she says.

'When it's an accident you're supposed to say sorry,' he whispers.

'That's right.'

'But he didn't say sorry to me.'

Paulette puts her hand on his damp cheek and he lays against it, tears caught on his eyelashes.

'You know what?' she says. 'Your grandfather loves you, Nellie, and one day, when he's ready, he will find a way to say sorry to you. And to me.'

'To you?'

'Yes, Nellie. Your mother is not the only person who got hurt in the crash. My . . . my friend got hurt as well. And when he got hurt, I got hurt. I got hurt bad, but it's not every hurt you can see with your eyes.'

'But you're better now, aren't you?'

She looks at the boy and she knows she could tell him a fairy story about forgiveness and hope with a happy ending. But Nellie would hear the lie in her voice.

'Sometimes,' she says. 'Sometimes I'm better.'

He sniffs and drags his sleeve across his face.

'How many times have I told you to ask for a tissue, Nellie? Come,' she says. 'You can eat this later. Let's see what's on the telly.'

14

In her dreams, Paulette is trying to get that big pot from the back of the cupboard, Granny's old heave-ho bucket of a thing that only appeared for weddings and funerals and swarms of visitors. It's stuck against something hard and, every time she moves it, it bangs against a piece of rock. What a rock is doing in Paulette's cupboard is a mystery in itself because it's the same rock Paulette used to jump on in the middle of the stream that trickled down the far side of Granny's house, slippery on one side, worn smooth by the feet of children from ancient times, warm brown feet on a white pitted rock that rolled down the mountain a million years ago. Still the banging and still that old pot with the warped lid and the red plastic knob refusing to budge. On and on it goes until Paulette opens her eyes and hears Maggie at her front door, fist on the glass.

'Paulette! Paulette!'

It's ten o'clock at night and Paulette comes to, surprised to find the world black and not bright and her feet bone-dry and cold where they'd slipped out from under the blanket.

She hauls herself from St Kitts all the way downstairs and opens the door. Maggie rushes through it.

'I tried the back door,' she says, but—'

'What is it, Maggie?'

'It's Kitty, she hasn't come home. I don't know where she is at all. I've rang around everywhere. Where in God's name could she be at this hour? We had words and she took herself off but that was after four. It's twenty past ten now. Where could she be?'

This is not a Maggie Paulette has ever seen before, with the voice of a girl, no joking in it whatsoever, the Irish accent so strong that Paulette realizes that Maggie must temper it every day, square off the edges and say English words the way the English say them, just like Paulette does, tucking her tongue up nice and neat so people can understand her.

She puts her arms around her friend as she sobs.

'Come upstairs with me,' she says. 'I'll get dressed. We'll find her.'

The roads are white with frost, a slick of ice on shallow puddles. The two women grasp each other's arms as they slip up the grove to the main road.

'Thank you, Paulette,' Maggie whispers, her breath making a cough of fog under the street lights. 'Gemma's on a sleepover, thank God. I'm glad she wasn't at home when Kitty and me were tearing lumps out of each other.'

'Was it that bad?'

'It was.'

They huddle together and cross the main road. Maggie keeps shaking her head and taking a deep breath. 'Bird's at his dad's, is he?' she says. 'You're lucky to have Garfield around. That's when you want someone else doing half the worry with you so you're not alone.'

Paulette grips Maggie's hand. She won't say anything about the loneliness of the weekends and how she wishes, just for once, Garfield would forget to turn up, God forgive her.

'Yes,' she says. 'Let's go up to the shops first. She might be there around the back. I've seen some teenagers smoking by the chip shop, down the alley by the pub.'

'I don't care if she's smoking,' says Maggie, lighting up herself. She cups her hand around the cigarette like a builder and sucks hard.

'No,' says Paulette. 'It's nothing these days.'

'And she's fifteen,' says Maggie more confidently, 'I'd been on the fags for two years by then. So, if she's a chip off the old block, that's no worry to me. None at all.'

She's talking plenty now and sounds more like herself.

'And I tell you what else,' she continues, 'if she's been drinking, I'll say nothing. Just let her come home and we can sort it all out. I was giving out and shouldn't have been. Aren't the young ones now a terrible worry, Paulette? I don't know that I'm prepared for motherhood and I've been at it a good long while with more to come. Ah, but Kitty is me all over. Gemma now, she takes after my brother.'

And on she goes until they reach the shops. But there are no teenagers behind chip-shop alley and no teenagers in the pub. There are no teenagers in the off-licence and not a single person braving the arctic temperature at the bus shelter.

'The park,' says Paulette. 'Maybe they climbed over the gates.'

It's *they* now. The mothers have decided that Kitty is being led astray by no-good friends, boys and girls who have themselves slunk out of the house to smoke and drink and flirt without a wristwatch between them and no regard for a parent's imagination.

They peer through the railings and listen for noise of laughter or screaming but the park is wide and black and deep and dangerous, and maybe, if she was in there against her will, they wouldn't hear anyway.

'Oh, Jesus,' says Maggie, her breath ragged. 'Where can she be?'

'What's the last thing she said to you?' asks Paulette.

'She told me to fuck off and she said, "Your boyfriend can fuck off as well."'

'What boyfriend?'

They're walking round to the other entrance in case someone forgot to lock the gates.

'Michael,' says Maggie. 'A guy from the Irish centre, a right good laugh, and he's not my boyfriend, not really. He comes round and we have a drink and he stays over if he can. And that's it.'

Paulette says nothing because Maggie's never mentioned no Michael in all the conversations they've had and she's been seeing him long enough to invite him into her bed. They rattle the chain and the enormous padlock. They grip the ice-cold bars and squint into the darkness. Nothing.

'Can you climb over?' says Paulette.

Without another word, Maggie has one foot on Paulette's open palms and another on top of the fence. She clings on like a chimp, like an escaping prisoner, swinging her legs up and over, dropping on to the grass on the other side. She groans.

'Maggie! Maggie!' Paulette wants to laugh. She cannot. 'Maggie!'

'We're fucked now, Paulette,' Maggie shouts. 'I've broken my back.' Maggie is rolling from side to side, holding her knee. 'And I've dislocated my hip.'

Paulette bites her lip. 'Can you walk? See if you can stand up.'

'Call an ambulance. Call all the emergency services, Paulette. I can't feel my legs and I've lost my shoe. I might have wet myself when I fell.'

Paulette makes a noise in the back of her throat to keep the giggle where it should be when a girl is missing and someone is trapped behind locked gates.

Maggie starts to laugh. 'Christ, how will I get back? You didn't think of that, did you, missus? Just threw me to the wolves.'

'Maggie, you have to stand up,' Paulette says. 'You'll catch cold. Go to the bandstand and see if she's there.'

Maggie hobbles to her feet and brushes at her jeans. She puts her shoes back on and says, 'What if I'm scared?'

'You?'

'First time for everything,' she says as she disappears into the dark. Paulette sits on the low wall and hugs herself.

She looks up and down the road to make sure no police are coming, although maybe for once the police would be a good idea. If it was Bird missing, she would have rung the police long time. And anyway, what's Maggie doing bringing a man into the house when she's got young girls? No surprise her daughter doesn't like the idea of a strange man in her mother's bedroom with nothing but thin walls between them.

She hears them coming before she sees them, Maggie asking Kitty over and over if she has anything to say.

'Like what?' says Kitty.

'Like sorry for a start. I've been out of my mind. Anything could have happened to you. I even called Gemma to ask if she knew where you were and now she's worried as well.'

'She hates him as much as I do,' says Kitty, and then they appear. Kitty with her arms folded, weaving and swaying, tipsy and sullen.

'Get up here on my hands,' says Maggie, knitting her fingers together, but Kitty jumps on to the wall and grabs the top of the fence. She's like a pole vaulter, flinging her legs behind her and landing soft as a gymnast on the low wall on the other side. She sees Paulette and starts walking away.

'Kitty, wait!' says Paulette after her but the girl saunters down the middle of the road without looking back.

It takes Maggie five goes to get out of the park with Paulette threading her hands through the railings and holding Maggie up until she can get a foothold, then, carefully, she steps on to Paulette's back and shoulders and she eases herself down on to the pavement.

It's not funny any more. They take off after Kitty, who disappears towards home. Maggie is calling her name over and over.

'Paulette, I'll give that girl a piece of my mind before the night is out.'

'Don't say nothing, Maggie. She's had a drink. Leave it till morning.'

'She's got no respect, that's her trouble.' Maggie's arms are swinging like she's going into battle. Paulette can barely keep up.

'Maggie, she's upset. When you get in, say nothing.'

'That's just it!' Maggie shouts. 'She's got no right to be upset. She's had me worried out of my mind because I dare to have a life of my own.' She stops suddenly and turns round. 'Or are you saying she's right? Is that it?'

'I didn't say nothing, Maggie. Just children can be funny about . . .'

'About what?'

'When you suddenly bring someone home and he's staying the night.'

'Suddenly?' says Maggie with her hands on her hips. 'Who said anything about suddenly? I've known him for years, and anyway, we can't all be fucking vestal virgins, Paulette, pining for a fantasy. And don't you dare sit in judgement on my parenting when you've spoilt yours rotten.'

Paulette stops in front of Maggie and shakes her head. 'Don't bring my son into this, Maggie. This is between you and Kitty. Nothing to do with me.'

The Best of Everything

'You just wait,' Maggie says, 'he'll break your heart,' and she strides off. Paulette watches her trotting after Kitty, shouting her name. She follows at a slow pace and when she gets to the edge of the grove she sees the lights on next door, upstairs and down.

At home, she puts the kettle on, makes a cup of coffee and adds in a tot of rum for the shock. Maggie so angry and Kitty running away like that. And Paulette ripped from her sleep and her good dream about her grandmother. And Maggie talking bad about Bird, who is sleeping somewhere else without a care in the world, who never brought a moment's trouble to anyone.

Early the next morning, Maggie stands at the back door with red eyes and black circles deep beneath them.

'Paulette, I'm sorry. I was out of order.'

'Yes,' Paulette says. 'Out of order and worried. You took it out on the wrong person, Maggie.'

Maggie takes her hand and holds it. 'Forgive me,' she says. 'And let me come in because I need to sit down.' She limps over to a kitchen chair. 'I've a million fractures and I think I caught bronchitis and acute sugar poisoning last night.'

'Sugar poisoning?'

'I took to bed with a tin of Quality Street and a packet of custard creams. I thought you'd have heard the munching through the wall. Will you put the kettle on before I die of consumption?'

15

It's Wednesday. Paulette runs for the number 18 bus that stands grumbling at the terminus with the doors open. It's a new one where you tap your bus pass on a machine. But Paulette hasn't got the new pass and she can't see anywhere to put the money down. The driver's an Indian man, white turban, beard, the whole works. He points to a metal chute and she drops her coins into the slot.

'Livery Street,' she says. 'I've put the right money in.'

'Which stop?' he asks, smiling. 'Livery Street is a long, long road. I could take you to the top of the hill but maybe you want to go up by the—'

'It's the same price, isn't it, no matter where I get off?' and she hears a curtness in her voice she didn't mean. He punches her ticket and turns to face the road. The bus starts before she can even sit down and she's jolted into a seat, untidy, embarrassing. She can't see his expression and she cannot apologize because all she did was answer his question and maybe he didn't notice, but all the same, it came out too sharp. She's tired, that's why. Last night she didn't sleep because of a little argument with Bird. Nothing much but the boy is ten now and using his lip like all boys do. Paulette is well aware that sometimes children fall into bad company and learn all kind of things but, all the same, it was unexpected from Bird.

It started when she went to collect him from the minder. Sometimes when she's on a certain shift, she's got no choice but to use childcare because Bird cannot walk home over the dual carriageway and cross main roads all on his own. It's just not safe. A girl got knocked down last year because the cars come too fast over three lanes and don't pay attention. So the childminder collects Bird and keeps him for just a couple of hours after school, one week in three. Paulette leaves work at five and goes straight to collect him but yesterday when she got there the woman told her Bird already left for home. She said he told her that his father had come to take him home and the woman believed him. Paulette didn't even stop to give the woman a piece of her mind and ask her why she didn't check but at the same time she wondered if Garfield had really come and taken him away. She sprinted all the way to her house, her heart hammering hard as she put the key in the door.

'Bird! Bird!'

He was in the kitchen, making a sandwich. One already in his mouth and another one he was cutting in half. 'Thank God, you're here,' she said, breathless. 'How did you get in?'

He pointed at the kitchen window he must have prised open, scuff marks all over the windowsill.

'You were late,' he said, barely able to speak for so much food in his cheeks.

'Bird! You can't come home on your own. You must wait for me. Didn't I tell you it's not safe with fools driving too fast. You can't cross that road on your own. And what is this nonsense about Garfield coming to collect you? You know that's not true.'

'I'm not a baby,' he said, putting the sandwich on a plate and getting a packet of crisps from the cupboard. 'Everyone else goes home on their own and I have to wait for her. It's stupid. Why can't I have a key? You've got a key, haven't you?'

Paulette folded her arms and reared back. 'What? Who do you think you're talking to? I said I will bring you home. And if I'm ten minutes late, you still wait. Do you hear me, Bird?'

Bird looked down at the floor. He held the plate with two hands. 'I don't like her food,' he said. 'She just sits down and smokes all the time. And all the other children are little. I look stupid when she picks me up.'

'You don't have to eat her food. I put a sandwich in your bag.'

'I ate that at lunchtime,' he said and then, quieter, 'Everyone will think she's my mom or something.'

'Bird, don't be ridiculous. She's white. When you start the big school, you can come home on your own. And anyway, that's not the point. You have to do what you're told.'

Bird raised his head and started eating his second sandwich. He went to the fridge and took out a carton of juice. He tucked it under his arm and went to leave the kitchen. 'Or what?'

Paulette put her hand out and stopped the boy from passing. 'Come again?'

'I said "All right".' He looked her full in the face, chewing and licking his lips.

'Go and sit down, Bird. And when you've finished eating, you can come and tidy this kitchen.'

He said nothing. He walked upstairs to his room where food is not allowed and she heard his door close.

On top of that, when she gets to work, Sister McKenzie says it's official. New rules mean everyone now has to do nights. Paulette's been half expecting it. She has avoided nights since she had Bird. By swapping shifts, doing extra when she can and cutting her hours back, she's managed to stay on days only even though it means less money at the end of the month. All the women auxiliaries are feeling the pressure, especially the ones like her with no man and young children at home, but the union says they have to accept it. Paulette has two options – no, three.

Option one, she looks for a new job. But well-paid jobs with holidays and benefits are hard to find. And at the end of the day, she's good at nursing. She likes people and she makes a difference. Option two, she gets a babysitter for Bird when she's working nights, someone to sleep over and make sure Bird gets to school in the morning. The boy is ten, but still. This is where Maggie would have come in if Maggie would offer, but every time Paulette hints at it, Maggie changes the subject. And Bird doesn't really like Maggie's house and he doesn't like Maggie's girls, says he's not comfortable there. The boy likes his own space. Or option three. She makes sure her nights are weekends only and asks Garfield to help.

So far, it's rare that Bird stays overnight at Garfield's house. They've only got two small bedrooms and the girl is in one. So, he only sleeps there when Garfield's woman is away with the child. But now Garfield is talking of getting a bigger house. They've saved up and put some extra on top of the money his mother left him. Says he's moving out towards the countryside and right at the same time that Paulette needs a babysitter. If the truth be told, whether she asks Garfield or not, Bird is going to be staying overnight once in a while anyway so she might as well bite the bullet and ask him.

Then, before she can say anything, Garfield breaks the news.

'I can't have Bird next week. We're moving on the Saturday and all day Sunday we'll be sorting the place out.'

'Oh,' she says, looking at Bird sitting in the passenger seat of Garfield's car, waiting for his father. 'That's come round quick.'

'But soon as we're straight, he can stay overnight. Spend a bit more time with his sister. Maybe stay a week at half-term and the holidays.' He looks Paulette straight in the eye to let her know none of his sentences finish with a question mark.

'All right,' she says. 'Just give me some notice.'

'I always do,' he says and takes a couple of steps down the path before he walks back to her. He keeps his voice low. 'Me and Angela got married on Wednesday. Registry office. Just the two of us, my sisters and Angela's parents. It was small. We didn't want no fuss because Angela is pregnant again and not feeling too good. It's another girl. We're telling Bird tonight so he might say something when he comes home.'

'Congratulations,' is what she answers with a good, broad smile. She waves at Bird and closes the door. She sits down slow in the kitchen. Garfield married. And another girl. Bird's sister is four years old now. Paulette hasn't met her, nor Garfield's woman, but Bird tells her the lady is nice, treats him good, so that's all she needs to know. Even at the registry office, brides wear a white dress, pregnant or not. And a veil sometimes. Paulette sees the little knot of guests on the steps throwing rice and confetti, Garfield holding the hand of his woman, his wife, the gold band on her finger. 'Say cheese!' The flash of the cameras and then a few drinks at home. Cutting the cake. Garfield got to the finishing line first.

As usual, Bird is happy when he comes home. When Bird tells her 'Becca did this' and 'Becca did that' it's all she can do not to tell the boy to be quiet, but it's just like Bird to be a good brother and show some interest in the child.

Then again, Paulette has to accept the facts. The reason she hasn't got a pair of baby girls is she just couldn't make it work with Garfield, that was that. Even without Denton's memory, Garfield and her were not right. She's not saying he's not a good father and maybe this woman really loves him. She snapped him up quick enough, almost as soon as Paulette gave him his marching orders. And now 'Angie', as Garfield likes to call her, is the one with the cosy family life, with a man to cook for and fuss over, someone to rub her back when she's pregnant and make mint tea to help with morning sickness. Paulette has to admit that the man has some good qualities, and sometimes when she checks on Bird sleeping she thinks she sees Garfield in him, but Bird's eyes are straight and his personality is completely different. He has light in his heart.

16

August. The beautiful summer just coming to an end. Saturday nights, when it's warm enough, Maggie comes round with a bottle of wine. Or sometimes she brings a small bottle of gin and an even smaller bottle of tonic for herself, and Paulette has Mr Appleton by the neck.

Gemma got a scholarship to a good school on the other side of town. The girl's an artist and the teachers told Maggie it was the right thing to do to let her go somewhere they would recognize her talent. So, Maggie's been paying out for the uniform, for school trips, for extra things she needs and bus fare every day. Maggie's daughter gets free school meals and a little grant from the council but it's not enough so Maggie's working at a launderette in the morning, cleaning in the afternoon and packing envelopes in the evening. They sit at Paulette's kitchen table with the envelopes in a box and leaflets on the table and their drinks between them, chatting about life and men and the future and the past.

Every so often they take a break outside and lean against the kitchen wall, heat still in it from the day. Because Maggie's girls are older than Bird, they're all right on their own, playing music in their bedroom or watching telly, but still Maggie leaves the back door open just in case. Paulette opens her door the same way and drags out two kitchen chairs on to the patio, listening out for Bird, frequency tuned to 'mother', and the two of them talk low so they can hear if they're needed. Rare for them to get interrupted. They ease their shoes off and splay their legs to get a little breeze on their sticky thighs. They sip their drinks, listening to Saturday-night radio, music to get you in the mood to go out for a boogie, but the two women just watch the ants going about their restless lives, they waft away a fly, they fan each other with bits of card. Sometimes, Maggie will suddenly get up and start weeding Paulette's two little pots, telling Paulette this one needs water or this one has finished blooming. Then she'll sit down and pour another gin and tonic, light another cigarette, and it's back to the envelopes.

Paulette empties Maggie's ashtray and puts it back on the floor between them.

'Sure you don't want one, no?' says Maggie, offering the packet of cigarettes to Paulette, same thing she does every time.

'No, no,' says Paulette. 'Haven't smoked since I got pregnant. Couldn't stand the taste and I wanted the baby born strong and healthy.'

Maggie taps her temple. 'I'd be very fucking unhealthy up here without the fags, I tell you.' She takes a long drag of her cigarette. 'And I've been smoking day in and day out since I was a girleen and my kids popped out all right. And neither of them indulges in the forbidden fruit as far as I know, but at this point, I'm going to assume I know nothing whatsoever about the two of them. Sly little vixens, they are. Twelve and sixteen now. Jesus. Where does time go? Is it speeding up or what?'

Paulette sips her rum and coke, rattles the ice against the glass. 'Some things feel like yesterday. Other things feel like a hundred years ago.'

'Know what you mean,' says Maggie. 'And Bird will be at secondary come September. He's going to Kingsley, isn't he? It's not bad there and at least it's nearby. Ah, the lot of them will be gone before you know it.'

Sometimes Maggie forgets that Bird is young and it will be a long, long time before he leaves home. Senior school first. Paulette has got him everything he needs for the new school year, uniform, coat, bag and shoes, trainers and pens and everything. Next week, she'll take him for a good haircut so, when he turns up, people can see he comes from a decent family. Garfield wanted to pay half, but she told him she had the money. Sometimes, he likes to push himself in where he's not needed. Sixth form next, because he's clever. Then university probably, with him coming home for them long holidays they get. He'll be twenty-one before she needs to think about him leaving her.

And Cornelius too, he'll be there, same school as Bird at last, the two of them in the same year but nearly seven months apart. Shirt & Tie better make sure Nellie is kitted out properly and not wearing no supermarket trainers or coat with the wrong logo. She could say something to him but she doesn't see him so much these days because Nellie comes on his own. And anyway, what would she say? 'Do not shame him or embarrass him, Frank.' Really and truly, it's none of her business.

'Might be moving,' says Maggie all of a sudden. 'Back home to Enniscorthy, God help me.'

'Only might or you really going?'

It's not the first time Maggie's said this. She gets down, same as Paulette herself. What woman doesn't want a little change of scene and a bit of a break from routine? You work, you cook, you clean and you bring up your children, you throw some crumbs to the wolf and you add all your bits of savings up so you can have a day trip come summertime and a drink-up at Christmas but, Lord Jesus Christ Almighty, now and again the routine can weigh heavy, heavy, heavy.

When Maggie stubs her cigarette out and doesn't light another one for a few minutes, Paulette knows it's serious.

'You see, sometimes,' Maggie says so quiet Paulette can hardly hear, 'sometimes you just get a yearning to belong, you know. England is better than Ireland money-wise and jobs-wise and schools-wise but my soul yearns to sit in a pub and know everyone else is like me. I want to talk my own fucking language and use my own fucking words and be totally and completely understood, you know?'

Paulette says nothing because the words don't matter and because Maggie knows the answer is yes.

'I want the craic. I want to be not different. I want to know what's beneath what people say because the Brits never fucking say what they mean, do they? It's like there's one sentence on top and an entirely different one hiding underneath and you only hear it a few days later when it's too late to answer back. And I want my kids to know who they are, for God's sake. Learn about their own history, not about that fat bastard Henry the Eighth who killed all his wives just because he could. Why do my girls have to know about him? Glorifying a woman-hating, all-powerful piece of shite who did nothing for no one. Why? And it's even worse when we do go home because they don't feel like they belong, and it breaks my heart.'

She's smoking now, talking a bit loud.

'I mean, don't you get homesick, Paulette? Because I fucking do.'

'Yes, Maggie,' she says. 'I know what you mean.'

Granny thinks it's a good idea. The minister thinks it's a good idea. Everyone thinks it's a good idea. People leaving St Kitts left right and centre because there are no jobs and Granny isn't getting any younger. Mrs Parchment in Small Heath has a room for them. Mrs Parchment, who Paulette has never seen and who has no first name, comes from Basseterre as well and takes Kittians into her lodging house in England for a small fee. Paulette is eleven.

'We only going for a little while, Sweet Pea. I'm a good seamstress and there's plenty work in England. Don't worry. It will be good for us. And when we ready, we come back.'

But when they come, Paulette can't keep count of the things she misses and the things she doesn't like and the things that aren't good for her. Never mind the cold, never mind the food, never mind the darkness and the noise, every time Paulette opens her mouth at school, there's someone there to laugh at her.

'Say it again!' says the girl in the playground. 'Go on, say it again.'

The only place she can speak is at Mrs Parchment's house but the old women are always talking together about people she doesn't know. Even when they go to church, where everyone is black, she's the odd one out because everyone has been in England much longer than Paulette and the children still make fun of her accent.

Soon, she learns that the more she keeps her mouth shut, the easier it gets. The less she mingles, the easier it gets. The quieter she is, the easier it gets. Paulette learns quick. You can nod and you can shrug. You can listen and see how other people talk before you open your mouth. You can take a back seat and don't push yourself forward. You can be clever but not too clever. Laugh but not too loud. And you can learn how to speak like a white girl, nice and slow with round letters and a narrow mouth.

But the little while stretches on and on. Granny goes back to St Kitts every couple of years and stays for months. When she comes back, it's always the same, how she misses her house and her garden and the sound of the river and that she's too old for the everlasting English winters. By the time Paulette is twenty-one, Granny has made up her mind.

'It's all right for you, Sweet Pea, you're young and you fit in,' she says, 'and you've got a good job now and a good future. And that's what we came for.' She puts her hand on Paulette's and squeezes it tight. 'I can't settle, Paulette. I'm going home.'

So, Paulette gets herself a little flat and makes friends and goes out dancing, and by the time Granny is back in her house with the shutters closed against the heat, no one would know how different Paulette sounded when she was eleven years old. No one would recognize the girl she left behind in her bedroom at the foot of the hill. No one would know that sometimes when she closes her eyes she can see the exact pattern on her blanket, the little blue knots of embroidery and the small mend in her crocheted coverlet. No one would know that all the English summers in the entire world would never make up for just one day from the childhood she took for granted. Light so white you had to hide under a tree, skies so blue, trees so green, the whole world bright like pirate's treasure, amber, rubies, sapphires.

17

It's November. She goes to church to remember her grandmother and because sometimes Paulette likes to sing a good English hymn. She says the Lord's Prayer like she was taught and squeezes her hands tight all the way through the blessing. Granny died before she could meet Bird but as sure as the sun rises, when the time comes, Paulette will be a good grandmother to her son's children. She had the best example.

The organ plays 'Praise My Soul the King of Heaven', one of Granny's favourites, and Paulette has to gulp a few times so she doesn't cry. The church is like cold storage. She sits near the back with a cruel draught whipping her from behind and the brutal ice of the stone floor creeping through the soles of her feet up into her chest. Two days later she gets a cold.

She calls in sick and stays in bed, wiping her sore nose with disintegrating paper hankies that turn to shreds on the bed. Paulette is never sick. Never. When last did she ever have a day off work? She can't even remember. She decides to succumb to the sickness and gives Bird money to go and buy her two magazines.

She reads every article. How to keep a man, how to wear pink lipstick and yellow shoes, 'Change Your Sofa, Change

Your Life'. She reads her horoscope twice. She underlines recommendations for books she will never read. She cries over an article about a woman who lost her new husband when he got cancer. She flips the magazines from back to front and as she clips her toenails short she reads the check-list for the perfect Christmas. When to buy your presents, when to order your turkey, when to make your Christmas pudding if you like that sort of thing and when is the earliest you can hang your Christmas decorations.

Paulette's never had another drawn-out Christmas dinner like the first one she had with Frank because the two of them go to Cornwall to the auntie's house every year now, thank goodness. When Nellie comes back, he tells her all about it, how he has to sit up straight and tell them everything he's been learning at school in such hard detail he wants to scream. He has to sleep on a camp bed in the conservatory, which gets cold at night, and then when it's time to go home, his auntie starts to cry and tells him he's a special child. If he's not out walking the cliffs, all Frank does is sit in a chair while people whisper in the kitchen about the disaster of the accident and how Frank should have been paying attention and, even though he's paid the price, it's ruined his life and it ruined his daughter's life and now it's ruining Nellie's life with no mother and no money and only Frank to bring him up. And on it goes while Nellie has to pretend he doesn't hear nothing because Frank likes him to be polite and invisible. Paulette might invite Frank and Nellie over in the dead time between Christmas and New Year. Make a nice dinner for them. Cold chicken and fried hake. Maybe try the new salad recipe from the magazine with apple and walnuts.

To be honest, over the years Shirt & Tie has changed for the better. Still looks like he's carrying the burdens of Our Christ and Saviour but, to give him his due, years now he's been looking after the boy properly, cooking, cleaning and doing the best an old man can do when he's in charge of a boy like Nellie with too much curiosity and personality for a child of his age.

Take the time Nellie nearly broke his neck climbing out of Paulette's bathroom window like SpiderMan. There's the boy clinging on to the guttering and the downpipe, laughing and screaming because any second he will break his little neck, and at the same time Frank comes huffing down the grove looking vex and embarrassed. The boy jumped the last five feet, caught his jumper on the hanging basket and nearly broke his ankles, still laughing, spiderweb lines drawn all over his face in black felt pen.

'Nearly!' he shouted at Paulette, rolling on the ground holding his foot. Paulette had to laugh.

'Nellie,' she said, 'one day . . .'

But Frank stood, hard and still as a statue, and poured more disappointment into one look than Paulette thought was possible.

'Get up, Cornelius,' he said to the child, quiet and terrible. 'Compose yourself.'

The Best of Everything

Nellie dusted himself off and smiled at Paulette but followed Frank home with his head down and his arms long at his side.

The next day, Saturday, and Paulette's on her own as usual, but she's got things to do at least which will kill some time, fetching things from the market in town where they sell fresh fish, snapper and hake. She wraps up extra warm.

And there he is again, at the terminus, the Indian driver she was rude to. He's got no turban, just normal hair cut nice, one grey stripe at the side. He lets all the passengers get off then closes the door and starts to read the newspaper. She is four minutes in the bitter damp with her lingering cold and by the time he opens the door she can't wait to sit down.

She watches him in the mirror. He's not old, her age maybe. And his eyes are light brown or dark green. When the bus gets to the shops on Livery Street, she gets up and walks to the front.

'No turban today,' she says.

'What?'

'You used to wear a turban.'

He frowns. 'Not usually,' he says, his eyes on the road. 'I was in mourning. It's over now.'

'Sorry for your loss,' she says and he glances at her while he's turning the steering wheel.

'Thank you.'

'Was it someone close?' she says and soon as she asks she knows it's too forward.

'My mother's eldest sister,' he says. 'She was an old lady.'

'Yes,' she answers but can't find anything else to say or any other reasons to keep talking and the conversation dies.

At the market, she dallies at the stalls, even the ones she has no business with, dog food, baby food, undergarments, premature Christmas gifts. All she buys in the end are the usual foods for the week and a treat for Bird and Nellie, chocolate chip cereal, bad for them in every way but the entire box will last less than half an hour and, anyway, once a week won't hurt.

She walks to the far corner of the market to buy plantain, sweet potato and yam from the Pakistani grocer and then she browses the long row of shops outside that sell more things she doesn't need, cushions and mops, paint, second-hand hi-fi systems, mortgages, elaborate funerals.

She's lost touch with the few mothers she used to chat to from Bird's old school and she realizes as she saunters between the shoppers that she'd like someone to meet for a drink or a cup of coffee. She should have brought Maggie with her but Maggie's always working and when she's not she's got a good social life at the Irish Centre, lots of people coming and going all the time. But it would be nice to sit in the window of a café with someone and drink an expensive hot chocolate laden with cream and marshmallows. She would lick the spoon clean and they could order cakes and stay there until it got dark and they could nip into the nearest pub.

She knows it's the bus driver that makes her waste her time in shop windows. She rearranges her thick scarf and takes off her hat even though it's so cold. She buys a lip gloss at the beauty stall and slicks it on thinly so it's not too noticeable. She pulls her belt tight as she calculates how long it takes for him to go to the end of the line and turn back. And she's right. It's his bus that comes.

When he sees her, he smiles. 'Back home?' he says.

She takes her ticket. 'Yes, back home. Make the dinner.'

'What else?'

'What else?'

'It's Saturday night. It's a dancing night, isn't it?'

The bus swings around the roundabout and she grips the handrail. 'Me? No, I've got a son to take care of.'

'I have two,' he says. 'Seventeen and nineteen.' He doesn't mention a wife. He has no need to mention a wife.

That morning, she stays there, up at the front, chatting with him until she reaches her stop. She tells him her name and he tells her his, and she walks home repeating 'Jasbinder' under her breath, the way she heard it on his tongue.

She begins to look out for him. And before she leaves work, she checks her hair and makes sure she doesn't smell of hospital disinfectant. She rubs in hand cream and keeps a little tube of lip balm in her pocket. Without budgeting for it, she treats herself to a new coat. Not expensive but not needed either.

Every time she gets his bus, she stands up at the front or sits on the seat nearest him and they talk and laugh. Even when the bus is full, she watches him in the mirror and sees him watching her back. She never pays these days.

She sees him twelve more times before he asks her. It's a treacherous day, the sort of day where you slip and make a fool of yourself. She inches her way slowly to the bus stop. The road is hidden under brittle layers of ice and, when he opens the door at the terminus, she sees he's wearing a woolly hat and gloves.

'I owe you a Christmas drink,' he says.

'What for?'

'Keeping me company,' he says. 'Makes me want to come to work.' She knows he is pretending to concentrate on his driving.

'Okay,' she answers. 'That would be nice.'

'You know the Golden Hind? Stephenson Street?'

'Yes, I know it.'

'What about Sunday evening? I finish at six, meet you at seven.'

'Tomorrow?'

'Yes,' he says. 'Tomorrow.'

18

What to do with Bird? If she goes out at seven she will be away for at least three hours, maybe more. She's never left Bird in the house on his own and even if Nellie comes round, two thirteen-year-old boys alone is not a good idea. Lead us not into temptation.

She could ask Maggie if Bird could sit round there for the night and she would ask no questions but, then again, Bird will be late getting into bed and him and Maggie's Gemma fell out when he called her 'Little Miss Fatty'. The girl is pretty as a flower but she must have said something to Bird for him to shout cruel things out of his bedroom window. Paulette made him apologize, but not even Maggie could make them spend more than half an hour in each other's company so that's that.

And then there's Garfield. When Bird has been at Garfield's from Saturday morning, he usually brings him home the next day by five or six. True, she could ask him to bring Bird home late, but it would have to be late late, like eleven o'clock, and he'd say something about Bird not getting enough sleep and then he might ask her where she was going and her face would give everything away. She doesn't want Garfield thinking she is putting some new man ahead of her child. But when all is said and done, Paulette is a free agent and she's got a date. And she's also got no choice. Frank.

Only rarely does Shirt & Tie come to her house any more, so if Paulette wants to see him, she will have to go and call on him at his house.

Last time Frank came it was a Wednesday in the summer. He came to the door to collect Bird to take him and Nellie to the museum and art gallery in town. A new exhibition, he said. Bonington's watercolours, he said, and 'some rather good modernist sculpture'. Paulette herself could have told him those two boys would rather go to a football match or the circus or even sit down and watch telly than take a slow walk with Frank round some dusty vases and statues with Frank telling the two of them how interesting it all was. She could just imagine it. Nellie would be wearing his hunted face, desperate to say something but keeping it to himself, and Bird would definitely think it was boring, too many facts and not enough action. What Paulette didn't want was Bird getting so fed up that he got cheeky and started to complain. She told Bird he would have to behave himself and what Frank was doing was a nice thing, but even so, when Frank came with Cornelius to pick him up, Bird was still upstairs getting ready, dragging his heels. The man was early as usual. Nellie ran up the stairs two at a time, so Paulette was left with Shirt & Tie.

'Come in, Frank,' she said.

Paulette brought him into the kitchen and made him a cup of coffee. Seeing as the man still couldn't fill his shirt collar, she cut him a good slice of bun, buttered it thick and put some cheese on a plate, placing it all on the table in front of him.

'Thank you,' he said and in ten seconds flat half the bun was in his mouth and the second half was waiting to load. Frank's relationship with West Indian bun was a serious matter. He could eat off a whole loaf if you kept cutting it and then he would dab up all the crumbs on his plate and still look like he could eat more. Paulette would have told him where he could buy it but there was no way Shirt & Tie would take himself to the Caribbean supermarket in town.

'How are things, Frank?' she asked as he ate but she kept washing up because sitting across from Frank was an ordeal when you could see the damage underneath the manners.

'Ah, quite well, I think. Better, I think,' he said. 'Keeping Cornelius entertained during the holiday is something of an ordeal, but you must have the same problem. And you're working, of course. If you ever need someone to look after Bird, if you ever run into difficulties, please do ask me. It's the least I can do.'

So, here is Paulette running into difficulties on Saturday afternoon and here is Paulette knocking the door of Shirt & Tie's house, which she has never been in since the first time, many, many years ago.

The front garden is tidy but the door still needs painting. The car is still under the tarpaulin and the grove still looks like it's run by burglars and vagabonds. Same thin curtains. When the door opens, Frank is surprised, she can see it on his face. He smiles and blinks before he remembers how to behave.

'Ah, Paulette, come in, come in. Please.'

She walks through the small narrow hall and into the living room.

'Do sit,' he says. 'Would you like tea? Yes, tea. I should make some tea.'

Then he's gone. Carpet has gone down since she was there and the television is bigger but everything else looks the same and the room looks empty in spite of the big settee and the pictures on the wall. But there's a new bookcase with books squashed on every shelf and a pile in front of it. She hears Nellie well before she sees him.

He clatters downstairs and flings the door open.

'What's happened?' he says, breathless.

'What you mean, what happened? I'm making a visit to your grandfather, Cornelius. People can visit, can't they?'

'Why?' he says, standing over her.

'You can't ask people why they come to see you, Nellie. You're supposed to—'

'You don't usually come here,' he says. 'What's wrong?'

'Cornelius!' says Frank, appearing at the door with a tray. 'Remember your manners.'

Nellie takes a newspaper off the coffee table and Frank puts the tray down. Cups and saucers with a little spoon on each, a teapot, a sugar bowl and a milk jug that matches the cups and a plate of biscuits, four in total. Paulette smiles.

'Lovely,' she says. 'Nellie, since you're so eager to find out, I came round to see if you wanted to stay the night with Bird on Sunday.'

'Yes!' He looks suddenly at Shirt & Tie who is perched on the edge of the sofa looking like he's forgotten something. Paulette hears him mutter under his breath, 'Sugar saucers spoons.'

'Can I go, Grandad? I mean, please may I go?'

Paulette holds up her hand. 'There's a catch, Nellie.'

Nellie looks from her to Frank and then at the tray. Then back to her. 'What?'

'Well, Frank, I was wondering if you weren't doing anything on Sunday evening if you could watch Bird for me. I've got a sort of social occasion and I won't get back until late so if Nellie came and stayed the night, you could come and maybe watch the television,' she looks at the pile of books he can't find room for on the shelves, 'or read,' she says. 'I mean, you will probably have eaten already but I could leave you some dinner. And there's bun in the bread bin for later if you get peckish. I bought one fresh.'

Frank pours the tea and passes her a cup and saucer, the spoon clinking from his shaking hand.

'Thank you,' she says. 'I shouldn't be back too late, maybe eleven or something like that. If Nellie brings his school uniform with him, I'll make sure they both get up on Monday morning, nice and early. I mean, if you're not busy it would be helping me out.'

Man's taking his time to answer and just when Paulette thinks the silence is too long, he seems to remember the question.

'Yes, yes. Of course. Yes. Delighted. That's no trouble at all and I'm sure Cornelius would welcome a change of scenery overnight. You can see for yourself.'

Nellie is smiling wide like she just gave him twenty pounds.

'Sunday night, Frank. Tomorrow. You sure? Can you come by six? I must be in town by seven.'

'We'll be there. Have no fear. I doubt Cornelius will allow me to forget, will you?' Shirt & Tie looks at the boy and Paulette sees in that look such tenderness and understanding of the boy's personality and the full share of life God gave him, bursting to get out.

Paulette gets in the bath on Sunday morning, puts some nice music on the stereo and lies there soaking. Her hair's in a waterproof headtie so the steam doesn't ruin it and the lemongrass bubbles come up to her shoulder.

What she must not do is run ahead of herself. Jasbinder said it was a Christmas drink. He didn't say nothing else and she mustn't expect nothing else. And yet she knows there is something else, she can feel it like strong rope tied from his heart to hers. Not since Denton has Paulette felt this way.

She can see how Jasbinder looks at her, desire in his eyes but not just that. Something more, something deeper. So, no. She mustn't get carried away.

What to wear, what to wear, what to wear? You think Paulette has man-eating outfits hanging up ready to be worn? She stands by the mirrored wardrobe selecting combinations. Jeans are always a good starting point but hers are high-waisted and pale blue, not the fashionable kind. Black trousers make her look like she's going to an interview and all her dresses are buttoned up and ready for church.

She goes back to the jeans and lies them on the bed. Puts a white shirt with them, a gold chain on the white shirt. A gold belt on the jeans. Black shoes and a black jacket. Small diamanté earrings. It will have to do. And anyway, she doesn't want to look like she's tried.

The day drags. She makes a good dinner for Nellie and Frank. Bird always comes home bursting from Garfield's woman's cooking. Sometimes he brings mutton, rice and peas in a Pyrex dish. The woman cooks her rice without coconut which is either laziness or obstinacy. One of these days, that Pyrex might fall and break when Paulette is washing it. Slippery hands.

She has a new half-bottle she was saving for Christmas that she puts on a tray with a glass tumbler and a packet of nuts and a packet of crisps. She makes sure there's ice there, runs the vacuum round the living room, plumps up the cushions. Cleans the sink and wipes the kitchen table even though it doesn't need wiping at all.

She's ready by half past five. She doesn't want to sit down to put creases in her blouse but if she stands up too long she will get tired and it's a good walk to the bus stop. Then thirty-five to forty minutes into town, more sometimes, then a ten-minute walk to Stephenson Street. She must walk slow or she'll be too early and look foolish.

Garfield drops off Bird bang on six o'clock just as Shirt & Tie and Cornelius are walking up her path. She watches from the living-room window. She opens the door and waves. If he sees her all dressed up, then too bad. He might go home and tell Angela that Paulette looked good.

The Golden Hind is half full. Music on the jukebox, not too loud, low lights, plenty of seats. It's a nice place. Everyone in their middle years. No pensioners and no young bloods. She walks straight to the bar, not looking around for anyone but looking like she's been there plenty of times. She orders a rum and coke but, before she can pay, Jasbinder is beside her.

'I'll get that,' he says to the barmaid.

He puts his hand in the small of Paulette's back and guides her to his table, a quiet corner, banquette seat with a high wooden divider between them and the rest of the world. He sits right next to her, close.

'I didn't know if you'd come,' he says and turns his glass around. 'I was hoping you would.'

'I said I'd be here,' she says but it comes out too sharp. She takes a sip of her drink and smiles at him. 'I wanted to,

Jasbinder.' She says his name out loud for the first time and he smiles.

'People at work call me Jimmy.'

He tells her about his day and the drunken hooligan who called him a lazy paki and the woman who asked him for change for a ten-pound note and then gave him lip when he didn't have it. He tells her about life at the bus depot and about his eldest son who doesn't come home at night because he's got into bad company and the other one who they might have to take to the doctor because he's depressed. *They.*

He tells her he noticed her for weeks before she noticed him and that he liked how tidy she always was and that he's seen her kindness, how she lets people get on the bus ahead of her, and another time she helped a girl with two children and a buggy, and then an old man who couldn't get up the step. He said she makes him laugh and whenever he sees her the whole day is better than it was before. He tells her she's dangerous because when he's thinking about her he doesn't concentrate on the speed limit and he's gone through rush-hour traffic from one side of town to the other and can't remember doing it because Paulette is constantly on his mind.

He tells her all this while they're drinking and laughing and talking about lots of other things but what Paulette remembers about that night as she sits on the top of the 61 bus on her way home is the kiss. She touches her lips where his have been and closes her eyes to make it last.

19

The house is quiet when she opens the door. She sees Frank on the sofa, nods at him to say she's back and creeps upstairs to check on the boys. Sleeping. Good. She left the heating on so the house is nice and warm. She throws her jacket on the bed and tiptoes back downstairs.

'Everything okay?'

'It's been quiet for an hour,' he whispers. He's sitting in the armchair next to the little lamp, no television, just him and an old book with a blood-red cover and a thousand pages. He inserts a worn leather bookmark and closes it. 'Was it a success?' he says.

'You got time for a little drink, Frank?' she says, walking to the kitchen. She sees the plates scraped clean, stacked on the side, and the bun demolished. She gets herself a tumbler and sits on the sofa in front of the tray. The bottle's been opened, two inches gone but enough left for the two of them. She pours two solid measures and hands him his glass, holds hers with two hands on her lap.

'Yes, it was a success. Sort of.'

'You look, may I say, very happy.'

'I haven't been out with anyone for a long time,' she says. The smile is automatic and uncontrollable. 'It was really nice.'

'It would be a cliché to say you deserve happiness, but you do.'

Paulette knows Jimmy will be home by now. Or maybe he's driving around looking for his eldest son like he said he would. There's a club up on Hunters Road, a bad place, where he thinks his boy goes and there's a girl in a Newtown tower block and a dumpling shop where they sell weed over the counter with the curry goat, he could be there. That's what happens if you don't keep a grip on your children. Or maybe Jimmy is lying in bed next to his wife. Her long hair, black and straight on the pillow. Does he touch it? Does he move it aside? Maybe his wife has stayed awake so she can ask him where he's been. Maybe she's asleep. Maybe they don't talk. Maybe he will lie in the dark looking at the same moon she saw on her walk home. He will turn away from his wife so he can think, undisturbed, about the woman he met in the Golden Hind. He'll remember the things he said and the kiss he gave her at the bus stop, leaning into her, kissing her so hard it took her breath away, his hands pressing her towards him, one on her back, one on her neck. She bites her lip to stop the smile.

He's watching her, Shirt & Tie, with his watery blue eyes and she thinks suddenly he might not be as old as he looks.

'Ever been in love, Frank?' she says.

The man seems to actually grow in his chair. Chest puffs out and he sits up straight.

'Anne,' he says. 'My wife.'

'She's . . .'

'Died several years ago. Twenty-two to be precise. I didn't have enough of her, you see,' he says, leaning forward. 'That's something I've known for a very long time. Not enough of her. We met at university, both reading English, and we married soon after we graduated. It happens that way, some-times, doesn't it? You meet someone and you simply have no doubts. That was Anne for me. She was quietly joyous. Yes, that's what I'd call it, she had a kind of tranquillity yet she was so alive, so bright. Happiness is not always something you read about in books, it can be a living, breathing, every-day experience.'

He looks at her with wonder on his face, lighter some-how, and then shakes his head and talks a bit louder, stronger, like what he wanted to say had been brewing for a long, long time. 'We bought a little cottage, quite a wreck really but we didn't care. It took everything we had, Grade II listed with a pretty garden, half an acre but quite wild and overgrown. We had plans for an orangery and possibly an orchard but we would have to save obviously. And so I didn't want children. Why would I? I was complete. She completed me, do you see? Every couple of years she'd talk about it. "What do you think about a baby, Francis?" Or "Do you think we might regret it if we don't have children?" But I thought it was an innocent enquiry, something akin to asking if we might take a cruise to Antarctica or visit the Taj Mahal. No, that's not quite right, not quite true. Part of me knew she was in earnest, but in all honesty, I was appalled by the idea. Just appalled. I'd have to share her, you see. I knew her capacity for love and I knew any child would have first call on it, naturally. And I worried I would end up with the scraps. What if one child became two or five? I could barely tolerate the thought. She was everything to me.'

He faces Paulette but his eyes are somewhere else.

'And then one day, Somerset I think it was, we were on a walking holiday, just the two of us, staying in a little coaching inn. Talbot Arms, I think, yes, Talbot. Off the square. I can see us that morning, getting ready to go out, putting on our hats and gloves by the door. I thought we might drive towards Burrowbridge, towards the river, and I saw that she wasn't listening. She'd heard some music, or rather we both heard it, but she seemed mesmerized and followed it, like there was a Pied Piper calling her, almost in a trance. Off she went and I followed. And there, at the end of the hall, in one of the public rooms at the back of the hotel, there was a woman playing the piano, Chopin, a nocturne, I think, and around her, five little girls in ballet costumes. The sun pouring through the stained-glass window. Little steps, all around the room. Practising. Very young. Pink tops and white skirts.'

He takes a sip of drink and begins to move his glass through the air as he speaks like he's writing it down. Paulette watches to make sure it doesn't splash because he's in the groove now, telling the story with no hesitation, more words than she's ever heard from him. Plain to see where the other half of the bottle of brandy went.

'What did I think?' he says even though Paulette said nothing. 'In that moment, nothing. Nothing at all. We stood at the door and saw the little girls, then we went for our walk. The Somerset Levels are quite beautiful in early spring. She was a great walker, very keen, and we would talk about the view or discuss our route, but on this day she was quieter than usual, although she was never one for great demonstrations or declarations but, yes, she was quiet. And I suppose I knew somewhere inside of me, possibly as soon as we saw the little girls, yes, right there and then, that she would have to have a child. I would have to say yes if I wanted her to be happy. And, of course, I desperately cared about her happiness. More than I can say. She was my wife.'

He looks down at his glass and throws what's left to the back of his throat. He shakes his head slowly and then nods like he's got some invisible friend asking him questions.

'I was thirty-five when Evie was born. And it happened exactly as I suspected. She fell in love. And my whole life changed.'

He shakes his head from side to side and smiles but it's not the kind of smile you ever wanted to see, too much sadness in it.

'Since then, my entire existence has been something of a farce. You see, after all her yearning, while my daughter is still very young, my wife dies. The thing she wanted the most, she is torn away from, and I'm left with the child. Me, the reluctant father working part-time and keeping house. Oh dear me, yes. Francis Bowen marooned, adrift in a half-finished cottage on an unmanageable plot and the scorn of a daughter who gets pregnant and dies. And then Cornelius arrives and I'm the reluctant father all over again. It's nothing short of comical.'

He turns the glass round and round in his hand and looks straight at Paulette like he just remembered she was there.

'On the day of the accident, that morning, at breakfast, Evie told me she was expecting and, in all honesty, I didn't believe her. She was seventeen. She looked perfectly normal and why wouldn't she? She was only two months, she said, possibly less. I thought she was baiting me and I told her she was being ridiculous. She liked to shock, you see. She smoked despite my protestations and swore and had several unsuitable friends that called at the house. She laughed and told me she didn't even know who the father was. "Evie," I said, "you must be serious." And she laughed again but I could see she was upset and worried. She was quite a sensitive girl underneath it all. I still didn't believe her and I told her I would call her bluff and we would go straight to the doctor. She refused. I insisted. That's how we were that morning. At loggerheads. In the end, I made her get in the car. I made her.'

He stands up so sudden he knocks the tray and Paulette has to reach to steady it.

'The weather was fine and visibility was good that day in case you were wondering. There was a bush on the corner that partly obscured the junction but otherwise visibility was good and I wasn't speeding. I did everything I could afterwards. The best care possible. I found somewhere for her, a rather lovely place, but they were unable to help in the end, though they did try.'

He takes a deep, ragged breath. 'Forgive me,' he says. 'You will want to get some sleep.' He walks to the hallway and takes his coat off the hook. 'I do hope Cornelius is no trouble to you.'

Paulette goes to speak but he holds his hand up. 'I would close the door quickly if I were you, Paulette. It's treacherously cold out here. Goodnight.'

He is gone and Paulette is stone cold sober.

20

Between Jimmy's shifts and Paulette's it's not easy finding time, but they do. If she happens to meet his bus she pays her fare and sits down. They don't talk out in the open. You never know who's watching. Then, as she gets off, he will say a little something to her like 'Take care' or 'See you next time' and she barely answers because she knows she is seeing him Tuesday at four o'clock or Friday at seven o'clock at the cheap hotel for a few hours, or at the pub, or his friend's house when the friend is out. But it takes months to arrange a whole weekend together.

The wind whips through Jimmy's open window, pulls at his hair, fluffs it up at the back. Paulette sways and bends with the motion of the little car dashing through the country lanes that curve and curl towards Burnham Overy Staithe. They picked the village at random as Jimmy read out the names from a map. It's a tourist town and it's out of season so there will be a pub and there will be a B & B. All right, so a black woman and an Indian man will stand out anywhere except the inner city but people will just think they've come to see the sea. Not that the two of them are desperate to spend their first night together, to sleep and to dream and to wake in each other's arms.

Jimmy is supposed to be with his friend picking up some furniture from Leeds, big job, takes two, might take all day, and Paulette doesn't have to say anything to Garfield because he thinks she stays in from Friday to Sunday, cooking and cleaning, with no life of her own.

The land becomes flat then flatter still and the sky so big and wide there's no end to it. The car cuts through villages and hamlets, fords a small stream and bounces through farmland. Paulette can smell the sea before she sees it. She strains to catch the first glimpse. It won't be the Caribbean but it's a long, long time since she saw the waves swirl up on to the sand and then draw back. Up and back. Up and back, forever.

Every so often, Jimmy puts his hand on her leg, on her shoulder, brushes her neck with his warm palm. Paulette is thin now. Love has devoured what few pounds she had to spare and left her hip bones sticking out, visible in her new black dress, sharp against her lover's belly. Her hair is short because he likes it that way. She knows this is not a romance film and the sun isn't shining and neither of them are twenty-one but the touch of him makes her a girl again and turns the March mist into everlasting summertime.

The first place they try has space for them and the woman is friendly.

'This is our biggest room,' she says, throwing the door open wide. 'Look there, between the houses. That's the North Sea. You can walk through the marshes, it's all sign-posted, then over the dunes and you'll find the best beach in the country as far as I'm concerned. Breakfast is seven until ten. Full English. And this is your key.'

They don't leave the room for hours.

The light has almost gone but they don't put on the lamp. There's a street light throwing patterns on the ceiling, the branches of a black tree outside, the warped angle of the window. Paulette traces her finger through the thick hair on Jimmy's chest. 'I could plait this,' she says. 'It would make a nice cane row.'

'You should have seen me when I had long hair,' he says. 'Right down to the back of my thighs. You'd be plaiting for a week.'

'I wish I had known you then,' she says. 'Will you grow it again?'

'Is that what you want?' He shuffles down in the bed until they're face to face. 'I would do it for you.'

He kisses her lips, her nose, her forehead. 'Tell me,' he says.

'What?'

'Tell me something I don't know, something about you.'

She knows she's gone quiet, that her breathing is shallow and her body is still. It's a long time since she spoke about her grandmother and coming to England and Denton.

She starts way back and skims over the bad bits, of being left out at school and how she never went back despite promising and promising and then her grandmother's death and

Garfield. She tells him about St Kitts where the sun shines bright, where she will take Bird when he's older, maybe when he leaves school before university so he can see where his people come from, and she tells him about the job she loves and how one day she might train to be a proper nurse and get her qualifications, then she stops suddenly.

'What?'

'I loved somebody once but he died,' she says. She takes a deep breath so she can carry on. 'He loved me and I loved him. We were going to set up home together and have children, the whole picture, house, car, kids, holidays, you know. I thought it was all settled. But then he got killed in a car accident. I've been waiting for him to come back.'

'Waiting for him?'

'I've been waiting to feel that same thing again. I remember it so well, Jimmy. The whole world is different, lighter. You have hope. I thought it had gone for good.'

'And it hasn't?'

'No,' she says, 'it hasn't.'

They get dressed and walk to the little pub at the end of the lane. There's a quiet hush when they walk in but there's music and enough politeness so that people don't stare at the black people venturing this far east in England. They order chicken and chips and drink too much. They sit close and try not to look like new lovers. They hold hands and try not to kiss. In the morning, they put on their coats and look for the sea.

The Best of Everything

It's twenty minutes away, further than it looks from the window, but worth the walk. It's wide and flat and grey and still and silver and powerful. The wind shoves them back to the dunes but they hunch and bend and press on across the long beach because Paulette wants to put her toes in the water like she used to, just in case, just in case, just in case that piece of sea meets up with the ocean that meets up with the still water in the little bay in Basseterre where the sea tickled Paulette's feet when she was a girl, where it might remember her.

There at the water's edge, Paulette takes off her nurse's shoes with the sensible sole and her thick tights, one leg at a time while Jimmy steadies her, and she runs towards the waves and screams as the ice water covers her ankles. And she screams again when it comes back. Jimmy is laughing at her.

'Come in!' she calls to him. 'Come in!' but he retreats from the waves, keeps his feet dry.

In the morning, when she wakes up, she watches him, his lips apart, his hands tucked under the pillow. She inches back the blankets and tiptoes to the cold bathroom down the hall. She smooths down her hair and rinses her mouth. She wipes the sleep from her eyes and goes to the toilet. She washes her hands and her armpits and creeps back to him. She pulls one of his arms over her shoulder like a fur stole and nestles in.

21

If Paulette is careful, careful, some weekends when Garfield picks Bird up on Saturday morning and if Jimmy isn't on shift, he parks at the top of the grove and walks down to her house. She watches for him so he doesn't have to stand at the door and lets him in quietly. She cooks extra, she fusses around him as he eats, she changes her sheets before he comes and puts them in the washing machine when he's gone.

But it feels too dangerous. It feels like Garfield might suddenly bring Bird home one day unexpected and the two of them would catch her out. Jimmy sitting on the sofa with a drink, tall and broad like Denton, good-looking with a sparkle in his eyes. And Garfield would know that she was sleeping with another married man and he would look her up and down and say she was a fool, just like he did before. Garfield knows her good. She wouldn't be able to lie.

And then it happens. Garfield rings on Saturday because one of his girls is sick and he has to take her to the hospital. He won't be picking Bird up until Sunday morning. Jimmy is due at six, only two hours' time. Paulette has no phone number for Jimmy and there is no way he can come to the house while Bird is at home. It wouldn't be right. He wouldn't like it. She would be embarrassed. He would tell

Garfield. It can't happen. Paulette runs to Maggie to tell her what's happened.

Maggie listens, propping her cigarette hand on the kitchen table and smoking like a labourer on a building site.

'So, what you're telling me is you're afraid your son will see that his mother is a red-blooded woman. And you're worried that Garfield, who you never even loved by the way, will know you have a boyfriend. Do I have it right?'

'Jimmy is married, Maggie.'

'Yeah, he's the one with the secret, not you. He hasn't got it tattooed on his face, has he? No. And anyway, you're entitled to a fucking bit of sex now and again, Paulette, for Christ's sake.'

'It's just easier if they don't meet.'

'Easier for who?'

'For me.'

Paulette doesn't say anything about Kitty running away when Maggie got a boyfriend. She doesn't remind her that the two of them had to walk the streets looking for the girl that told her to fuck off but it's on the tip of her tongue. It's easy to talk brave when you're not in the firing line.

Maggie winces as the smoke gets in her eyes. She picks a thread of tobacco off her lips and says, 'Right. He's due at six, is he? Leave it to me.'

At a quarter to six, Paulette watches from her window as Maggie walks to the top of the grove with a cigarette and a shopping bag. She loiters almost out of sight at the spot where Jimmy always parks. She stands for a while, then sits on someone's garden wall. Then she stands up suddenly and bends down to speak into a car window. The midnight-blue Escort she's been waiting for. Paulette sees Jimmy drive away and Maggie walk off to the shops.

Paulette stands at the bottom of the stairs and listens to Bird playing music in his bedroom then she sinks down on to the sofa and closes her eyes.

'Thank you, Jesus.'

But that only happened once. Usually, Bird is at Garfield's on Saturday nights and Jimmy comes round, parking at the top of the grove so as not to arouse suspicion. He can't stay the whole night without questions at home so he leaves before midnight, kisses her before he opens the door and he's gone. And then midweek they always find time to have a drink in a faraway pub or a meal in a restaurant, kissing in his car before he takes her to the bus stop.

He rings her nearly every night from a phone box to say hello, to ask her how she's been and say he's thinking about her. Once or twice Bird has answered and Jimmy pretends it's work ringing about her shift. Paulette has to keep her voice natural and just make the bare arrangements to see each other.

And then the phone is silent. She picks up the receiver fifty times, listens and yes, it's still working, but the hard disappointment of the dialling tone makes her stomach cramp. Jimmy doesn't seem to be working his usual shifts any more. She's worked earlies, lates and nights and one day she even waits for five buses to pass until she feels stupid and the cold rattles her bones. And Paulette doesn't know which street he lives on even if she had the nerve to go his house, which she does not.

Maggie is useless.

'He's fucked off, Paulette. I'm sorry, but it's the truth.'

'He wouldn't do that. Something's wrong.'

'Here,' she says and hands Paulette a can of stout which is as bitter as cabbage water. She gulps it down.

'He had trouble with his kids. Maybe one of them had an accident.'

'An accident that cut off all Jimmy's dialling fingers?'

'I don't understand it. Maybe—'

'Ah, come on, now, Paulette, my love. The next thing you'll say is maybe he's ill. He is not ill. He is not putting a plaster cast on his son's leg. He has not developed amnesia. He has got a severe case of Wandering Eye. He's found himself another woman, would be my guess. Or he's lining one up as we speak because that's what they are like. Men treat women like life rafts in the ocean. You don't let go of one until you've got your arm around another. There was a woman before you and there is most certainly one after you.'

Paulette closes her eyes and feels Maggie's hand on hers.

'I'm sorry, love. Really sorry, you know. It's a blow to the old ego and no mistake, but listen, if he's fucked off then all he's done is brought it forward by a few weeks or a few months. He's married so he was going sooner or later, wasn't he? Better he goes before you're in too deep.'

Paulette studies the black-and-gold label on the side of the can and wipes the condensation off with her thumb.

'Christ, Paulette,' Maggie says, shaking her head. 'You haven't fallen for the prick, have you?'

When Paulette starts to cry, Maggie lodges her cigarette in the corner of her mouth and flings both arms around Paulette's neck.

'They're all flea-infested curs,' she says, 'without a bare scrap of decency from Adam onwards. Dogs, the lot of them.'

Later that night, Maggie comes round with the rum and gin so they can hold a wake. 'That's what you do when someone dies,' she says. 'You forget their misdemeanours and celebrate the good times, and there were good times, weren't there, Paulette?'

She nods.

'And he's dead to you now, so say goodbye for once and for all. Cheers, my love.'

Then, on the thirty-seventh day without him, when she's been not sleeping and crying into her pillow and dragging herself around the ward like a sleepwalker for twelve hours, she comes out of work and there he is, smoking a cigarette, sitting on the concrete wall that surrounds the hospital. His back is hunched, his beard is touching his chest, he hasn't seen her.

Maggie said he would be in touch and that if Paulette has half a brain she'll tell him where to go. Maggie said he'd have good excuses, ones he'd had days to prepare, and she must thicken the wax in her ears against them. Maggie said men have a thousand lies but only one truth. And the truth is, they come first. They always come first. Maggie said he would be back and here he is.

Paulette stands at the automatic doors of the hospital while they open and close behind her. Open and close. Open and close. She could turn round and go out the back way. She could sit in the staffroom for a couple of hours or do some overtime. Sister McKenzie said they were short-staffed and she'd be very grateful. But instead her faithless feet take her to him, stand by him until he looks up from the low wall and says, 'Sorry.'

22

Thursday morning. No work today because Paulette has volunteered for the weekend night shifts again. Why not?

She's in the kitchen with the radio on. Some bomb somewhere on the other side of the world killed some people. The woman prime minister that was going to make a difference to Paulette's life has made no difference whatsoever. Paulette's purse still needs feeding and Bird is getting bigger every single day. Weekends now start on Friday according to Bird, and Garfield comes straight from work, beeps the horn outside and the two of them go off. Doesn't bring Bird back until Sunday night. She can hardly get a word out of him. Yes, he's done his homework, yes, he's eaten, yes, he's got some new top or jeans or something from Garfield or this aunt or that uncle and yes he had a good time, thanks, Mom. Bird goes straight to his room and she doesn't see him till morning.

Once upon a time when dinosaurs walked the earth, Paulette would have liked that extra Friday night for herself. She was seeing Jimmy then, eking out hours, counting minutes and relishing every single moment she had with him. But Jimmy has gone, long time.

When she saw him outside the hospital, he said somebody told his wife and his wife went to her father and her father went to Jimmy's father and before he knew it there were seven men from his family standing in his front room asking him what he was doing running round town with another woman and a black woman at that. That was seven months ago.

He's not driving her bus any more, he tells her. He was forced to put in for a transfer to a different garage. Forced. He tells her someone had it in for him and gave his wife chapter, verse and illustrations. He tells her he can't afford to leave his wife while their son is still acting like a gangster and not coming home at night. And how would she manage the other one who has some kind of learning disability, hardly talking, won't come out of his room? No, he can't leave his wife to cope on her own. It would kill her.

Paulette can be killed, though. Oh yes. Paulette can have her heart broken not once but twice by men who didn't love her enough. Oh yes, Paulette can bear everything the world throws at her. And at the same time, no! No, Paulette cannot have two baby girls and a man who buys an engagement ring in secret and stands up and says 'I do' in front of witnesses and then plans a big reception party in secret and springs a surprise on his new wife. *Ta-da!* And Paulette can't show off her wedding ring and put 'Mrs' in front of her name. No, that can't happen to someone like Paulette. Even Maggie got married and she's got a tongue like a razor blade and teeth the colour of old leather.

The yam is peeled, the plantain is peeled, the sweet potato is peeled and sitting on the side and the chicken is browning in the Dutch pot but as God is her witness Paulette cannot think why the fuck she is making a big pot of food when all she wants to do is go to her bed and never come out again.

Some lying fool on the radio is singing about how he can't live 'if living is without you', and she bangs her hand on top of the radio buttons over and over until the man shuts his mouth. Then she hears the door knock.

She wipes her hands and goes to the front. She can see it's police through the glass. It's also Nellie.

The policeman looks eighteen tops, like he got his badge last week, no smiles, nothing.

'Yes?' she says.

'Sorry to disturb you. Do you know this boy?'

Nellie with his big eyes and his rucksack in his hand. She can see that same chest heaving like it could break.

'Yes, he's mine. Why?'

'He is?'

'I said yes. Nellie, go inside and wash your hands.' Paulette folds her arms and looks hard at the force-ripe policeman who doesn't believe a white boy can belong in a black woman's house.

'He's been caught at Kang's Minimarket on Hanover Street this afternoon with another youth causing trouble.'

'What other youth?'

'We're yet to apprehend him. He ran off.'

'What colour was this other youth?'

'I beg your pardon?'

'Black or white? The other youth. Black or white?'

'We're led to believe from the witnesses we've spoken to that the other youth may have been a white boy but we are—'

'Right. And?'

'Well, Mr Kang is prepared to let it ride if he stays out of the shop. And we're inclined to let it—'

'Good,' she says. 'Is that it?'

She closes the door and walks into the kitchen. Nellie is stirring the Dutch pot, moving the chicken around with a wooden spoon.

'Don't tickle it, Nellie. Move it quick or water comes out. It's frying not boiling.'

She watches him for a few minutes. He's smiling.

'What?' she says. 'You think police at my door is funny?'

'You said "he's mine",' Nellie says quietly.

'Was it Bird with you?'

'No,' he says. 'It was a boy from school. And we weren't doing anything, just—'

'I don't care, Nellie. I really don't. But do not bring police to my door again. I don't like it, I don't need it and I don't want it. You hear?'

She edges him out of the way and takes the spoon off him. 'And you cannot be mine because no child of mine would spoil food in real time,' she says.

When all the food is in the pot, vegetables boiling, chicken browning, callaloo ready to steam, she tells him to sit at the kitchen table. She makes him a sandwich and gives him a drink.

'Listen good, Nellie. Sit up properly in your chair when I'm talking. When you first came here you used to lie on the sofa while Bird was on the carpet playing with his toys. You used to lie down and half close your eyes and I used to say, go asleep if you want, and you always used to say—'

'Only if you sit by me.'

Paulette sees the little child now, alive and kicking in the teenager. The long eyelashes and the golden hair, worry in his eyes. She could put her hand on his face and he would incline to it and close his eyes, purr like a cat. She puts her hand to his cheek now and shakes her head.

'Nellie, I am sitting by you now, like I used to, and I'm telling you, if you do not fix up, if you are not careful, if you do not listen to what I say, you will get into serious trouble one of these nights and you will not be sleeping on my sofa. You will be sleeping in jail. Do not go down that road. You hear me?'

He nods and smiles. 'He's mine,' he says.

She sends Nellie home before Bird comes back from school because she hardly sees her son these days. After school, he always brings a friend home with him, either Nellie or new people, good studious boys, and sometimes a girl called Leah. Leah is blonde with long, straight hair down to her waist and big eyes like a barn owl. Small, quiet and clever. She knows how to be polite and she knows how to get Bird's attention. Paulette's been in the kitchen listening while the two of them watch telly or she's upstairs straightening her bedsheets while they're in his room. And Paulette keeps a 'door open' policy, don't worry about that.

Clever little Leah never knows the answer to her homework question. Makes Bird explain it to her and then she says, 'Wow, Bird, thanks for telling me.' Or she asks him which page to look at in the textbook and he sits close and shows her. 'Thanks, Bird. I can see it now.' Yes, the girl knows what she's doing.

Bird comes home and, for once, he is alone. And he's in a bad mood.

'I'm hungry,' he says, lifting the lid on the pot.

'Needs another hour. I'll make you a sandwich, sit down.'

He throws his bag on the floor and slumps in his chair.

'What's wrong?' she asks, folding her arms. Sometimes, the boy really looks like his father for true.

'Nothing.'

'Take your coat off and tell me.'

He wriggles out of his coat and puts it on the back of the chair. 'Everyone's got Nike and I've got these,' he says, looking at his feet.

Paulette sighs. 'Not again, Bird. I am not paying one hundred and ten pounds for trainers. I haven't got it. And neither has Garfield. He's got children to bring up.'

'Mom, the sandwich,' he says. Paulette gets out bread, cheese and ham, and starts. 'And no one wears Adidas any more,' he says. 'I look stupid. Everyone at school's got Nike.'

'Not everyone, Bird,' she says. She pours him blackcurrant juice and puts it all in front of him. He takes a massive bite.

'Everyone,' he says.

'Those boys didn't have Nike, the ones that came last week.'

'Yes, they did! How would you know?'

'Nellie doesn't have Nike?'

He coughs and splutters, swallows hard and pounds his chest with the flat of his hand.

'Nellie? Nellie? Mom, Nellie?'

'Bird,' she says, passing him some kitchen towel, 'don't make fun of your friend. It's not nice.'

'But Nellie, Mom?' He shakes his head and goes back to his sandwich.

She watches him eat, the perfect dome of his head, the long, beautiful fingers and his broad shoulders. Time has done its work on the little baby in the cot with the yellow gingham cover, fast work and no mistake. Her baby will be a big man one day soon. To be honest, he already is. She hasn't got him for long. What does she go to work for if not to make him happy? No one can say she spoiled him because she never had the money but she promised him the best of everything and that's what he should have. No one can say the boy takes things for granted or lives in luxury. Anyone that looked at her boy would see a well-brought-up, clean young man from a good family, from a mother who spared nothing to give him what he needed. He looks up and catches her looking.

'Shall I ask Dad?'

'No,' she says. 'I'll see what I can do. I'm not promising anything. Go and do your homework.'

23

Bird is fifteen. Leah is his girlfriend now. Garfield was keeping a party for one of his girls and told Bird he could bring her to the house, went and collected her from her home and everything. Leah was well behaved, so Garfield said, and ate all the food she was given. She brought a nice present for Bird's sister and a bunch of flowers for Garfield's wife. The girl might be clever and cute but all the times she's been coming to Paulette's house, flowers have never appeared.

Nellie comes round on a Saturday sometimes when Bird is at his father's or out with his girlfriend. He's got his own key now in case Paulette is late from work or in the bath. He doesn't ring first. Just knocks the door, uses the key and comes in. To be honest, Paulette is glad of the company. The two of them watch old films on the telly and Nellie tells her the end before it's even halfway through.

A cowboy comes into the scene and before he even speaks, Nellie says, 'He will die,' or 'He did it.' Two gangsters are hiding the loot and Nellie says, 'It will be gone when they come back.' The boy can ruin a good story with his clever ways. Sometimes they watch quiz shows or cook with Nellie chopping or stirring or adding salt, or Paulette is cleaning the kitchen while he sits and chats his nonsense: what he's going to be when he leaves school, how school is crap and doesn't matter, why the teachers don't like him and so it goes.

He never talks about Shirt & Tie, never complains about his grandfather and their poor way of living. Whatever else Frank has done, he's brought the boy up to have respect for his family and Nellie's loyalty is a testament to the boy's good heart.

One day, Frank comes to the door.

'Hello, Frank, long time no see. Come in,' she says. The man has aged hard, hard, hard. Fully grey now and wearing the same anorak he's had since Noah's time, which has been washed so often it's as thin as he is. He doesn't look right at all.

She makes him coffee and cuts him a piece of bun. He doesn't touch it and that is a first.

'Are you well, Frank?' she says. 'Everything all right at home?'

The man turns his coffee by the handle like he's looking for north.

'Cornelius has been in trouble at school. It's rather concerning.'

'What kind of trouble?' she says. What a white man calls trouble at school is definitely not what black people call trouble. Probably the boy got seven out of ten instead of full marks. Paulette's not worried.

'Well, it's rather difficult. As a matter of fact, I wanted your advice.'

'Put it plain, Frank.'

'Violence.'

'When you say violence . . .'

'Fighting.'

'Fighting who? Tell me what happened.'

Frank knits his hands together and doesn't stop talking for a full half-hour. And it comes to this.

One boy, a white boy, said something to Bird about him being black, something like 'You're standing in the shade', and added things that Frank calls 'expletives' but he won't say exactly what. He doesn't have to because Paulette knows every single one of them words, nothing could surprise her. Anyway, Bird pays no attention because a) it's nothing he hasn't heard before and b) the one thing Paulette and Garfield agree on is you don't box anybody down unless you really have to and c) nine times out of ten, name-calling is not a boxable offence. But before Bird can even respond, Nellie says something to the boy about him being stupid, says he's so stupid he can't even spell stupid. Asks him to try but instead the other boy tells Nellie that, behind his back, everyone calls Nellie 'Mark'. Nellie asks him what he means and it turns out it stands for 'Mark Down' because everything Nellie wears is cheap. Then bam! The two of them are rolling around on the floor. The teacher comes. Everyone says Nellie started it and Nellie himself says, 'Yes, I did,' instead of blaming it on the racist. And in the middle of the day Frank is called to the school. Nellie will not back down. Nellie will not apologize. Nellie says he did the right thing and he will do it again so the school tells him he's suspended for a week.

Two things trouble Paulette about the incident. First of all, some little fucking racist calling her son names. She's a good mind to go to the school first thing Monday and find out who it is and pop to the boy's house with Garfield. And secondly, why didn't Bird come and tell her himself so she doesn't have to hear it from Frank?

But Nellie with a temper does not surprise her one single bit. And her heart swells when she thinks of Nellie smacking the racist boy upside his head for bad-mouthing his friend.

'So, he's off school for a week?' she says.

Frank nods.

'What are you going to do?'

'I intend to make him do some chores around the house. I intend to make him reflect on his behaviour. What do you think?'

Paulette tries not to smile as she imagines how that conversation will go. Frank with his long English sentences and Nellie with his eyelids heavy, waiting for the man to finish. Nellie will be Nellie and no amount of chores are going to change that.

'Yes, Frank,' she says. 'That's a good idea. Make him reflect. And send him round to me for a couple of days. Let me find him some jobs to do.'

Monday morning, Nellie knocks the door after Bird has gone to school. He's wearing old clothes, the colour leached out of them, baggy jogging bottoms, loose at the knee, and a sweatshirt that's too small. Bird's clothes can't fit him any more because Bird's been growing like a tree, big and strong, outstripping Nellie by three inches, and anyway, Bird wouldn't like it. He takes off his old coat and throws it on the sofa.

'Is that where your coat goes, Nellie?'

He picks it up and hangs it in the hall while she watches.

'Don't forget who you're dealing with, Nellie. I'm not one of your teachers, you know.'

She makes him mop the kitchen floor while she stands back and watches. Then tells him he must vacuum the sitting room and plump up the cushions, empty the bins, wipe down the skirting boards, sweep the path. And the boy works like he's on piecework, like someone who would rather be doing housework than anything else in the world. And as he works, they talk.

'First thing, Nellie, is thank you for standing up for Bird. Second thing, no one asked you to stand up for Bird so you should have minded your own business. And the third thing is, you can't go round hitting people.'

'Because?'

'Because you'll get into trouble.'

'I don't care.'

'Try to care, Cornelius. Try to care. Even when you don't feel like it, you have to try to care and you have to do the right thing. That's the way of the world, Nellie. Everyone trying to get along with everyone else, best as they can. It's only one life you have, you know. You don't get another one if you mess this one up. You have one single time on earth and you can spend it in trouble or you can spend it happy.

You have to choose. And when you choose, make a plan, make it happen.'

'What did you choose?'

Paulette watches him wiping down the front of the kitchen cabinets and making a very good job of it. 'Guess,' she says.

He turns round and looks at her. 'My grandfather says you're the best person he's ever known.'

Paulette smiles. 'Finish up and we'll make corn porridge for lunch.'

She shows him every step, the milk and cornmeal, sugar and nutmeg, the condensed milk. She stands over him while he stirs it.

'Keep stirring, Nellie, even when you turn off the gas, keep stirring for a little while. The bottom of the pan is hot. It can still stick.'

She dishes him up a big portion, twice hers, and sits down in front of him. Watching Nellie eat is one of the purest pleasures of Paulette's life. He concentrates like he's on a high wire because corn porridge is a serious business and when he scrapes his spoon around the bowl and the porridge is finished, he sits back and puts his hands on his belly, what little belly he has.

'God,' he says.

'God has nothing to do with it, Nellie. You made it with your own two hands. You got a flair for it. You could make that your plan for the future.'

'Maybe I'll get fat,' he says.

Paulette picks up his bowl and clears the table. 'Not if you do all the jobs I've got in store for you, Nellie. And not if you take after Frank. Come, you got ironing next.'

'Splendid,' he says in Frank's voice and he gets up from the table like an old man. 'I'd be utterly delighted.'

Paulette shakes her head and laughs.

Saturday night and Paulette is at Maggie's house. Maggie's new man has left to go back to Ireland with his latest fancy piece so they're holding another wake. Paulette has the rum and Maggie is trying out a new vodka with lemon in it. Paulette has curry patties and Maggie has a box of Quality Street. They both have their slippers on and because Paulette has grown her hair she can fix in her big rollers, nice and tight. The telly is on with no sound.

Maggie says she's given up the fags so the Quality Street are taking a beating. She speaks with a mouthful of toffee.

'Here's to the future,' she says.

'I don't know how you can eat sweets and drink at the same time.'

'Necessity is the mother of invention,' she says. 'Now toast me.' She has her glass held high and a fierce look in her eyes.

'To the future,' says Paulette.

'And to the death of love.'

'To the death of love,' says Paulette but before they can chink she moves her glass. 'No, no, come on, Maggie. Make it positive.'

'To the death of the man himself, then.'

Paulette laughs. 'No, no. To better days, my granny would say. Better days.'

'You believe that as much as I do,' says Maggie but says it anyway. 'Better days.'

One hour later and Maggie is searching the kitchen drawers for a secret stash of tobacco she thinks she hid for desperate times. Paulette can hear clattering cutlery and clanging saucepans. She hears Maggie rifling through the bin.

'I knew it!' she says in triumph. 'You don't have any rolling papers, do you, Paulette?' she calls.

'Nothing like that, no.'

'What about Bird?'

'Nor him.'

'Nip home and see.'

'He doesn't smoke nothing, Maggie.'

'He's a dark one, that boy of yours. You never know.'

'I'd know if he was smoking, Maggie. I would smell it. What about your girls?'

'The two of them sleeping over with some friend or other. I have a feeling I'm being lied to but it's no worse than I did at their age. In fact, it's miles better. And anyway, I'm in the mood to forgive tonight. Well, them two at least. Ah-ha!' she shouts.

She sits back down and rolls a cigarette. She sucks hard on it and blows perfect rings with her chin in the air.

'Now, that to me looks like a wispy noose. Can you see?'

'Or the halo of an angel, maybe,' says Paulette, squinting.

'It must be yours, then. Not mine,' says Maggie. 'You'd do anything for anybody, Paulette. We have a saying, "In life, you should be the candle or the mirror. Either be the light in the room or reflect it." And you're both.'

'Maggie, you're drunk.'

'I'm not. And anyway, it's true. You're good and I'm not. I'd take that noose and put it around the bastard's neck. Slap the horse on the arse and see him dangling.'

'Maggie, fill your glass, man. This is a wake, you said. And at a wake, a West Indian wake anyway, you're supposed to remember the good times.'

Maggie is quiet for a few moments, counting to five under her breath. 'Right!' she says. 'That's done. Now what?'

By the end of the night, by the end of the drinks and the sweets, by the end of reminiscing and resolutions, the two women are slumped, leaning into each other because of the dip and sag of Maggie's settee.

'I have got to go, Maggie. But I can't move.'

'Do. Not. Move. I will fall. If I fall, I will suffocate on the cushion.'

Paulette struggles forward, gives up, leans her head back against the sofa and laughs. 'We're stuck,' she says.

'Listen, right. You can sleep here. When I can feel my legs, I'll get you a blanket, when I can remember what a blanket is.'

'No, no, no,' says Paulette. 'Nellie is coming in the morning. He has to help me clean the windows. Punishment.'

'Is he a waif or a stray? Not that I know the difference. Him and the old man, what's going on there?'

'Oh, that's a story for another day. Help me up.'

'Paulette, neither of us is in a fit state to help anyone. Stay where you are. You are the best pillow I ever bought. Better. Better than the best pillow I ever bought.'

'Thank you. I appreciate that, Maggie. I really do. I am a pillow.'

Maggie sighs. 'So, who is he, the nice boy who will be wielding the chamois leather too early tomorrow morning?'

'You wouldn't believe me if I told you.'

'Go on.'

Paulette takes a deep breath. 'He's the son of a girl who died who is the only daughter of the man who crashed a car when she was in it and who killed the love of my life at the same time.'

'Son of the daughter of . . .'

Paulette starts to titter, just a few little laughs that turn into a full bellow. Maggie isn't laughing. 'I don't understand.'

'Nor me,' says Paulette between her giggles. 'Nor me!'

24

Paulette's birthday is in October, good time to have a little open house if the weather's good or go out for a nice dinner, maybe sit down and think about what you did last year and what can change in the future.

This year she will turn forty-six so it's getting harder and harder to convince herself she still has some youthful years left. But, as Granny would say, old age is a privilege denied to many.

She's going to book a day out for her and Bird, just the two of them, something like a cinema trip and then a restaurant. He's big enough now to come out at night and behave like a man. Fifteen years old, tall and strong and clever. Good reports every single time. Leah is still in the picture but Paulette doesn't think it's serious.

Instead of waiting outside in the car, Garfield comes to the door that Friday night. She notices now how Garfield and Bird have a little secret language. It's like a code they don't share with her. Garfield will say something to Bird like 'Night Hawk' and Bird laughs and says, 'Never in this World, Soldier.' All right, so it's from a film but Paulette can't find a video called *Night Hawk* no matter how she tries. Garfield stands at the door and just as Bird is about to leave Garfield pulls out two pieces of card from his pocket.

'And look, Bird,' he says.

'No way, Dad.'

'Leicester Square premiere.'

Bird starts firing guns at Garfield, who throws himself against the wall like he's dead.

'I was working in London last week,' he says, 'so I went there specially to see if they would let me buy two tickets. Couldn't believe it.'

Bird has them in his hand now. 'No way, Dad. No way.'

Garfield looks at Paulette. 'It's next week, Sunday. He'll be late home.'

'Sunday?'

'Yeah,' he says. 'Me and him can get something to eat afterwards so don't cook for him.'

'What is it?'

'*Spawn, Alien Warrior!*' shouts Bird.

'Get your things, Bird,' says Garfield, and when Bird runs upstairs, Garfield frowns. 'What's wrong? It's his favourite film. It's an all-day thing, his cousins are going as well. I've paid for the tickets.'

'It's my birthday, Garfield, I was going to—'

'Shit!' he says. 'I forgot.' And the way he speaks she knows it's true. Last year he stopped off and made Bird buy roses for his mother with a bottle of sparkling wine and chocolates so Garfield doesn't mean no disrespect.

Bird is coming downstairs with his bag. 'Nellie can come and keep you company, Mom. Tell Nellie to come.' The way he says it, like it's the best idea he ever had.

'No, it's all right,' she says. 'I was going out with Marcia anyway. I was going to ask you to keep him a bit longer in case I was late. So don't worry. I've got plans.'

In the end, when Garfield comes for Bird on Friday night, he brings her a card as usual and a box of chocolates, and just before Bird leaves he puts a little gift bag and a sealed card in her hand.

'You have to open it on Sunday, Mom,' he says. He kisses her on the cheek. 'Happy birthday.'

She hugs him close, feels him let go first. Used to be she would peel his arms from her neck. She waves them off and blows a kiss. The car disappears at the end of the grove.

She puts both cards on the mantelpiece and the gift bag next to it. It's very small. Jewellery. He must have saved up hard for it. She puts the television on and eats her dinner in front of the news.

Sunday, nine o'clock in the morning, the door knocks. Paulette thinks about not answering. She's not dressed because why? Might just soak in some nice bubble bath and scrub the hard skin from her feet. Or maybe put on a hair treatment and then some nail polish and take herself off to the West Indian Community Centre on Spring Street where there's a dance. She's bound to know someone when she gets there. She can catch up with people she hasn't seen for years. Put on a nice frock and some high heels. Catch a little groove. Maybe she might meet a man. The idea fills her with dread.

More knocks again, louder. She pulls her dressing gown tight around her waist and makes sure her headtie looks neat. She opens the door. Nellie. The boy rarely comes at the weekend or bank holidays without being invited because more often than not Bird is with his father, and if for some reason he's at home, then Paulette wants her son all to herself. And anyway, he must spend time with his grandfather. But the sight of the boy with a square box tied with ribbon and an envelope bigger than his own face makes a lump in her throat.

'Happy birthday,' he says, smiling. 'The latch was on so the key wouldn't work.' She brings him in and when he sees the empty living room he says, 'Where's Bird?'

'His father took him out for something. He'll be back later,' but she can't look him in the eye when she lies the same way he can't with her.

'Oh,' he says, 'if you're having a party or something, I'll go,' but he doesn't move.

'You want a drink?' she says.

'Aren't you going to open your present?' he says.

'Oh yes, yes.'

The ribbon slips off easily. She eases the sellotape from the paper and then takes the lid off the box. It's a silver bracelet with flowers around the edge in blue and pink. It's got little yellow beads and a tiny bumble bee for the clasp. Very terrible and lovely.

'Nellie, it's beautiful,' she says. She opens the card, big, pink and glittery. *To my friend, Pea*, it says. *Happy Birthday*. And inside Nellie has written his name next to Frank's.

'It's from both of us,' he says. 'But I chose it.'

She bites her lip and puts her arms around him, 'Thank you, Nellie.' But when she tries to pull away, he holds her close. He's way over height now, a boy still but the hold is strong. A clear ten seconds goes by. She leans back.

'You're a good boy to remember,' she says and she doesn't care if she has water in her eyes and she doesn't care if he knows Bird isn't there to give his mother his good wishes.

'It's easy,' he says, 'you're like my mom,' and this time, for the first time, she doesn't correct him.

Paulette sits him in the kitchen. She gives him some cold chicken from the fridge because Nellie can eat day or night. It disappears as she heats up a bowl of West Indian soup that he tackles like a veteran, sucking meat from the bones, halving dumplings against the side of the bowl. She smiles.

'Bird tells me you got into trouble again, Nellie.'

'What did he say?'

'Never mind what he said. I want to hear it from you.'

'It wasn't my fault this time.'

'You're already on a warning, Nellie. This is the third or fourth time. You can't keep fighting people every time some-body does something you don't like.'

He doesn't look up, carries on eating and speaks to the bowl.

'It was an accident.'

'That's not what I hear. You know the saying, "Tell the truth and shame the devil"? Well, if you want to be a good person you have to take responsibility for what you do whether it's good or bad.'

He sits back and looks off into the distance. The boy is good-looking without a doubt, but he always needs a hair-cut, always needs better clothes and better care. If Nellie was hers, she would dress him in good-fitting jeans and quality shirts with long sleeves, or sweatshirts like all the kids are wearing. She would keep his hair so short you would be able to see his face properly and she would make that boy shower twice a day. He's getting big now, hormones ripe to the nose. By rights, he should have a man to speak to about sex and girls and keeping himself fresh and clean.

'Yesterday,' he says, 'I went out with Grandad to the hills. He's got some new tablets and he's not so sleepy. Anyway, he loves going walking and sometimes I don't mind going with him. But really I only go for the mint cake. I knew he had some in his bag but he said I couldn't have it until we got to the top. I was well tired, man.'

Paulette smiles at the boy's phrase.

'Anyway, it starts drizzling and it got really slippery on the rocks and there was nothing to hold on to. I said we should go back but he just keeps going and telling me all the time, "It's good for you, it's good for you." All I want is the mint cake. Have you ever had mint cake?'

Paulette shakes her head.

'In the end he had to help me up the last bit. The view at the top was amazing, but all the time he's telling me, "Don't stop, Cornelius, don't stop," and he's telling me where to put my feet and do this and don't do that. Instructions all the time. I hate it. I can't help it. I just really hate it. And that's what the boy at school was doing.'

'What did the boy say?'

'He told me to fuck off.' He waits to see her reaction and when she can't bite back the smile, he says, 'I had to make him see the error of his ways, as Frank would say.'

'Nellie,' she says. 'Nellie, you have to behave yourself.'

He carries on eating.

'Anyway, you're back at school and they're not taking it any further. That's the main thing.'

Nellie looks up from the bowl, his spoon in mid-air.

'Speak if you have something to say, Nellie.'

'I don't like it when people tell me what the main thing is.'

Paulette picks up the saucer where he has laid his lamb bones neatly, picked clean and dry. 'Well, what do you think the main thing is, then?'

'My grandfather has a main thing for him. Bird has a main thing for him. You have one for you. And I have one. The main thing is different for everybody.'

'Boy, you always have the answer for everything. Maybe you will be a teacher when you grow up or get a good job like your grandfather had.'

Nellie stops eating. He puts his spoon down and wipes his mouth with a piece of kitchen towel.

'I'm not like him. I'm not like my mother either, apparently. He says he doesn't know who I'm like. Maybe my father. But he doesn't know anything about him. So, I'm a mystery.'

'Well, you're good enough for me, Cornelius. And you're good enough to do the washing-up. Come.'

25

Bird's sixteenth birthday. Garfield says he's taking him to Manchester because there's family over from Montserrat who want to meet him and he can have a party with everyone, cousins, aunties, uncles. It's a whole weekend thing.

The Barn Owl is also invited. Paulette is not. She wants to say to Garfield he better make house rules when they get there because Bird is not having his future ruined by getting a white girl pregnant. And Paulette is not having the girl's father come to her door making noise. And also, can he make sure that amongst all the partying and meeting people, Bird is revising because Bird is not having his future ruined by falling behind at school neither. If any kind of misfortune comes to Bird, it will be on Garfield's watch, not hers, so he better make sure he has his two eyes fixed on their son at all times. Not his daughters, not his seldom-seen family and not anybody else. On Bird. Sometimes, even thinking about Garfield and his bragging mouth makes her kiss her teeth so loud she gets face ache.

Barn Owl is still flirty-flirty and Paulette still isn't too worried about it becoming long term but she notices a little break in the friendship Bird has with Nellie. When the three of them are in the same company, which is rare, she sees, as sure as eggs is eggs, Nellie is jealous.

The three of them are sitting out the backyard with pop and crisps. Paulette is seasoning chicken, the onions smarting her eyes, the smell of thyme and garlic on her hands. She's pretending not to listen to their conversation, looking busy and preoccupied, but the back door is open and her ears are good.

'Fantasy sandwich,' says Bird.

The girl, who has a laugh like a knife on concrete, says, 'I like Coronation Chicken with extra mayonnaise.'

Then Nellie comes in. 'Why have a fantasy about something you can go and buy for a quid?'

'White lion and hibiscus,' says Bird in a faraway voice.

'You can't eat a white lion, Bird mate. There's not even a shop that sells lion meat,' says Nellie.

'Exactly. It's a fantasy, Nellie. Yeah? We eat lamb and beef, don't we? Why cows and not lions? Yeah. It's unattainable like – like Madonna. See what I mean?'

'I love Madonna,' says the girl but Nellie cuts across her.

'All right. Moondust.'

'Don't be a wanker, Nellie man.'

'What?'

'You can't eat moondust. It's got to be edible.'

'Oh, right. Edible but unattainable. Right.'

'Something you could eat if you could catch it.'

'A rainbow, then. Or the flu. Chicken pox.'

'And eat it, Nellie. And eat.'

The girl laughs again and Paulette can hear the change in Nellie and feel the temperature drop.

'I've got no idea.' Nellie says the words short and tight.

'Ask me,' says Bird.

'No, forget it. Anyway, you just said yours was lion meat.'

'That was just an example.'

Nellie sighs. 'What is your fantasy sandwich, Bird?'

'I'm not sure. There's so many. How many can I have?'

'A hundred.'

'You're not taking this seriously, Nellie.'

'Fuck off, Bird. You're doing my head in.'

Bird and the girl start laughing together. 'You're so easy,' says Bird. 'You take everything too seriously.'

'Yeah,' says the girl. 'Too seriously.'

Paulette peeps out the window and sees the set-up. The girl practically sitting on Bird's lap with one arm draped round his neck and Nellie hunched over with a piece of long grass in his hand, making patterns in the dirt.

'Nellie!' Paulette shouts. 'Come here.'

He comes into the kitchen with his face vex.

'Leave them,' she says. 'Help me with this.'

He already knows how to rinse rice and put the peas to soak. He already knows how to skin a chicken if she wanted one doing and how to brown it too. He already knows how to soften the skin of plantain and pick the bones from salt-fish. He already knows how to grate the fresh coconut and squeeze out the water. She passes him a good piece of yam and a sharp knife.

'Peel this and four potatoes. And some sweet potato there, look.'

His head is down, his hands work quick. There's no need to speak to Nellie like you might have to with other children but she wants to take his mind off the lovebirds in the garden.

'How is school?'

'All right.'

'You behaving yourself?'

'I got an A in English.'

'Good. You always know how to explain yourself and you've been ahead in your reading since you were little, so that's no surprise. But you're sixteen now, Nellie. You need to start planning out your future. Bird wants to stay on into sixth form. You want to do that as well?'

'Nah, I'm going to join the army or the navy.'

'Oh? Well, you better start practising taking orders before you wind up in a court martial.'

'How many potatoes did you say?'

'Four. And how is Frank?'

'Paulette,' he says, 'Frank is Frank.' He mimics her perfectly down to the stance she has when she's cooking. She shoves him with her elbow.

'And how are his new tablets?'

He straightens himself up, adjusts his school tie and hunches himself over. 'Ah, well, Paulette, I'm so pleased you asked, actually. Allow me to divulge some details. You see, my new medication is somewhat stronger than the last batch, if you follow my meaning, and if I may be blunt, they give me an awful case of the shits.'

Paulette laughs. 'Listen,' she says. 'Don't mind Bird out there. He's just showing off.'

'You know what else, Paulette? Bird is Bird,' he says in her voice and later on she remembers how he said it, like he knew Bird better than she did. But right then, with him standing up like a big man making West Indian soup with his West Indian accent with his lip turn down and his side-eye, she can't help but laugh. Soon as the dinner is cooking and they're sitting at the kitchen table, when Bird and his girl-friend have gone upstairs to be on their own, she sees that same dark look come over his face.

'Listen, Nellie. Don't worry about all the giggling and kissing. It will wear off.'

'Everyone's got a girlfriend except me. And everyone that's staying on to sixth form are all in a gang.'

'You could stay on if you wanted. Frank would be happy.'

'God!' he shouts. 'I know! He keeps going on about it. But I can't. And I don't want to. And he never fucking listens to me!'

'Nellie, watch your mouth.'

'Sorry. It's just . . .'

'Just what?'

He turns his face up to the ceiling like someone wrote the answer on the lightshade. He closes his eyes and Paulette can see the quiver on his top lip and the blood flush his face. 'What happens when he dies?' he says quietly.

'What?'

'My grandfather. He's really old. And he's sick. What happens to me when he dies?'

'Frank isn't going anywhere. You think seventy is old?'

He looks at her with his black eyes. 'I'll have no one,' he says.

'Nellie, "when" is a long, long time away. And when it comes, you'll have all the answers and you'll be a grown-up person with your own life. Anything can happen. Stop worrying. And if you frown like that, it will be you looking seventy before your time.'

He goes home before the soup is done. That night, when the house is quiet, when Bird is in bed in soft sheets and clean pyjamas with his fresh shirt hanging on the back of his door, she thinks of Nellie and feels bad that she didn't say more, that she didn't put her arms around him and make him a promise. But if there's one thing Paulette knows good, it's that promises can break easy as a china cup and nobody knows what the future will bring.

26

Summer holidays soon come. Bird has finished his exams, praise the ever-living Lord. All Paulette has done since March is remind the boy to revise, make sure he gets to bed at a good hour and feed him up. Garfield's contribution is to tell Paulette he wants Bird off the television and off the Nintendo game thing and to not let him out with his friends and to put some kind of time limit on Barn Owl's visits. 'Flying visits,' he says because he thinks he's funny.

Paulette had to remind him that it was him and his wife who bought Bird a little sixteen-inch television for his room, making extra work for her going up to check it's revising he's doing not watching films. When Barn Owl is in the house, it's hard to tell the difference between the girl's shrill giggling and the canned laughter on a game show. More than once, she's had to take the television out and put it in her own bedroom until Bird behaves himself. And Bird gets cheeky when he's cornered and it's Paulette getting most of it directed against her, but then again, he's under pressure. Finally, June comes and it's all over.

On the last day of school, Bird comes home early. Flings the kitchen door open and says, 'Mom, guess what?'

'What? Bird, don't pick at the food, it's not ready yet.'

'Nellie stole a car.'

'What?'

'You should have seen it. He stole a car and drove it past the school gate. Everyone was outside because it's the last day and Nellie pulls up outside the school with this other kid and bangs on the horn. *Baaaaaaarrrpppp!* Man, it was so loud.'

'Nellie can't drive.'

'Oh yes, he can. Mom, I'm starving.'

Paulette motions to the cupboard where she keeps biscuits and cakes. 'Only one, Bird, and then go and get changed.'

Bird leans against the sink and shakes his head. 'Man, you should have seen him. I bet he gets caught.'

'When was this?'

'Just now, soon as the bell went. We were all outside and saw him. He looked like he was crying or something.'

'Why didn't you stop him, Bird? He's going to get into trouble.'

Bird throws the chocolate wrapper in the bin. 'Me? What could I do?'

Paulette sits at her kitchen table and reads the free paper. She's not sure why she reads it these days, nothing but bad news and gossip. Sometimes, they're advertising local jobs. She sees an advert for someone to work in a greengrocer. She knows the shop, a nice old-fashioned place where they have a tidy display outside and shelves of tins inside, where the man wears a white apron like it's 1955 and weighs everything out on a big mechanical scale. Trainee, it says. And the wage is good.

Maybe Nellie should apply. Keep the foolish boy out of trouble. What is he playing at stealing cars, acting like a badman?

That evening, she can't rest because Nellie hasn't come round for a long time now. Maybe the boy really has got himself arrested or been in some kind of accident. She rings Frank's house but no one answers. She puts the telly on but can't settle. The news comes on showing all kinds of strife in the world and she gets a bad feeling about that boy, same feeling she had when he was so small, when he held out his cold, cold hand. 'Pleased to meet you.' How many times has she rocked the boy to sleep and fed him and kissed him and held him close? How many times has she watched him playing and watched him laughing and felt some kind of tremor in her consciousness? Something isn't right and no one can tell her different.

She puts her coat on and calls to Bird to get ready.

'Where we going?'

'To look for Nellie. See if he's at home or he really has got into trouble. I hope I find that boy in his own house where he should be.'

'Why do I have to come?' says Bird, dragging his feet. His hands deep in his tracksuit trousers.

'Because he is your friend from childhood, Bird. And you don't turn your back on your friends. And if he's in trouble or if something's going on, maybe you can talk to him.'

'Me? No one can talk to Nellie, Mom. He argues with everyone at school, even the teachers. You don't know him.'

The thing is, Paulette does know him, and that's what's got her walking the streets at night. They cross the park to Shirt & Tie's house and knock the door. Nothing. But Paulette can see a light on somewhere. She lifts the latch on the back gate and sees through into the kitchen. Bird is behind her. There's someone in there. She walks quietly up to the back door and opens it.

'Frank?' she says.

But it's not Frank. It's Nellie. He's standing under the cold naked bulb of the kitchen, wriggling and struggling in a black, sparkly dress. A silver butterfly brooch on the shoulder suddenly drops to the floor. Nellie is wearing his school trousers with the dress on top, tight and stretchy, pulling across his naked chest, and he's fighting to get out of it. On the table in front of him are a pair of girl's black shoes and a tartan skirt.

'Fucking hell, Nellie,' whispers Bird, giggling. 'Nah, man. I didn't know you was into this stuff, man. Wicked!'

Paulette is quick. She bustles Bird out of the kitchen door and locks it behind him. 'Go home,' she says. 'Now! Go!' And she puts her finger on her mouth to tell him to be quiet. She draws the curtains so he can't see in and, when she turns back to Nellie, he is ripping the dress off, red in the face, breathing heavy.

'Nellie, calm down, calm down. Don't tear it. Look, let me help you. Quiet down.' She pulls the dress up over his head. 'One arm at a time, Nellie. Not so fast.'

It comes off in two pieces in the end and, as Paulette puts

it carefully together on the kitchen table, she sees a small suitcase on the floor with lots of other clothes in it, a small make-up bag and some cheap jewellery.

Nellie is panting. He flops into a kitchen chair and puts his head on his arms on the table. She cannot see his face but she can hear him. Great gulps in his throat like his heart will break. Paulette puts her hand on the back of his head and strokes his hair, damp from sweat.

'I was just trying it on. That's all,' he says.

'Nellie, it's your business. Nobody else needs to know. Come, look. Your school jumper, Nellie. Put it on.'

He grabs it and shoves his arms inside. 'I was just trying it on to see,' he says.

'Yes, yes. I know. Sshhhh.'

He sits up quickly. 'It's fucking Frank! Always saying I'm like her. Arguing and stuff. Answering him back. Every fucking day. All my fucking life. And I just wanted to see for myself. It's my mom's dress! Not mine. And it's not his either. I just found it and I wanted to – wanted to . . .'

Paulette looks at the suitcase. 'Those are your mother's clothes?'

'Yes! He took it, Frank did, he took that from the home where she died and he kept it under the stairs. I knew it was there and I just wanted to see if—'

Paulette sees the bloom of damp and mould on the side of the old case and now can smell the stale fustiness of the airless cupboard.

'Nellie,' she says. 'Sit up. Sit up. Come on. Sit up and tell me what happened. And tell me about driving cars around. What's going on?'

He wipes his nose on the sleeve of his school jumper. His face is a mess, red and blotchy. His eyes are the same.

'Everyone thinks he's like this proper person but he's not. He's a mess, man. And he's seeing some fucking counsellor that keeps telling him to talk about his feelings, so he keeps getting all the papers out and going over and over the accident. With me! I mean, come on! The fucking detail, man. What she was like when she lived in the care home. How her head was, like, mashed in one side and shit like that. I can't remember! I was like three when she died. He goes on and on about it till I feel like I'm going mad. I don't want to know. He forgets that's my mother he's talking about, you know! It gets on my fucking nerves!'

Paulette sits dead still. She puts her hand on his arm and squeezes. Nellie sniffs.

'He always tells me to behave when I'm not even doing anything wrong. All I was doing was asking him for some pocket money, and he said we don't have money for things like that, and I said why. Everyone else in my class gets pocket money. You give Bird money, don't you? And his dad gives him money as well.'

Paulette nods.

'At first, he didn't say anything, but then he said when my mom was in the accident she went to this place, a big massive place by the lake, The Cedars or something like that, and he said he sold his house to pay for it because it was some kind of special expensive treatment or something where they said they would make her better, but they fucking didn't.'

His face is dry now. She can see the anger still bubbling up.

'Every time he tells me about my mom, it's different. Sometimes he says she was cheeky and didn't do as she was told. So, I'm like her, then. But other times, it's "Oh, she was perfect, she was beautiful, she just made a mistake." And I'm nothing like her. Them times, I'm like my father, who- ever that is, some kid at her school or some boy from the area. Who the fuck knows. Nobody. So, obviously when I'm doing something wrong, then I'm like my father. Mr Fucking Invisible.'

Paulette shakes her head. 'Nellie, that's hard.'

'It's not hard! It's impossible and it's fucking bullshit! We even did it in biology and it's nurture not nature.'

'What is?'

'What you're like. It's about what happens to you when you're growing up. You can't catch badness off anyone. You just can't. So if there's something wrong with me, it's his own fucking fault. He should have let me get adopted. Did you know that? I could have got adopted if he'd said yes but he didn't so I have to grow up in this shit place with him.'

'That's because he loves you, Nellie.'

'Yeah, right. He just felt guilty cos he fucked it up with her. That's all it is. Guilty conscience. Anyway, I said I want some trainers, that's all, just some proper fucking trainers, man. Money doesn't grow on trees, he says. No shit, professor. I'll tell you what does grow on trees, though, yeah? Manners and reading and sit up straight and shake hands and Latin and fucking documentaries. Yeah, nuff of those everywhere. He went to school in World War fucking Two. He's got no idea what it's like now when you're wearing trampy clothes and these fucking trainers.'

He rips the shoes from his feet and launches them across the room. They bounce off the kitchen cupboard. 'And you know what he said? He said all the rest of the money's saved up for university. "Your future has to be accounted for, Cornelius." Fucking hell, Paulette. You don't know what he's like. I keep telling him I'm leaving school, and he keeps saying no I'm not. He keeps telling me about the future when I can make something of myself because my mom was clever and didn't get the chance to make the most of herself. Honestly, you should hear him. He's not right in here.'

Nellie screws his finger into his temple and keeps jabbing it until Paulette holds it and tells him to stop. 'Nellie, calm down. It's hard right now but—'

'And anyway, what fucking future? I don't care about the future. What about now? What about what I want?'

Nellie is up now, walking round the kitchen in his thin socks, walking round Paulette's chair, picking up a milk bottle and putting it down again, picking up a fork and a knife and waving them around. Vex.

'And then I remembered he said he had some of her things. I asked if I could see them and he said when I'm older and I said why and he said because I was still a child and if I wasn't a child I wouldn't be breaking the law. I said I only took the car for like ten minutes and he asked me where I learned to drive in the first place and I said some of the other kids showed me and he said I was a disgrace to the memory of my mother and my grandmother. Grandmother? Grandmother? He's bringing her into it now, someone I've never even met! "Despite my greatest efforts, I find you cannot be trusted, Cornelius." Blah blah blah. I told him to fuck off and he walked out of the door. I knew where her things were, in that cupboard under the stairs, because he's been taking out the papers from the court case and reading them to me. Jesus. No one knows, man. No one knows.'

He drops into the kitchen chair opposite Paulette and she holds his hand while he cries, not even trying to hide it any more, not even wiping the tears off his face. Paulette runs her thumb across his cheek.

'I found the suitcase,' he whispers, 'and I opened it. It's just . . . I just wanted to see how big she was and what sort of person she was and I was only going to look. She was only eighteen when she had me and I was thinking what she would be like. You know, before the accident, and maybe if she was alive, she'd be my friend or something. I mean, not my friend . . . I was thinking . . .'

'What?'

'I wanted to feel close to her.'

'Of course you did. Nothing wrong with that, Nellie.'

'I'm not a freak or nothing, Paulette. Now everyone will know.' He puts both hands over his face. Paulette peels them back.

'Nellie, you leave Bird to me. He will keep his mouth shut or be sorry about it.'

She makes him look at her, puts her face close to his until he looks back. 'What you want to do with your mother's things is your business, Nellie. What you have to do, you have to do. Stop crying. If you want to feel close to your mother, it's your business and no one else's. If Bird tells anyone, he will be in trouble with me. It's not a mistake to love someone, you know. It's natural. Come.'

She bundles the boy up in her arms and holds him close. She can feel his shoulders shake and feel the heaving of his chest. 'Nothing wrong with you, Nellie. You know that, don't you? Other people is other people and you are you. And even if you want to wear a different dress that doesn't belong to your mother, that's all right as well. It's cloth, Nellie. Nothing more than cloth, just cotton and threads. It's not a sin. Don't pay no attention to anyone who makes you feel bad about yourself.'

She makes him look at her again. 'Except stop stealing cars. You didn't get caught by the police?'

He shakes his head.

'You're lucky. But someone will tell them if you're not careful. And someone might tell Frank.'

And right then she hears Frank behind her.

'I beg your pardon?' he says. 'Tell Frank what?'

The man's face is red and sweating and his shirt and tie is all crooked like the first time she saw him in the park. Man looks like he's had a good drink in a bad place.

'I was just calling to see Nellie about coming round tomorrow because—'

'You needn't cover for the boy. We have had some considerable disagreement about his behaviour whereupon he resorted to profanity and aggression. I'm afraid his true nature is coming to the fore.'

'Look, Frank. You can't say that. It's nothing to do with me but take it easy for tonight. I think Nellie has had a shock and you don't want to—'

At that moment, Frank sees the dress. 'What's this? What have you done?' Then he sees the suitcase and falls to his knees like somebody about to pray.

'Don't touch her things!' he shouts. He picks up the dress and holds it to his chest. 'How dare you!'

'Frank, Frank. Calm down. This can't help. Sit down and quiet yourself. You're a grown man.' Paulette pulls Frank up and puts him on a chair.

He clasps the dress and the shoes and the tartan skirt to his chest and speaks quiet and slow to Nellie.

'These things are most precious, Cornelius. I told you! This is the last vestige of my daughter. Don't you understand? There is no explaining your actions these days. This – this – going off the rails and breaking the law. It's intolerable, do you hear? What will become of you?'

Paulette can smell beer off him and he's trying not to sound drunk with no success.

He carries on, Shirt & Tie talking like he's in a Shakespeare play, laying too much blame on the boy and not enough on his own self. Paulette has a good speech of her own waiting on her bottom lip ready to spill. Who brought him up, she wants to say? The house so poor and so dry not even a lampshade in the kitchen. No food on the side. No little bit of softness or colour. No wonder the boy wants some excitement. A young boy like Nellie, feeling embarrassed about how he lives and what he has to wear. All right, all right, so he's in the wrong, but don't talk so much nonsense, Frank. A man of big years losing control of himself in front of the boy. What kind of example is that? But instead of pouring petrol on the flames, Paulette puts the kettle on and makes a cup of coffee for Shirt & Tie and a drink of squash for Nellie, cheap economy squash, not the proper brand Coca-Cola all the kids like.

'Drink this,' she says to both of them.

She waits until Shirt & Tie has his hands on the cup before she says, 'I'm going home, I've got my son to look after. But, Frank, take my advice and calm yourself down. You've been drinking. And listen, Nellie hasn't done nothing wrong. You have to give the boy some leeway. School's not easy for him. The child is a good boy and you love him, I know that. But you have to put yourself in his shoes a little bit. He's got no mother and he's confused and he's hurt. You listening, Frank?'

Frank says nothing and he stares at nothing, his eyes full of water and pain. She takes one long look at the two of them, sitting on their separate chairs in the stark kitchen with the naked bulb hanging above, and she shakes her head.

'Enough words have been said tonight, Frank. Go upstairs to your bed and sleep it off. Nellie, come home with me.'

'No,' he says. 'No, thank you. I don't want to see anyone. Thank you.'

She moves his hair aside so she can see his face. Polite to a fault. 'Everything is all right. Don't worry about anything. Tomorrow is another day. Come and see me if you can't sleep. I'll be up.'

She walks home the long way so she can think. She tries to put the jigsaw of Frank and Nellie together, his wife and her death and the girl pregnant and the accident. And the baby Frank must have had to fight for. Paulette knew from time Nellie was going to change her life. She knew from the minute the child put his hand in hers, like God was winking at her, saying, 'Watch him now, Paulette!' Not one single soul on this earth could say Paulette hadn't done her best by the boy, fed him, clothed him, scuffed him when he was out of line, advised him, hugged him and done everything short of be a mother to the boy. That special place was reserved for Bird and Bird alone. And yet, there is an extra chamber in Paulette's heart and in that place lives Cornelius Bowen and there's nothing she can do about it.

27

Two days later, Shirt & Tie is at the door. Paulette was half expecting him after the kitchen scene. When Paulette got home that night, she called Bird down from his bedroom and sat him on the settee.

'I hope you haven't told anyone what you think you saw, Bird.'

He smiles and shakes his head. 'Man, it was—' but the look Paulette gives him clamps up his mouth. She sees him calculating how much leeway he has with her but on this subject Bird is on ice so thin it can't hold him. She puts her finger close in his face.

'You think you know everything about life, Bird. Let me tell you something, what Nellie was doing was natural when you grow up without a mother. You don't know nothing about that, do you? Because you've always had me and you will always have me. Nellie is lonely, Bird, and when you're lonely you will try anything. Some people live different, which you will discover one day. In my eyes and in the eyes of God, you don't pass judgement on things you don't understand and you always come down on the side of mercy.'

Bird bites his lip. 'Okay, okay.'

'Who you speaking to, Bird?'

'Yes, Mom.'

'That's better. Don't let me hear you been running your mouth with your friends or that big-eye girl you got there.'

'I finished with Leah.'

'Why?'

'She kept coming round when I told her not to.'

'Well, good. And don't talk to nobody else about him.'

'Yes, Mom.'

Paulette loves her son more than life itself but she is no fool. Bird only has to tell one person in confidence and word will spread. Whatever Frank thinks, it's a good thing Nellie is not going back to that school for sixth form.

So, when Shirt & Tie turns up, she takes him into the kitchen, makes tea and puts some biscuits on a plate. Even though Paulette is tired and upset and worried about Nellie, she tells Frank to sit down because Paulette knows the man is about to tell her something.

'It's about Cornelius,' he says and picks up a biscuit from the plate. He taps it on the table because the two of them know he doesn't need no biscuit but it's something to do with his hands.

'Yes,' she says. 'What about him?'

'I feel it's only right I tell you about him, about his history so to speak.'

Paulette looks at him full in the face, telling him to carry on.

'You see, my daughter was pregnant when the accident happened—'

'You told me that already, Frank.'

'Yes, and when Cornelius was eventually born I don't think she was actually aware of what was happening to her as the brain injury she sustained was rather severe. Traumatic. She was unable to care for herself and she was beset by seizures, rather severe ones, as I say. She was in residential care and died when Cornelius was three years old. Shortly after I first met you, actually. The news was unexpected and I'm afraid I took it rather badly. I rather fell to pieces.' He's tapping the biscuit harder now.

'Sorry,' says Paulette and she's back there peeking through Frank's window, the curtains apart, him sitting there on the sofa crying. That's what was going on that day. Nellie crying for the mother he could hardly know and Frank not even able to come out of his own grief and comfort the boy. She remembers her breath misting on the window and the look that passed between them all.

'She was only twenty-one years old. She died so suddenly that I couldn't get there in time. Hence, she died alone.'

There's a catch in his throat, water in his eyes. The biscuit has broken in half. Paulette puts her hand on his for a moment. 'That's hard, Frank.'

'I was rather ill afterwards – actually, I was rather ill before because of the accident itself. I had a breakdown, you see, and then just as I thought I might recover, her death compounded my already fragile . . . well, you may already be aware I went to prison, for the death of—'

'Denton,' says Paulette. 'For the death of Denton.'

She feels a sudden shift in the air. There's something not right about sitting in her nice clean kitchen with all her pots and pans and dinner in the oven and everything just so except that the man sitting across the table is the man that killed Denton. And again, she is flying across the park and pushing this same man down on to the grass and feeling more hate for him than she thought she could ever feel for another human being. She thinks of him drunk in his own kitchen while Nellie was crying, throwing himself on the kitchen floor, acting like all the bad things in the world only happened to him, putting too much drama in a situation that was already bad.

'My case went to Crown Court,' he says, 'Death by Dangerous Driving, and I pleaded guilty and I was of impeccable character and it had been an unfortunate series of events so, all in all, it was a short sentence, relatively speaking. Nine months.'

Garfield's told her all this. She remembers the who and the how and the when and the short, short time the judge thought Denton's life was worth.

'My barrister was very good and explained to the court that I may have been in shock at the news of Evie's pregnancy and, of course, we had had words. I was thinking, right at the moment of impact, I was thinking of my wife. I saw her quite clearly in my mind's eye and how devastated she would have been. Not with Evie, you understand, but with me and my response, and she would feel I had let her down. What she would have said to me. That's what I was thinking. *Anne, darling*, I thought. *What am I to do?* And Evie was in the back seat and she was shouting at me and I remember thinking to myself, *Anne, where are you? I'm lost.* Yes, I was thinking about Anne. A moment's thoughtlessness on my part. Just a few seconds of inattention. Then all of a sudden I was in the middle of the road and my whole life changed.'

'Yes,' she says. Paulette would give anything for the man to stop tapping the biscuit. It's too loud and it's making a mess.

'Anne was only forty-five when she died and Evie was ten. She was my responsibility, mine alone. And while my wife was a natural mother, I'm afraid I wasn't a natural father. But I was learning. That's the thing. I had begun to love her, properly, as a father should. I thought I had a second chance. That was it. A second chance to make it right. Do you see? And then she told me she was pregnant. I had no idea. None. She was a slight girl and I found it very difficult to believe.'

Paulette nods. 'Yes, you told me, Frank.'

'So, shortly after Cornelius was born, I found myself in prison. My sister was good enough to put herself forward to care for him until I was released, but I had to fight for him. And fight I did. I used it all up, everything I had left, all my emotional reserves, to make sure I got him. He had clung to life. He had survived in spite of everything and I had to have him. Because he was my chance to put it all right. Everything I had done wrong would be put right if I could just have the child.'

Paulette plaits her hands together as she listens. The old man telling her his life story with himself right plum in the centre as usual. What about Nellie? What about Paulette? What about Denton himself, mangled up in the driver's seat with the steering wheel lodged against his chest and his heart never beating again in his whole life?

And still he carries on.

'I've had some considerable time to reflect on things as you might imagine. To begin with, my daughter sustaining such horrendous injuries at my hands was extremely difficult for me. The guilt never quite subsides. And then my going to prison when my barrister thought the sentence might be suspended was quite a shock.'

A shock for him? Difficult for him? Paulette leans back in her chair and remembers, like it was last week, the minutes and hours and days of her grief, and now the man is raking it all up again like he's the victim. His soft voice and his long words, talking like she wasn't even involved, like she's a neighbour and he's chatting over the garden wall. Nobody realizes what Denton's death did to her and, despite the wife and the kids and the lies, when he died something changed deep down, some kind of fracture that time didn't seem to put right. If Denton hadn't have been snatched from the earth, her life would have run along different tracks, smooth and straight.

And somehow, and as God is her witness she can't say exactly how it happened, the man who caused her all this misery is sitting six feet away making a whole heap of biscuit crumbs on her good fucking tablecloth.

She puts her hands up and shakes her head. 'Frank, Frank.'

'What I mean to say is, I had rather a difficult time, on top of which—'

'We all had a difficult time, Frank, if you remember. And while we're on the subject, your grandson is having a difficult time as well. The boy's in pain and you need to step in before it's too late. I think he's getting into some bad company. Maybe you can take him to your sister for the summer holidays and—'

'Yes, yes, yes, of course. You see, Paulette, I simply wanted to explain a few things about the exact circumstances of how we come to be in this position. I think it's important.'

She looks up. 'No, Frank. I'm telling you something important as well. Nellie needs you.'

'Well, yes. Naturally. But what I mean to say is, although I was given nine months, I was actually in prison for only four, and during that time, with a little research, I found a place called The Cedars in Downham Valley, which was developing a new treatment. Frightfully expensive but such a caring place so I had little alternative . . .'

Outside, a few doors away, there's a dog barking. The people keep the dog chained up and all day it barks and tries to get attention. When it gets tired, the barks turn into yelps and whines and still nobody comes for it. Paulette hears the dog now and all she wants to do is go and break the chain off the wall and let the dog go free. If she could rescue that dog, Paulette feels, she would be able to put the whole world right. And still Frank is talking. She stands up quickly.

'Frank, you don't hear me? All that is history. Yours. Not mine. Go and tell somebody with qualifications who can help you. It's not me that should have to listen to it. I don't want to hear what you got to say about the accident. You don't think it might be painful for me to remember how the man I loved got killed?'

'Yes, yes. That's it, you see. I have spoken to my counsellor and that's why I would like to explain. I think you misunderstand, I only—'

She shakes her head and walks to the kitchen door. 'I misunderstand? Listen, Frank, I got sorrows of my own. You don't notice, do you, Frank? You don't notice, you don't say sorry and you don't care.'

He gets to his feet and opens his mouth to speak but Paulette holds her hand right up to his face.

'Go home, Frank,' she says.

He doesn't move. 'Ah, I see I may not have chosen a good time. I am so sorry for distressing you. It may be that—'

Paulette kisses her teeth, long and hard. 'What did I just say?'

They both see Bird at the same time, standing at the door listening.

'You heard her,' he says with a hard voice. A man's voice now.

Bird takes two steps backwards, leaving a space for Shirt & Tie to leave the kitchen. He shuffles carefully past Bird. 'I'm sorry,' he mutters.

'Get out,' says Bird.

Paulette hears the front door close quietly.

'You all right, Mom?'

'Yes,' she says. But she worries about what her son heard. She can't remember what she said out loud and what she only thought. She's not sure what he already knows about Denton, or what Garfield has told him, and wonders if he realizes she never loved his father, that he was born of second best. She wipes her eyes and takes a deep breath.

'You sure you're all right?' he says again.

'Yes, yes.'

Bird leans down and kisses Paulette on the cheek. 'I never liked him anyway,' he says.

When Bird has gone, Paulette sweeps Frank's crumbs into her hand and flicks them into the bin.

28

Paulette is ten years old, sitting on the hard bench of St Barnabas Chapel, early Sunday morning, swinging her feet. It's cool inside, the shutters are closed and the light is dim. Granny is wearing her best shoes, the ones that pinch her bad foot, but sandals are not allowed, not on Granny and definitely not on Paulette. Granny always sits with both hands on the Bible and Paulette must do the same. 'Keep your hands on the Lord's words and you cannot get in trouble, Sweet Pea.'

Paulette loves the hymns but when the service starts she tunes out and still gets the gist if Granny asks her later. Instead, you can look at the stained-glass windows and wonder if you could draw it with your pencils or you could wonder what you will have for a snack when you get home and if Granny might make conch fritters or if there's any sugar cake left. And she wonders who might come to their house after church for sweet cold lemonade with the bits floating on top. If it's Miss Cardin with Marlene or Judith, they'll take her to swim in the river. But if it's Mr and Mrs Powell, she will have to stay and serve the drinks while the adults talk about the sermon.

Then, just like someone opened a door, she feels a drop in temperature. She looks at Granny, who is searching for a scripture in the Bible and so is everyone else. The minister raises his finger.

'And what does it say at Matthew chapter twenty-five verse thirteen? Watch therefore! For ye know neither the day nor the hour wherein the Son of Man cometh. When you least expect it, says Our Lord Jesus. When you are thinking about something else, when you are making your plans, when you, with your prideful self, think you can dictate the direction of your own destiny, then! Then, the Lord will strike. Pay attention, each and every one of you!'

It was as if the man had looked into Paulette's faithless heart and found her mind wandering when it should have been on the serious business of praising the Lord and keeping watch. Sometimes, says the minister, you're looking in one direction and life catches you from behind.

It's only a matter of days before things get serious with Cornelius and somewhere in the back of her mind Paulette was marking time, waiting for it. When she looks back, she wonders if she could have done something else. Maybe she should have taken the boy when he was offered to her or let the boy come live with her from when he was small. But Bird has always come first, which is exactly as it should be, and her son is studious, kind, polite and well behaved. And despite all she has done for Nellie, she hasn't changed a single thing. He still has a sharp lip, a dark sadness and completely perfect manners. But them manners are only sheep's clothing and Nellie is beginning to show his teeth.

If she had to pin it down, she would say it started when Nellie got drunk on the street. Maggie sees him and comes to tell her. She stands at Paulette's front door with two bags of shopping.

'Just now, up on Hanover Street, by the bookies.'

'What was he doing?'

'Well,' Maggie says, putting down her shopping and lighting a cigarette, 'he walks straight into me, weaving all over the street. "Watch it!" I said to him and I pushed him away because I was about to topple over myself. He tells me to fuck off and gives me the finger. And then, while he's all impressed with himself, he knocks into someone else and someone else and starts singing and bellowing like a banshee.'

'Jesus,' says Paulette.

'Last I saw of him, he was running between the cars at the traffic lights, banging on the roofs and the bonnets, making a right bloody nuisance of himself. One bloke got out and started chasing him and he ran off. Anyway, there's nothing you can do. He'll be long gone by now.'

'Thanks for telling me, Maggie. Like you say, I can't do nothing.'

'That's the length of it, Paulette. I'll see you.'

Nellie isn't finished yet. Two days later, he steals a car. How does Paulette know? She knows because Bird is in the car with him. Nellie persuades Bird to get into an old beat-up car belonging to one of his fool-fool friends. A car so loud you can hear it from Scotland. A patchwork-looking car somebody sewed together at a welding shop. How does Paulette know? Because as soon as she got in from work, Maggie ran round and told her the car screeched down the grove, parked outside her house and Bird got in. It drove off fast, skidding and weaving, and Maggie thought it was going to crash. It was late afternoon and Maggie was waiting all day for Paulette to get in from work.

Paulette is heartsick. She is weightless. She stands at her front door waiting for the car to come back, screech or no screech, loud or quiet. It must come back so she doesn't have to ring Garfield and tell him. It must come back before she gets a phone call from the hospital to say her son is lying on a bed with a broken leg.

One hour feels like one week. And it's two long hours before the phone rings and it's Garfield. Yes, there has been an accident. He's at the police station. He's bringing Bird home now. He's all right.

She's standing by the front door when they pull up. Garfield shoves Bird inside and steps in behind him.

'What you say, Bird?' says Garfield.

'Sorry.'

'Sorry what?'

'Sorry, Mom.'

Garfield kisses his teeth. 'Go upstairs and wash off the stink of that police cell. I can't look at you.'

Paulette wants to put her arms around her son but not now, not in front of Garfield. Bird walks past her and Garfield closes the door.

'What did I say, Paulette? What did I say?'

'What happened?'

'Oh! Oh! You don't know your son's been riding round in a mash-down car with that white boy you keep in your house?'

'I was at work.'

'You sure you was at work and not out with your fancy piece while Bird was wrapping himself round a tree up in Downham Valley?'

'Garfield, I was at work. What happened?'

'Let me tell you. It was you brought that old man into your house and introduce his grandson to Bird, right? You. It was you who thinks it's all right for a boy who wears women's clothes and takes cars and gets drunk on the street at sixteen to be sitting in your kitchen like he's family. You. Well, that same boy makes Bird get in a stolen car and he says he's going to find his mother. And you know his mother is dead, right?'

'Yes, I know.'

'Yes. So, the boy is crazy as well as everything else. He takes the car right up to some big, deserted hospital in Downham Valley and breaks through the security gate, tells Bird how she died in the building and it was his fault. He rides around the house like he's on a racing track and sets off the alarm. Police come and he makes them chase him right out to the motorway.'

Paulette's hands are gripping one another. 'Is he all right?'

'Bird, you mean?'

'Of course I mean Bird! Is he all right I said?'

Garfield shakes his head. 'You saw him just now! Paulette, it's only by the skin of his teeth we've still got him with us.'

He drops on to the settee, throws his head back and closes his eyes. 'Jesus God Almighty.'

'What happened?'

'Just give me a minute, all right. Just give me a minute.' Garfield starts rubbing both hands over his face like he's washing with soap and water. Because she knows him good, she recognizes this is instead of being angry and instead of saying something harsh.

'You want a drink?'

'Yes, yes, get me a drink.'

Paulette pours two inches of Appleton's in a glass and hands it to him. He's shaking.

'Fucking police,' he mutters. If Paulette wants the whole story she is going to have to be patient. She cannot go upstairs and see to Bird, she cannot ask Garfield any more questions, she cannot get upset and she cannot try to defend Nellie who, whatever is wrong with the boy, has now overstepped the line so far she's not sure he can step back. Anyway, sit down, Paulette, and wait.

After a few minutes, Garfield starts.

'That white boy can get in trouble all he likes because he's white. You think Bird can afford to get his face known by police? What you think they see when they look at Bird? Thief. Burglar. Robber.'

'What happened, Garfield? Can you tell me properly?'

'I am telling you – if you could just listen, you would hear it.'

They lock eyes with a lifetime of unfinished arguments rearing up like a pack of wild dogs. Paulette is first to look away.

'Yes, sorry. What were you saying?'

'I'm sitting at home. I get a phone call from the police. They said they are at some hospital I never even heard of. Bird is there. He's not hurt. I have to come straight away. Before I can even find my keys and leave the house, they ring back and tell me instead I must drive to the police station because Bird is fine, it's the other boy who needs stitches in his head.'

Paulette bites back any questions she has about Nellie because now is not the time. But Garfield sees.

'No, Paulette. It's not that boy you should be thinking about. Bird could be locked up right now with junkies and child molesters and in court tomorrow morning.'

Paulette feels her blood run like ice. Garfield is up on his feet now, pacing the room, his lips thin and hard.

'So, I get to the police station and they said Bird is locked up and he gave my name. Am I his father, they ask. Yes, I am. They tell me they're not sure what they are going to do with him. Then they leave me an hour in reception. No word, nothing. I ask to see him. I ask to see him. I ask again. Wait, is all they say. Eventually, one renk piece of lard comes out with a face like a bulldog. Asks me if Bird has ever stolen a car before. I said Bird can't drive and the man laughs. He asks me if Bird has ever been in trouble with the police before. I say no, officer. He goes away. I wait again.'

Now, Garfield is fake laughing, the cold laughter she used to hear from him all the time.

'You know what they said? They said, "We've seen other cases like this when boys like your son start running amuck. It's how riots start." That's what they said. I had to keep my mouth quiet. Riots? What does Bird have to do with riots? So, I said to the officer, it was the other boy driving and he shook his head. Both boys ran off when the car crashed and the arresting officer said it looked like the black boy was the driver.'

Paulette is shaking her head over and over. 'I can't believe it,' she says.

'Well, you better believe it. Anyway, eventually, another officer comes and says I have to wait to see what the other boy says, and if their story holds up, Bird could get off with a caution. Four hours altogether. He comes back after four hours and says yes, the white boy said he was the driver.'

'Good.'

'Good? You think that's good? You think it's good I had to debase myself in front of them? Yes, officer, no, officer, three bags full, officer. Please, Mr Policeman, he won't do it again. Please, Mr Officer, if you could just be lenient this time. They made me wait right until now to give me their decision. There is me, Garfield Lynch, in a police station in a country village twenty miles from civilization. I don't even know where I am. And I'm thinking I'm going to have to leave Bird there till morning and then see him in court and get him a solicitor and watch him get three months and sent to a young offenders' or prison. You know what that feels like, Paulette? Me, a black man, to have to sit in reception in a redneck police station and beg for my son?'

'You did it, though, Garfield. Thank you.'

He walks straight up to her face and all the rage he didn't spend on the police is spilling out.

'Thank you? You speak like I'm doing you a favour. He is my son, Paulette. Mine. I'll tell you exactly what is going to happen so listen good. Bird isn't spending one more day with that fucking white boy. Before we know it, Bird will be eighteen and eighteen is when they treat you like a big man. And big men go to prison. Yeah, the officer told me that today. Sometimes even seventeen. So any more run-ins with the law and that's it. Do you hear me, Paulette? Bird's life would be over. Done!'

He stares at her, lets it sink in.

'You didn't believe me when I said it would end up serious, did you? You didn't believe me when I said there was something wrong with that boy from day one and it was plain and simple ridiculous you even had that man and his child in your house. I never understood it. Never. Now look what's happened.'

He walks to the window and looks out. She knows him good by now and sees him reeling in his temper like he's catching a fish. There's a little grey in his hair these days, making him look distinguished if that is even possible. Good thing the police could see he was a respectable man. Thank God for Garfield.

He runs his hands over his face again and then turns to her.

'Sit down. We have to talk.'

He finishes his drink and rolls the glass around in his hand.

'I was going to tell you this next week but I'm telling you now,' he says. 'Me and my wife and the girls, we're going to Texas for two years. The company got a big contract out there and they're taking the whole crew, sorting visas and everything. It's a golden opportunity, once in a lifetime. And Bird is coming with me.'

Paulette goes to open her mouth but he puts his hand up.

'Two years. He can finish his education there. Get some qualifications, get away from here. I already looked into everything. And listen, this is not just because of tonight. It's something I was going to tell you before anything like this happened, but now? Now, I am certain it's the right thing to do. Bird is coming with his father, Paulette. And his sisters. The whole family is going, all of us together. First of September.'

His voice changes to one of reasoning and common sense, softer now with all the cunning of a stalking cat. He leans forward.

'You know as well as I do, he needs to break away from that boy and that won't happen as long as he's here. And what is here for him anyway? He's too clever for that school. You know that. You said it yourself. He needs something to aim for. Something big. He's got nothing here. He can come with me and make a fresh start.'

Paulette stares at him. 'I can move house,' she says. 'I can move to Shawcross Heath. Get a transfer off the council.'

'A transfer, Paulette. How long you think that will take?'

'I'll talk to Nellie and I'll talk to his grandfather—'

'Oh, the same grandfather that came to the police station while I was there and talked nice to the officers in his good English? And they talk all nice to him and explain everything that was happening. "Slap on the wrist," they told him. Maybe a caution, but nah, nothing serious for the white boy. Fifteen minutes. Yes, fifteen minutes is what it took for the man to walk out. He takes his boy with five stitches in his head and they just walk out. That same grandfather you will have a talk with? The one who didn't even wait to see what happened to Bird. Walk straight past me waving to the woman on reception. Him?'

'Bird could go to a different school.'

'Paulette, Paulette, stop,' he says.

'There's other—'

'Other ways?' His words drop like granite. 'You have a better idea of how to give the boy a future, Paulette? Think about weekends. If I'm not here, what is he doing with himself on Friday, on Saturday night, on Sunday when you're working nights? All weekend he's alone or, worst still, out on the street. With Nellie or a different friend, maybe even a worse friend, or a girlfriend and the next girlfriend. And the girl is in his room where you can't keep an eye on him and, before you know it, he's smoking weed full-time with a pregnant girlfriend and working in McDonald's for a handful of shekels. Even if he goes to sixth form at that school, he still lives here in this house and the no-good boy can come round as soon as your back is turned. Is that what you want?'

'Garfield, I don't know if I—'

He takes her hand like he's got good news for her. 'You can visit,' he says. 'Often as you like. No one is keeping you from your son if that's what's worrying you. He'll love it.'

'You've told him already?'

'Tonight, on the way here. I told him and he wants to come.'

He says it so final and so sure. He says it like him and Bird are already sitting on the plane without her. He says it like she's a dog with its foot caught in a trap and the only way to get free is to bite the leg clean off. He says it like its final because he knows she will say yes because she loves Bird more than she loves herself.

'We need everything ready by the end of August because we fly out on the first,' he says. 'Make sure he stays out of trouble until then. You think you can do that?'

He closes the front door quietly. Paulette hears his car pull away. She stays on the sofa until Bird comes down and puts his arms around her. Kisses her on her cheek.

'Did he tell you?' he whispers.

She says nothing because Garfield has outplayed her, because he laid the trap from long time and because, once again, she can't get in between him and Bird.

'America, Mom,' he says with a boy's excitement. 'America.'

29

For days now, Bird has been talking about 'the US' as he calls it. She hears him on the phone, the pitch of his voice, the new easy drawl so he sounds like the boys on the videos. From trainers to sneakers. From pavement to sidewalk. From hello to hey.

Paulette had already booked a week off work for the summer thinking her and Bird might spend some time together but that can't happen now. All them hours will be spent thinking of what to do, how she might change things, find a way out. She could just say no, plain no. She could just refuse to part with her child. She could take Garfield to court; say he was trying to kidnap his son. But if the police asked Bird, she knows exactly what he would say.

Tired? Paulette never knew tiredness nor heartbreak like it. The very next day after talking to Garfield, she gets up early and goes to the council and tells them she wants to put in for a transfer to Shawcross or one of them areas. The woman behind the desk might as well have laughed in her face. Two years, that's the waiting list, maybe three. Unless there's over-crowding. How many children does Paulette have? One. All right, any disabilities, any difficulties, any special reasons? No, nothing like that. Just the twenty-four-hour dread of giving up her son in six weeks' time and that doesn't count.

She goes to a financial advisor she found in the paper. The man was nice and helpful and told her she could maybe get a mortgage, but her age would be a factor and she would need a big deposit and then maybe she would be able to get herself a little one-bedroom flat, not Shawcross or a nice area like that but maybe somewhere nearby, if she could possibly get a sympathetic bank. Maybe. And if she ever missed a payment, they would take the flat off her straight away. Was she aware of the risk of that kind of debt?

She goes to a housing association. They want to know why she wants to move so quickly and if she has rent arrears. Unless she's overcrowded or her house has rats or mould or cockroaches, she will need better reasons to move. However, if she wants a swap to a worse area with fewer bedrooms, then maybe something could be done.

She rings her second cousin in Manchester who she hasn't spoken to in a full year or more, but he says he doesn't have no space because he has his woman and their three children living with him which Paulette would have known if she had kept in touch.

She looks at flights back to St Kitts. Who is left there? Nobody. There were no jobs when she left and who is to say there are jobs now. If her grandmother was alive, God rest her soul, Bird would be sitting on that porch with the white-painted wood, peeling a little where the sun catches it, the red flowers in the metal pot, the front door mat swept clean. And right this very minute, Granny would give him a style of dressing-down you don't get outside of the West

Indies. And when she'd finished with Bird, she would turn to Paulette.

'Matthew chapter twenty-five verse thirteen, Paulette. What it say? Watch therefore! For ye know neither the day nor the hour. You didn't see it coming, did you, Paulette? You didn't heed the scriptures, Sweet Pea? Now look what happen. Signs and portents all around you from day one but you couldn't see.'

And Paulette would lean on her grandmother's lap and she would cry, and all the time Granny would be stroking her hair and telling her how she would make everything right if she trusted in the Lord and did as she was told.

'Yes, Granny,' she would say, yes, yes, yes, and then Granny would bring out coconut cake and carrot juice to assist them in making their plans.

There she is, working to save money for Bird's future so he can go to university and get set up in life and, while her back is turned, Nellie takes her son and drives him round the streets like a drunk man until he's arrested. And yet! It's Bird who spends hours in a police cell. Not Nellie. Oh no! Shirt & Tie has the accent and the education and the skin colour people respect. Nellie gets run out of every shop in the precinct because he's stealing, Nellie gets into fights with boys two years above himself, but it's Bird who nearly goes to court.

All the evidence was there for Paulette to see. What about the time Nellie came to her house with the police? That should have been a warning bell as loud as a trumpet. But no, Paulette doesn't think nothing. What about Frank telling her that Nellie was fighting and got suspended from school? Paulette thinks it's funny. And Nellie stealing a car that time. Couldn't she for once think about how it might affect her son, how he might think it was exciting and want a piece of the action?

Cornelius Bowen is angry with the world and he wants everyone to know. But Nellie was not Paulette's business. Paulette's business was Bird and keeping as much clear water as possible between that juvenile delinquent and a decent go-far boy like her son.

Looking the wrong way, Paulette. As usual.

Sleep is a stranger to Paulette. Peace of mind is something she can't even remember, like the music from the ice-cream van you hear far off and you wait and you wait but it never comes down your street.

No matter how tired she is, jobs in the house still must be done, so the washing machine goes on. The oven goes on. The iron goes on. She cooks, she cleans. No one seems to understand, not even Maggie.

As soon as Paulette saw Maggie, she said, 'Bird is going to America with his father for two years,' and Maggie smiled and said, 'Oh, that's grand! When? Exciting for him.'

Nothing about how it would affect her or how would Paulette manage or feel without him. Paulette said she couldn't stop and talk and just went inside.

Bird is at his father's under house arrest. When he comes back to Paulette, she must do the same. And every day when she goes to work, Garfield picks him up and takes him home to look after his sisters, to stay indoors and do as he is told.

Over and over, she replays what Garfield said and how he worked his plan. He had it all mapped out even before Bird got in the car with Nellie. He was plotting from time, maybe even years before. All he had to do was get Bird onside before Paulette had any idea. Clever.

When she feels the panic rising up in her chest, she says, 'Two years, only two years, just two years, two short years.' She takes a deep breath and gets on with whatever has to be done in the house.

The door knocks and, when she opens it, it's Nellie and Frank standing there like this is just a normal day.

'Yes?' she says. You think she's moving aside for the two of them to come into her house? 'What do you want?'

Yeah, they look surprised all right. Frank starts because the man was never short of a word when it suited him.

'Cornelius has come to apologize.'

Nellie has a little wound in his forehead no bigger than a fingernail. Black eyes, bruises on his face, the whole works.

'Yes,' says Nellie, not looking at her but studying the pavement like he wrote his apology there and he's reading it slow. 'I am really sorry. It was all my fault.'

Paulette folds her arms. 'You think you have to tell me it was your fault, Nellie? You think I don't know my own child?'

'I think what he means to say—' starts Shirt & Tie but Paulette cuts in.

'I know what he means to say but it's not enough, you see, Frank. Sorry makes no fucking difference whatsoever now. It's his fault and it's your fault. It's not my fault but guess who is going to suffer. Not you and not him. Just me. Just me and my son who won't have his mother by his side for two years in a foreign country.'

'I'm sorry, I don't understand,' Frank says. Nellie has the good sense to keep his mouth shut because he knows Paulette good.

'That's it!' she says, stepping on to the path. 'That's it! You don't understand! You see, Frank, my boy is leaving me, going clear to the other side of the world because you don't understand. You don't understand how to look after your grandson. You don't understand how to pay attention when you're driving a car. You don't understand what is important to me even though you eat my bread and drink my wine. You don't understand how life shapes up for a black boy in this country when he gets arrested. You got a clue about any of them things, Frank? Do you? Tell me?'

You damn right the man can't answer her. What could he say? But more to come.

'From day one, I don't know what the two of you are doing in my life,' she continues. 'For some fucked-up reason I took pity on you, but then Paulette is a fool, everyone knows. Grade-one, top-of-the-class fool.'

Frank opens his mouth, but Paulette points her finger right near the man's eye socket.

'I warned you. Didn't I warn you? Didn't I say if you don't look after that fucking wild animal, something would happen? But I notice it don't happen to you, does it? No, it don't happen to white boys and white men. It happens to me. Bird is going for two years. America. Yes, you didn't know that, did you? You think they invited me to come? No, they didn't. There's nothing here for Bird. That's what his father said. Nothing here. Only me and I don't count.'

The two of them standing there, shocked out of their conscience. Paulette is mighty. She is righteous. She has heartbreak and grief and loss on her side. She has motherhood and generosity on her side, she has forgiveness and a thousand dinners and hospitality and goodness on her side. And what do they have? One killed a man and the other nearly killed himself.

'Paulette, I am so sorry,' says the old man.

'Yes, sorry,' says Nellie. 'I didn't think.'

Paulette kisses her teeth so hard and so long, she sucks all the air out of the space between them. 'Let me tell you something,' she says, walking towards Frank and poking him in his scrawny chest. 'You wait how many years to say sorry to me? So many times you could have said sorry for ruining my life but only now when it affects your grandson can you say sorry. When you can't come inside and fill your belly in my kitchen. Well, sorry isn't good enough. Sorry is never good enough. Sorry don't make everything right, mister. Sorry never turned back time and sorry can't mend me.'

Frank is backing away and Nellie has his head down, walking with him.

'Don't ever come to this house again,' she shouts. 'Not you and not him. Nellie, you hear me? You are not my child. I don't love you. I don't even like you. I don't need you and I don't want you here. Neither of you. Don't come back, you hear me? We done. You are not mine.'

She sees the wince of the boy like someone kicked him in the head. She would remember it later.

She waits until they've gone, standing on the path in her slippers. She gets her breath back, turns round and walks slowly back to her quiet house.

You couldn't call it crying what she did then. A lot of it was silent and a lot of it was howling, but she had to stop in case Maggie came round. All Paulette wants is to be on her own with Mr Appleton, who never once let her down. And then, after two days, it was time for work. Rent and electricity don't business about some black woman's broken heart. Television licence people don't care if she's hurting, they want their money same way.

30

She does everything in a positive frame of mind, buying everything Bird needs so he can turn up respectable at the airport and when he opens his suitcase nothing but clean, fresh and new clothes.

And Nellie? One evening, she's sitting watching the telly when she hears a quiet knock on the door. Bird flies down the stairs and opens the door, which is rare for him at the best of times. She can hear voices. Nellie. The boy has the cheek to come back round to talk to Bird. Paulette gets up and goes to the door and gives the boy a look that tells him to shut his damn mouth because if it wasn't for him . . . but before she can say anything, Bird is doing some high-five nonsense and slouching against the open door.

'Yes, mate! U. S. of A!' he says.

'Where?' says Nellie.

'Texas, mate. With my dad. Four weeks and I'm outta here, sucker! Yeah!' says Bird. He picks up an imaginary rifle and takes aim at Nellie. 'Pow!' he says. 'The land of the free and the home of the brave.'

Nellie looks at Paulette and she nods. 'Oh yes, your friend leaving you, Nellie. Who you going to drag into trouble now?'

His smile is false. 'Fucking amazing, mate,' he says. And Bird is rattling off the details when Paulette eases Bird aside and closes the door right in Nellie's face.

'Go and tidy your room, Bird, and don't come down until it's done.'

That night, like every night, Paulette cries when Bird can't see her and then tells herself off in the morning when her face looks like an old cushion. Bird tells her she looks tired, asks her if she's sick, but she tells him there's a bug going round the hospital, staff and patients alike.

On the actual, horrible, dreaded and awful day, Garfield collects Bird and his suitcase and his rucksack, checks on his passport and the money Paulette has given him. She tells him, for the tenth time, that he can show the school his reports and the certificates from swimming and football even though Garfield says it's different football they play in America. She kisses Bird. She reminds him he's been brought up good and not to disgrace himself.

She sees Bird and Garfield exchange a look. She hugs Bird. She hugs Garfield and begs him to look after their son and says they must ring from the airport no matter what time and ring her again when they get to the house they're renting in Dallas. She's looked up Dallas on a map and she's been to the library to find out what she can.

She waves at the front door and watches father and son walk down the path and drive away. She waves even when they are out of sight and holds tight on to the front-door handle and the smile she fastened to her face.

She goes inside and straight upstairs. She strips Bird's bed and puts on clean sheets so when he comes back it's all ready and waiting because you know what? Sometimes things don't work out, Garfield. Man thinks he has all the answers. Thinks he knows Bird better than she does, his mother who knew from the womb when the boy was tired and when he was hungry. So don't be so confident, Garfield, it wouldn't be the first time you've been wrong. Two years is a long, long time.

She thinks of the way Bird skipped out the door, excited to be going away, and Garfield triumphant, father of three kids, wife, career, foreign country. Garfield has been working on Bird for years, she sees that now. She thinks of Bird and Garfield's secret language and the way, yet again, things have happened behind her back.

And yet! And yet! Don't underestimate good home cooking and a mother's love. In spite of himself, the boy might get homesick. America is not for everyone, not for black men anyway. Processed food is all they eat over there. Burgers and pizza. Who knows what's in the future. Yes, it could all go wrong. If and when Bird starts to miss his home, he'll find things just as he left them and his mother waiting.

She goes to Texas for a visit. Of course she does. Bird rings her every Sunday and tells her what he's been doing. His life sounds full and he's made some friends with some boys on the same street. School is keeping him on his toes because they don't have the same subjects over there or the same way of learning but, if she knows Bird, he will rise to the top. When he rings, he always says, 'Love you, Mom,' something he never used to say when he was at home so at least he's missing her.

She leaves it eight weeks, counting every day, and then takes her savings and goes to the travel agent in town to buy herself an open ticket. The travel agent books her a hotel in the good part of Dallas, the Fairfield Inn, three stars and a free breakfast. The photographs look very nice. She tells Garfield the day and time the flight gets in and tells work she will be away for two weeks but if all goes well she will stay another two at least. And if they need nursing assistants there, who knows.

She shops for a nice new wardrobe and gets her hair pressed. She gets a manicure and good coat and a scarf like the one she saw Princess Diana wearing. She makes sure she's stopped the stupid crying at night because it's putting ten years on her eyes and twenty on her outlook. Think positive! She's going to see Bird and she's getting a good holiday into the bargain. That's the way to look at things, not by saying she misses her son like he's oxygen itself.

Her new suitcase has wheels. She bought a big one and a small one that hooks over the handle. When the plane lands, she's proud to skim them silently across the polished floor of Dallas Fort Worth International Airport. DFW Garfield called it on the phone because he likes to put Paulette in her place from time to time.

Bird is there to meet her at the airport. Just him on his own with a smile that cleaves her heart. She's already decided she won't cry. He looks so good in his short-sleeve shirt with the sun on his skin, in his close haircut and big trainers like any other American boy in the airport. He has definitely grown, maybe a full inch, and he's filled out like a man. And he's driving legally with a full licence. A nice open-top car.

He gives her such a long and hard hug she can hardly breathe. And they stand there for a full five minutes until she pushes him back to look at him all over again and put her hand on his face because she wants to know it's real and true. And it is. Just her and him for the long drive to where they live in Duncanville.

'Oooh, it's hot!' she says as soon as they are on the road. 'Is it always this hot at seven o'clock in the evening?'

'Yeah,' he says. 'Hotter sometimes.'

The roads are wide, wide, wide, with a whole heap of traffic and yet there's her son driving like it's nothing. She puts her hand on his shoulder.

'You passed your test already, Bird? That was quick.'

'Yes. It's better here. Everything's automatic. I passed first time. No trouble.'

'I'm so proud of you, Bird.'

'Curtis,' he says.

She looks at him.

'No one calls me Bird here. It's Curtis.'

'Even your father?'

'Yeah, he said Curtis is a man's name and it's on my birth certificate so it's better to use it here, so people don't get confused.'

'Oh, I see. Curtis.'

He takes her to the Fairfield Inn, carries her luggage for her and, when they are up in her room, he tells her the plan for her fortnight. Him and Garfield have gone to a lot of effort. A nice spa day and a family day, just the three of them, and then some sightseeing and some nice meals and a few days to laze around the pool at the back of their house. Yes, Bird's gone to a lot of trouble for his mother.

'Dad said don't go asleep otherwise it will give you bad jet lag for the rest of the holiday.'

'I know, I know. I've been working nights now for years, Curtis. Don't worry, I know what to do.'

'I'll pick you up at ten tomorrow morning, then.'

He goes to walk away but Paulette calls him back. 'Wait,' she says and walks over to him with her arms outstretched. 'You're in too much of a hurry to give your mother a hug and a kiss?'

He puts one arm around her shoulder and kisses her cheek.

'I'm parked out front, Mom. They'll give me a ticket. And I've got extra math then baseball practice.'

'Yes, yes, you told me. Go on then, quick,' she says and when he's gone she looks out of the window to see which way he went.

Yes, she must stay awake for another two hours at least. She goes downstairs to the bar and orders a nice rum. The place is half empty, but the bartender is nice, asks where she's from and how long she's staying.

'Not sure,' she says. 'I haven't made up my mind.'

31

Bird is late the next morning and she's waiting in the lobby when he comes.

'Traffic,' he says.

'Never mind, Bird,' she answers, 'I was just—'

'Curtis, Mom.'

She gets in the car and puts a headscarf on this time because of the wind from the roof being down.

'Whose car is this?' she asks.

'It's Dad's. It's great, isn't it? He lets me borrow it if I get good grades.' He taps his temple. 'Clever.'

Oh, Garfield is clever all right. Got his boy and got him behaving himself and sounding like a grown-up American. Got him a new name and a whole new country. Got him all to himself.

The roads become narrow and more homely, until the streets look like they do on the telly with low houses and front lawns. She keeps up the talk to her son, making sure she drops in a Curtis here and there to let him know she heard what he said.

He suddenly swings right and pulls into a long drive.

'Home!' he says. Home is what he calls it now and he opens the door with a key. Garfield's woman holds out her hand and introduces herself.

'Angela,' she says. 'It's good to meet you at last, Paulette.'

Yes, that's right. Paulette has been avoiding her for years and the woman has done the same. She's not pretty-pretty but you can see she takes care of herself and Paulette is glad she bought herself the silk neckerchief and patent-leather shoes. Garfield has taken his daughters to a birthday party so it's just the three of them, Paulette, Bird and Mrs Garfield.

The room is set out nice and very clean, flowers on the table. Everything is pale blue, even Mrs Garfield's dress. Her hair is natural, set in waves with a hairband in pale blue silk to match her outfit. Bird goes into the kitchen to make some coffee while Paulette offers chit-chat about the long flight and the weather and the bad food on the plane, and after a while the woman shouts towards the kitchen.

'Curtis? Bring the cake.'

Bird comes in with a tray set out nice with cups and saucers and a milk jug and small plates just like Paulette taught him and she feels proud in front of the woman for Bird's manners and behaviour.

'He's a good boy,' Mrs Garfield says and something in her voice makes Paulette vex.

'Oh, I know,' she answers. 'He has been since the day he was born. Always.'

When Garfield comes home, to give the man his due, he greets her properly and asks all the right questions about the hotel and the flight. Pays her attention so Paulette doesn't feel stupid in front of his wife.

Then he's full of news about the job and the area and his daughters, who Paulette will meet later, and he tells her she's looking well and she's going to have a good time. He tells her Curtis usually has homework and sports practice because he's trying to catch up with his friends and then he has chores around the house but he'll spend as much time with her as he can. Thank you, Garfield.

The rest of the day, they all go to a shopping mall which is the biggest thing Paulette has ever seen, with restaurants right inside and a cinema complex with a bowling alley and more shops than you could see in two city centres put together. All air-conditioned, spotlessly clean. They only covered half of it before it was time to go back to Garfield's house for a barbecue in their back garden. Garfield has a swimming pool now but he says everyone has them and it's nothing special. The way he says it lets Paulette know it's special to Garfield, yes indeed.

Garfield tells her his two daughters are playing with the next-door neighbour and Paulette wonders if he is keeping his girls out of her way so she can have Bird all to herself.

The barbecue is on, meat sizzles, children laughing in the background and crickets chirping in the distance. She eats a burger six inches high, she eats fries and coleslaw with chilli in it, she eats a frosted muffin which was too sweet by fifty per cent and she drinks three cocktails. Sweet soul music is on the stereo and Mrs Garfield is keeping the conversation jogging along with stories about American celebrities and gossip about the neighbours and the price of food and things you can't get hold of and dealing with the heat. Paulette can't dislike her.

By eight o'clock, Mrs Garfield is tidying up and Paulette is mashed. She's sitting next to Garfield on the deck with a long drink of ice-tea with a little rum in for a sweetener. It's nearly knocked her out.

'You've got a lovely home here, Garfield,' she says.

'Yes, it was a good move,' he says.

'How is he doing at school? How is Curtis doing?'

'Like I said on the phone, better than I expected. He just got straight down to it, good grades, decent friends, black and Hispanic boys from good families, one of them right across the road there. And he passed his driving licence first time. I give him an allowance every week but he has to earn it.'

'Good,' says Paulette and wants to remind Garfield he didn't say any of this on the phone and neither did Bird but she keeps her mouth shut. What she can see is the boy is happy and filled out and, if he keeps it up, he will be success-ful in his life. Later on, maybe next week, she's going to find a recruitment agency and make enquiries about nurses in Dallas and what she might have to do to get a job. She won't tell Garfield or Bird but she wants to have a plan just in case Bird looks like he might stay past the two years.

'Can you drop me back to the hotel, Garfield? I can hardly keep my eyes open.'

'Yes, let Curtis do it. He needs the driving practice.'

'I'll go and tell him,' she says. She steps through the patio doors but Bird is not in the living room. She listens and hears music coming from somewhere and, more importantly, she can hear Mrs Garfield clearing up dishes in the kitchen. She's been meaning to talk to her, to Angela, and say a little woman-to-woman thank you, one mother to another. A few words about it being hard to have someone else's child in the house, she's done it herself and it's not always easy. And also Paulette would like to say she has always been grateful to Angela for being nice and kind to her precious son and for making her welcome into her house today. Paulette must remember to buy a little present next time they go to the shops. But as she gets to the kitchen door, what Paulette sees stops her Christian thoughts. There's Bird by the sink taking one of the dishes out of Angela's hand.

'Leave it, Mom,' he says. 'You take it easy. I'll do it.'

Paulette turns to stone. Mom, is it? Two months and all of a sudden this woman is Mom? Or was she Mom from time, from when he was a little boy? Oh.

They didn't see her. She eases back from the door silently and goes to the toilet down the hall. She washes her shaking hands and puts her face straight and not pained. She smooths back her hair and then goes to the kitchen and coughs before she enters. She says thank you to Angela for such a lovely time and asks if she can help with the tidying.

By the time she's finished, Bird is jangling the car keys up by the front door, eager to take her back to her hotel.

*

247

The two weeks are a daze after that although Paulette puts on her best Elizabeth Taylor Oscar-winning performance so no one knows the bleeding wound she's carrying.

On her last night in Texas, they're all in a Mexican restaurant, Garfield, his woman, his girls, Bird and Paulette all together, and Paulette has a funny experience. She looks at the two girls, pretty little things with good manners, and she realizes how much like Bird they look. Same round cheeks and mannerisms, same way of talking which is Garfield's way of talking.

And suddenly, it's like she's sitting at the table and sitting above the table at the same time. What does she see? A nice family. Man, wife and three children and an auntie visiting from abroad. All of them making conversation and being extra polite for the auntie who doesn't visit very often, pushing the boat out, ordering extra food and cocktails for the distant relative. Yes, that's the picture. Paulette on the outside, looking on. She can't eat much after that, says the food is too spicy.

Mrs Garfield notices and tells her to come outside and get some air. They walk out of the front door and around the back of the restaurant where there's a little bit of shade and Mrs Garfield gives her the glass of water she brought off the table.

'You all right, Paulette? You've been quiet this evening.'

'Yes, yes,' she says, 'just not used to the heat.' She fans her blouse up and down and dabs her forehead with the back of her hand.

Mrs Garfield shakes her head. 'Oh, yes. I'm still not used to it yet but it's better than an English winter, isn't it?'

'You can say that again,' Paulette says.

They stand side by side looking out over the parking lot, the heat shimmering patterns on the horizon. Invisible birds chirping over the motorway hum. A waiter in a red bandana comes out and tosses some black bags in a big grey dumpster. It clangs shut. 'Ladies,' he says.

When he's gone, Mrs Garfield moves in close and puts her hand on Paulette's arm.

'I just want to say how pleased we are to have you here for a visit, Paulette. Garfield and me will take good care of Curtis, don't you worry. And his sisters love having him around full-time.'

Paulette covers her hand with her own and squeezes to say thank you because she doesn't want to get back into the crying business in front of a stranger.

32

The evening flight to Heathrow feels shorter on the way back, and now she doesn't care about arriving anywhere in good condition the drink is free-flowing. She buys a little bottle of vodka at Duty Free and puts it in her bag for the plane. Sip, sip, sip. Vodka is like sandpaper, you put it on anything and it smoooooooths it all out. Smoooooth.

She falls asleep, wakes up and collects her luggage. She gets in line for a taxi. Nice smooooth taxi. Expensive taxi. Private cry-in-the-back taxi.

When it pulls up outside her house it's morning-time, cold and damp, sweet and familiar. She opens the door, flings her big suitcase inside and rings Maggie's bell. The kids will be at school by now.

'The wanderer returns,' says Maggie, putting a cup of coffee in front of Paulette, 'and the wanderer didn't sleep by the looks of things. You all right?'

'Maggie, it was hot like a furnace,' says Paulette and takes a big packet out of her little carry-on case. 'Bought you these.'

Maggie opens the plastic-wrapped cigarettes. 'Jesus, Paulette. Two hundred! That'll keep me going for a good week.' She kisses Paulette on the cheek. 'And you had a little tipple on the plane, right?'

Paulette winks at her. 'Twice what I wanted and half as much as I needed. No, wait. Half as much as I wanted and twice what I needed.'

'What was she like, the wife?'

Paulette thinks of Mrs Garfield trying to be kind and *Curtis* this and *Curtis* that and *Let me help you, Mom* and the woman's hand on hers.

'Yes, she made a big effort. Bird is happy, that's all I care about.'

'It was that bad, was it?'

Where to start? She skips over the detail and goes right to the end of her holiday and starts there. 'You know what, Maggie, I went and found a recruitment agency and asked them what I would have to do to be a nurse over there. It's not impossible, you know. I must have a sponsor but they need nurses so it looks like I could get one. I didn't tell them I'm an auxiliary but I think it's the same thing so I could go if I wanted. Sell up everything and go.'

'No!' says Maggie, throwing her hands in the air. 'No!'

'Well, I'm just thinking at the moment.'

Paulette has the next day off work so she spends it in bed, messing up the blankets with her twisting and turning, twisting and turning around the things she saw and the things she heard. Bird, sorry Curtis, in the bosom of his new family looking like he's been there all his life bathed in pure, everlasting sunshine and swimming-pool water. His two sisters looking up to him, their eyes and his eyes the same, his new 'Mom' in powder blue. *Bring the cake in, Curtis.*

She wakes and sleeps while the rain beats hard against the windowpane. It's only four o'clock in the afternoon and outside is nearly black. She puts a blanket over her shoulders and goes downstairs. She pours hot water into a mug with lemon and honey, adds a tot of rum and, as she's walking out of the kitchen, swipes the bottle of Appleton and lays down on the sofa. She pulls everything in, her feet and head, her knees and shoulders, the hopefulness she had before she got on the plane, her plans and all her foolishness, pulls it all in and sips her hot toddy, topping it up from the bottle as night comes.

Her lasting memory of Garfield is him in the Mexican restaurant, people chattering in languages she doesn't understand. The smell of frying meat and strange spices, guitar music and the drone of air conditioning right over their table. There he is, sitting at the head of the table with his new stainless-steel designer glasses and his hair short and grey at the temples giving him the wise-man look he always wanted. All of them, his girls and his boy and his wife, looking at him as he points to the menu and tells them about what to order and what is best and what will be too hot and what will suit their palate like he ever went to a fucking Mexican restaurant before in his whole life. And when he looks at her, he might as well have said, *See, Paulette. See what you've been missing.* She can look back on her time with him and see what happened as clear as glass.

The Best of Everything

Paulette hurt him really bad, and all this time when she was thinking it was done and dusted and the two of them were on the same page about Bird, he was plotting how to hurt her back. Let Paulette bring up the boy when homework needs doing and clothes need washing and dinners need making. Let Paulette bring up the boy when the hard years arrive and she's getting the curled lip. Let Paulette do twenty-four-seven monitoring of each kiss he gives the Barn Owl so it don't turn into something else in nine months' time. Let Paulette bring up the boy when she has to watch him like a hawk and make him do his homework and get in the shower. But soon as Bird is moving into manhood, and she's making plans about his future, one single little slip, just one, and there is Garfield coiled around the child like Satan in the Garden of Eden offering him the sweet fruit of America. And what can Bird say? He says, yes please, Dad, because he knows no better. Revenge is what Garfield wanted and revenge is what he's got.

The bottle of rum is nearly finished but she has a couple of miniatures left if she needs more. She's hot now and throws the blanket off. She lies back against the cushions, props her feet on the armrest and raises her glass to Garfield, the Chess Master. He has outmanoeuvred her, played the long game and won the prize. Well done.

It's two o'clock in the morning when she wakes up with a stiff neck. Her glass has fallen on the carpet and, when she rolls over to pick it up, she's got pins and needles in her arm where she's been lying on it. She stumbles up to bed, dragging the blanket behind her.

The next morning, she takes the two buses to work. They are short-staffed on the maternity ward so Sister McKenzie tells her she has to help out there for the whole day. Soon as she gets there, a woman gives birth to twins, pretty little things, boys, but one is too small for safety and goes straight into neonatal intensive care on the next floor. Paulette sees the mother clutching her one baby while the other is taken away, pain and worry all over her face. At the end of her shift, even though she is bone tired, Paulette goes to the special unit to see the child. The mother is there on her own, sitting on a chair by the glass, not even allowed to hold the baby it's so weak. And by the look on her face, so is she.

'Which one is yours?' asks Paulette, even though she already knows.

The woman taps the glass with one thin finger. 'Him. Robert. Robert James.'

'Lovely name,' Paulette says. 'He's got a brother, hasn't he, a twin? Just look at him, I can see he's looking better than he did this morning. He was a bit pale, wasn't he? Now look. He's got a good bit of colour on him.'

For the first time, the woman turns round and looks Paulette full in the face.

'Do you think so?'

'Oh yes,' Paulette says. 'Oh yes. Definitely. You didn't see me but I was in the room when he was born this morning. I could see you was worried when he didn't cry and the doctors took him away but you know what? When they do that, it's because they know how to handle the situation. They know what they're doing.'

She puts her hand on the woman's shoulder and squeezes. 'He's a fighter,' she says. 'He's strong. And he's going to be just fine. You'll see.'

The woman nods and puts a hand over her mouth instead of saying anything and Paulette knows what she's thinking. She's thinking that if she lets go and really starts to cry then she might never stop. She's thinking, now is not the time to panic, not the time to fall apart. She's thinking she must hold on and be strong these next few days, because if she's lucky there are years and years and years when this baby will need her, and his brother will need her too, and she must be there, strong, all in one piece.

The next day, Paulette's back on the maternity ward and it's so busy she doesn't get to see if the woman's baby is any better. It's just screams and cries and flowers and chocolates and grandmothers and grandfathers and 'here is your baby' and 'ooh, he looks like you' and so many comings and goings that Paulette is exhausted more than usual when she gets home. She goes into Kang's to buy a packet of crisps and a half-bottle of rum but the brands they have aren't what Paulette likes. Never mind.

These days, Paulette's house is as quiet as a graveyard. It used to be she didn't mind the weekend to give the place a good tidy, moving the sofa to vacuum underneath it. Turn the cushions and plump them up, wipe the windowsill and make the house fresh. And the reason she didn't mind was because she knew Bird was coming back on Sunday night, coming home to her, and the waiting time was sweet. What good is a tidy sitting room if there's only herself to see it? Maggie is kitchen-folk so she doesn't count.

Still in her coat, she goes straight upstairs, peels off the brown check dress that reminds her of labour pains, newborn babies and joyful celebrations that don't include the invisible auxiliary nurse that comes into the birthing room to mop up the blood, strip the bed and make it ready all over again. The same nurse who brings the new mother a cup of tea and a piece of toast, fills the water jug and makes the blanket sit right.

Her uniform drops to the floor and she gets into bed. There's a glass on the bedside cabinet. Clean enough. She pours in a little inch from the bottle and takes a sip. It's not bad. She opens her crisps and, careful not to make crumbs, she eats them one by one, and to be fair to such a humble snack, when you're hungry, the salt hits the spot.

Tomorrow she will turn the heating right down because if she comes in at this time every day and gets straight under the blankets, she can save money. What is the use of burning gas to heat a house just for her?

And if she takes the tiny television out of Bird's room and puts it at the end of the bed on the chest of drawers, she can watch the news and her programme about redecorating your house. And she noticed if you take out a magazine subscription for a Christmas present it's cheaper than at any other time of the year. Well, the present will be from Paulette to Paulette. But which one? She smooths the pillow behind her head and leans back to think.

33

Paulette is running down the emergency ward at work but no matter how fast she runs and how many beds she checks she can't find who's ringing the alarm. Every bed is empty. Every ward stretches on for fifty feet and there's no one else around, no Marcia, no Tanya, no Sister, no doctors, no nurses, just incubators with red lights flashing above them, red lights getting brighter and louder and brighter and louder because somewhere there is a baby in distress and only Paulette can save it.

Seven a.m. She pulls herself out of her nightmare and mashes her hand on the electric clock and it falls to the floor. The evil twins of rum and heartburn been playing with her all night. She groans loud and turns her face to the wall. Ten more minutes.

By the time she gets to work nearly half of her shift is done. She must report to Sister McKenzie, who says she had to ring in for cover because with the winter flu and lots of people being off sick, they're already short-staffed. She asked Paulette what happened and how come she didn't ring in so Paulette said she got ill in Texas and couldn't get out of bed and, since she's now on her own, there was no one to ring in for her. But because Paulette's attendance sheet is white as snow, Sister McKenzie doesn't complain too much.

'Just don't make a habit of it, Paulette, and think of the other nurses who have to cover for you and work twice as hard,' she says. 'And actually, you look terrible. Are you sure you should be here at all? If it's catching, go home.'

At the nice off-licence on the high street by the park, Paulette buys proper Appleton's and stocks up for the week. Then home. Then bed. Then a small dish of nuts with a drink. Then telly. Then seven a.m. Then work. Then home. Then bed. Then half a chocolate bar with a small drink while she watches a film about a man who gets trapped in the wilderness. Fool. What's he doing in the fucking wilderness in the first place? You deserve what you get, Clint Eastwood. Then a little drink. Then the rest of the Clint Eastwood double bill where he shoots up half of San Francisco and sleeps with the other half. A man's film.

Then seven a.m. and seven a.m. and seven a.m. and so it goes until, two weeks before Christmas, the postman comes.

She's got a parcel to sign for from America. She rips open the packet standing there in the hallway. There's a card inside, small but heavy, and in Mrs Garfield's handwriting it says, *Lovely to see you, Paulette. Come again soon. Merry Christmas from all of us.* Everyone has signed it, including Curtis.

She places it on the mantelpiece then tackles the package that came with it. She peels off the sellotape and brown paper and the Christmas paper underneath and finds inside a framed photograph. There she is with Bird sitting on the deck at Garfield's house in the blazing sunshine, Paulette in her new sundress and sunglasses with her hair done nice and

Bird with his tight T-shirt and jeans, with his new haircut, both of them smiling. Paulette has a cocktail in her hand and Curtis has his arm around her, face straight at the camera. The glass in the frame is made of clear plastic for safety. She kisses Bird and places the photograph on the mantelpiece next to the card.

She's in the shower and dressed in twelve minutes flat. She runs to Kang's and buys a whole heap of the sweets the girls said they missed. She goes to the post office and changes fifty pounds into dollars for Bird. She dashes to the proper newsagent and buys a gift box, brown paper and sellotape, she buys a thick marker pen and two cards, one for Garfield's family – a snow scene in an English village – and another one, red silk and padded, that says 'To My Son At Christmas'. By the time she gets home, she's tired out. She got light-headed crossing the park and even though it was freezing cold she had to sit down for a few minutes to gather herself.

Two women walking past looked at her funny and one of them said, 'You all right, love?' Paulette nodded, then the woman bent down and picked up all the sweets that had fallen off the bench on to the wet path.

'Thank you,' said Paulette and made herself get up and walk nice and brisk along the path. When did she last eat properly?

Then, the rest of the morning, she takes her time and packs everything up safe and neat, writes the cards out carefully and writes Bird's new address in big black letters on the outside. Return to sender at the bottom.

The Best of Everything

Paulette didn't figure on the fierce rain that comes from nowhere just as she's about to leave the house. She's got on her hat and coat standing at the front door with the parcel in a carrier bag when the clouds part to let out enough rain to float the Ark and, with it, darkness so thick, she would need a torch to get to the post office.

She closes the door and puts the parcel on the kitchen table. She makes a cup of coffee but doesn't take her coat off because rain like this can sometimes dry up as quick as it came so she sits down to wait.

How much the parcel will cost is something she refuses to think about. She'll just have to pay it. She's surprised she didn't think about cards and presents before but then she's been busy at work and taking a little tot at night to help her sleep so it's not surprising it slipped her mind.

She hears it then. Somewhere, something is ticking. Paulette doesn't have a grandfather clock and she doesn't have one of them old-fashioned things you put on the wall that shows the time and the weather. She looks around and, as it gets darker, the ticking gets louder. She puts all the lights on.

She stands up. Someone could be playing a joke. She thinks about Nellie and if he's come in and planted a bomb and as soon as she has the thought she can't get it out of her head. It would be just like the boy to do something ridiculous and blow up the whole street.

She goes from the living room to the kitchen and back to the hallway but it's not there. She stands dead still because Paulette is getting frightened now because the ticking could well be in her head or it's the ticking of her heart telling her her days are numbered. She puts her hand on her chest. Nothing. She puts her fingers in her ears but the ticking is not in there either. She walks back to the kitchen and looks at the hob and there it is. The old clock Paulette uses as a kitchen timer. *Tick. Tick. Tick.* She never heard it before when the house was full of life.

She lets out one long ragged sigh of relief and takes out a glass for a little drink to steady herself. A person could go mad living on their own.

She'll post the parcel tomorrow.

34

Christmas on the horizon. Three days to go. The weather draws in quick; evening starts in the afternoon and morning comes late. Seems like Paulette lives her life in the twilight. She's been popping in on Maggie at the weekend, started to have a cigarette once in a while with a little drink to take the edge off the evenings, too long and too quiet.

As soon as Maggie opens her door, Paulette can see Maggie's face is set hard.

'Come in,' she says.

Paulette sits at the kitchen table and asks her what's wrong.

'Kitty's at it again, different fella this time but I don't like the cut of him.'

'Bad boy?' says Paulette, pouring two drinks.

'No, but an arrogant little shit. Comes here telling Kitty about getting out of the ghetto as he calls it. Talking like he knows everything about everything. Big ideas. Big plans that don't stand up to a minute's scrutiny. Cheeky little rip. He's the one with that bloody ridiculous orange car. And an earring of all things. And there's Kitty lapping it up. I can't stand that kind of eejit. Talking down to women.'

Paulette hands her a glass. 'At least he's got ambition, Maggie.'

'Ambition? Sounds to me he thinks he's better than my daughter. And I'm not having that. Ghetto, for Christ's sake. Talks like a bloody gangster.'

'They all do it, Maggie. It doesn't mean anything.'

Maggie looks at Paulette and shakes her head. 'It means plenty, actually, Paulette. I know my daughter and she's already got a touch of the aristocracy about her. Too wrapped up in herself. You know yourself where that leads.'

'What do you mean?'

Maggie shrugs. 'Look at Bird. This new boyfriend reminds me of Bird when I think about it. He couldn't wait to get away, could he? Five minutes in America and he's playing the big man and forgotten all about you.'

Paulette never even told Maggie about the 'Mom' business, but even so, Maggie knows Bird only calls once a week and that Paulette sits by the phone waiting for it to ring.

'Bird has not forgotten about me, Maggie. And he's only there for two years.'

'For Christ's sake, Paulette. For once in your life, catch on to what's happening. Bird's sitting pretty over there with his father, a good father I might add compared to some. Why come back? And anyway, Bird's had the wool pulled over your eyes since he was a baby. You think the sun shines out of his arse but he's as selfish as they come and loves himself into the bargain. I would have done differently with him if he was mine.'

Paulette puts her glass down, careful, careful, careful.

'What did you say?'

Maggie looks away. 'Nothing. Just that Bird isn't the golden boy you think he is, that's all.'

Paulette stands up and throws the rest of her rum to the back of her throat. 'I never told you how to look after your children, Maggie. Don't tell me nothing about mine.'

'Well, someone has to tell you the truth,' Maggie shouts after her. Paulette slams the door on her way out.

Saturday the next day. Paulette didn't even really go to bed after what Maggie said. She lay on top of the blankets with her anger to keep her warm because Paulette never said Bird was a golden boy and no child is perfect but Maggie had been storing up them harsh words for a long, long time and fired each one like an arrow where it would do the most damage. Paulette goes over and over all the perfect sentences she could have said to Maggie to hurt her back but it's too late now because she will never speak to her again as long as she lives. Sleep or no sleep, Paulette goes to work and does the night shift, dragging her feet and sitting down whenever she can.

She waits for the bus, leaning on the shelter. Really and truly, if it was softer she would lie down and close her eyes. She cranes her neck to see if she can see the number 18 coming from afar and sees instead the little church near the corner where she used to go every so often to sing a good English hymn. Her feet carry her there all by themselves.

There's hardly any congregation because it's the nine-fifteen service, old ladies mostly and a few homeless-looking people. The church is warm and the minister walks among the congregation at the beginning. Doesn't take him long to get to Paulette.

He says welcome and that it's nice to see her again. He squints his eyes and says he remembers her from a trip to the seaside, many years ago, with some children and an older gentleman.

'Frank,' she says.

He asks after her family, assuming Frank is part of it, and she doesn't put him right. Just tells him everyone is well and then when he goes to shake her hand Paulette holds on to it. She wants to tell him everything that has happened to her since the seaside, since her granny died, since Denton and Bird, and she wants to ask him if God has any wisdom about what she should do with the rest of her life and what scriptures might ease the cancerous pain that seemed to be spreading all through her body. From the look on his face, she realizes she's holding on too long and nothing is coming out of her mouth and the minister has other people waiting to speak to about problems bigger than hers, so she smiles and says, 'Thank you for asking.'

The service begins, she listens to the hymn, closes her eyes for the prayer and thinks her own thoughts. Nothing to rush home for after all.

For the first time in her life, she wishes she could drive. She had the chance to learn so many times but never had the confidence, especially after Denton got killed. But now with a car she could take herself places, seaside, cities with good shopping and old buildings. She could go and visit friends she hasn't seen for twenty years, people she lost touch with, go to carnivals and exhibitions. Take night classes and different courses. Might not be too late to learn new tricks.

Cookery was always her expertise. What if she changed career and learned high-class cordon bleu, got a job in a professional kitchen? Or even set up on her own to do catering for weddings and funerals? Get some flyers printed and rent all the equipment. Saucepans, baking trays, industrial mixer. It would all cost money.

Maybe St Kitts is where she will go. Granny's grave is there and her mother's and the father she only saw a few times. The bones of her ancestors are all waiting for her and maybe she would feel more at home in her childhood home. But jobs are hard to come by still and she would have to make new friends, something Paulette has never been good at. But it's something to think about.

Marcia has told her to come by over the holidays. 'Everyone's coming, Paulette. You won't be the only guest.' She tells Paulette how many people there will be, her kids, her sister, her brother and his kids, her husband's parents and Marcia's mother, so she won't feel like she's intruding.

She'd planned to go to Maggie's but that's not going to happen now. She's done with the woman, and anyway, Paulette has heard Maggie's celebrations over the years. They start quiet, then comes the music and the dancing and then late-night arguments and slamming doors, then music again and laughing until the early hours.

And then there's Princess Alexandria Hospital. Every year it's the same. Sister McKenzie asking who can work Christmas Eve. Who can work Christmas Day? Who can work Boxing Day? Here I am, says Paulette, and signs up for three whole nights of overtime and three whole days of sleep. She's back in Sister McKenzie's good books.

Then the service is nearly over and she's singing 'Oh Come, Oh Come, Emmanuel' to the church organ. She has a few words with the lady sitting next to her. *Nice service, yes it's cold, yes.* Then out into the biting sleet. She changes her hat to the big woolly thing she bought on the market but even with the hat on, scarf on and gloves on, she can feel the drop in temperature.

In the centre of town, she waits for the second bus, the one that takes nearly an hour, through the inner-city council estates, past the high streets and terraced houses, out through the suburbs and way beyond to where she lives, almost past the city limits.

The big cathedral in the middle of town is all lit up, the huge Christmas tree outside decorated with fake snow and coloured lights. There's music coming from inside, calling the faithful to worship. Paulette's done her duty already this morning but something draws her to the magnificence, the towering greyness, looking proud and permanent.

She gets to the door of St Philip's. She's walked past it a hundred times, five hundred maybe, and never been inside.

People are hurrying past her, families and couples chatting to each other. Everyone seems to know everyone else and Paulette feels out of place. Maybe another time.

But as she turns to leave, she sees a woman coming up the path wearing a navy-blue coat and hat. Older than Paulette, better dressed, coming at a good stride, one arm holding on to a young man, taller still than his mother, the two of them composed and dignified, walking with purpose, completely in step. The woman's face is soft and calm, not so different from the first time Paulette saw her.

Paulette can't go in and she can't go forward without bumping into them. She just stands there in her big coat and hat and scarf and puts her head down. Paulette knows she is forgettable, and she hopes that after all these years the woman might not remember.

Paulette is only twenty-nine, so she doesn't need to hold on to anything to sink to her knees. She holds her bouquet in one hand, a wooden cross in the other, and just buckles down on to the grass. The grave is still raised up with dirt, no headstone, just a marker that says 'Denton Fitzpatrick' and the date he was taken. Fresh earth, fresh death, his body somewhere down there just under her feet. Paulette's whole body shakes.

She tucks the cross in the soil and lays the flowers where she can. There's not much room because there are wreaths and bouquets and 'DAD' spelled out in silk roses. Even though

Denton was only buried yesterday, everything is soaking and the petals are bruised.

Cloudy day. Not one scrap of sunshine and the day coming to an end. Paulette didn't dare come early but after six the churchyard is locked up so in the end she had to take a chance. They buried him right in the corner where the cemetery has spread out to cope with new deaths and the everlasting circle of life. Granny would say, 'Let what comes, come, and let what goes, go. No use fighting it.'

They took twenty-two days to bury Denton because there was a post-mortem and police enquiries. Garfield told her everything. As soon as they released the body she had to beg Garfield for details of the funeral, where and when, and he only told her after she promised not to turn up at the church and cause no trouble. Like it even crossed her mind, Paulette wearing the stink of disgrace. She wouldn't disrespect his family. All she wants to do now is say one last prayer for Denton before he passes from this life to the next.

Her knees are wet. She won't stay long. She tries to remember the best words for the occasion but there is nothing whatsoever in her mind. She can't remember anything to recite for sorrow, for forgiveness or for love. All she can think of, kneeling in front of Denton, next to the church of the Holy Sepulchre with rain weeping down the spire, is the Lord's Prayer.

'Our Father who art in heaven, hallowed be thy name. Thy kingdom come, thy will be done, on earth as it is in heaven. Give us this day our daily bread. And forgive us our trespasses, as we forgive them that trespass against us.'

She has a little break because she can feel her throat getting tight.

'And lead us not into temptation, but deliver us from evil. For thine is the kingdom, the power and the glory. Forever and ever. Amen.'

'Amen,' says another voice behind her. She turns round and, without nobody telling her, she knows this is Denton's wife.

Paulette scrambles up to her feet and tries to stand straight. It's not easy because the land slopes down to the path and they didn't bury Denton at the right angle.

The woman looks her up and down, sees the earth on her clothes, her tear-streaked face. 'Paulette,' says the woman. It's not a question.

'Yes.'

'I thought so. I heard about you.'

'I'm sorry. I'm really sorry. I didn't know.'

The woman takes two steps past Paulette, close enough to touch, and starts tidying the flowers and rearranging the wreaths. Paulette's feet can't move. She stands there watching for a full two minutes. Nothing hurried about Denton's widow, nothing wild or out of place in her plain black dress and black wool coat with a little fur collar. She looks controlled, like one of them people from the Royal Family that know how to behave when tragedy strikes, brought up to know how to walk and what to wear. And there's Paulette who's barely put a comb through her hair for weeks, wearing her work coat and unpolished shoes.

'You can go now,' says the woman and Paulette picks her way through the headstones and goes home.

She hasn't changed much in nearly eighteen years, but even if she had, Paulette would know her anywhere – tall and slim, a light-skinned woman with freckles and dark brown hair. Mrs Denton Fitzpatrick. Grace to her friends. And this must be one of Denton's sons, plain as day. Paulette turns her head, studies the noticeboard in the vestibule announcing Christmas sermons and choir services, she keeps her face half hidden by her scarf so the woman can walk past without seeing her.

But as she draws level with Paulette, Grace Fitzpatrick leans a little, moves in towards Paulette and catches her eye. They both stand still. It's a moment, half a moment, ten clear seconds, but Paulette is seen again, caught out again in her shabbiness with no son to guide her to worship.

Then Mrs Fitzpatrick walks on and Paulette puts her head down and scurries away.

35

January comes hard for Paulette. No tinsel, no coloured lights, no peace on earth, nothing. She posted the parcel too late for it to arrive on time but Bird said it didn't matter because they had so much to open on Christmas Day itself. He rings nearly every Sunday evening and it goes like this:

Hi, Mom, it's Curtis.

Yes, I'm fine.

Yes, I was top in math.

They don't do that here.

Yes, they're all right. Everyone's good.

No, I went out with my friends.

You don't know them, Mom, just friends.

I don't know.

I don't know.

Not really.

I don't know, I'll ask Dad.

Yes, I'm great. Really.

Dad says they send their love. He's asking what the weather's like.

Okay, then.

Yeah, I'll remember.

Love you, Mom.

Bye.

Sometimes he asks about Nellie and Paulette says she hasn't
seen him, which is true. Still, on January 10th she remembers
it's the boy's birthday. Seventeen.

She's got no plans to send him any present and she's
got no plans to send him any card either because, as God is
righteous, the boy can't be forgiven. And yet without really
thinking, she gets off the bus early and walks to the end of
Shirt & Tie's street. She stands and looks for a few moments.
Everything's the same, just like it was the first time she ever
saw it. Curtains half open, car under tarpaulin, the rest of
the street looking like the set of a documentary called *Don't
Live Here*.

She hasn't been home for two minutes when the door
knocks and she knows it's him. It knocks again and again and
Paulette stands in the kitchen in the dark and eases the bottle
of Appleton's from the cupboard. She pours a little half-inch
while, in her mind's eye, she sees the stance of the boy at the
door, head down, his ear to the glass, thinking about using
his key and having the good sense to think again.

And still she listens to the knocking. She could open the
door and tell him not to come again and tell him how good
her son is doing without his bad influence and tell him it's
Curtis now and he doesn't know Curtis and will never see him
again. And she could tell him what it's like in the evenings for

Paulette and how when she puts a cup down on the kitchen table she finds it there three days later with a bloom of white mould on the cold, cold coffee, and how her house smells of rum not chicken and she doesn't even make enough rubbish to fill the kitchen bin.

Then the knocking stops and Paulette goes up to bed.

Easter is when she plans her second trip, end of March. She's got enough money for the plane and that same hotel. She starts dropping hints in February. She tells Curtis to ask Garfield what is a good date. She tells Curtis four Sundays on the trot until Garfield himself comes to the phone.

It's tricky, as he calls it, because they're moving house Easter weekend. It's not a holiday in Dallas but that's the week they complete on the house. Yes, yes, buying not renting. Time to make the investment. Yes, yes, better area, better school for the girls, better pool, better everything except a better time for visitors.

What about the following week? Hmm, says Garfield, it will take a while to get the house straight. Or the week after that? Let me think about it, is Garfield's answer. But yes, it's better if she comes another week, comes another month, comes another time.

Paulette puts the phone down, slow, slow, slow, but stands over it and takes stock. True, she could get on the plane herself and just turn up and demand to see her son whether they're moving or not. She could postpone the trip for two weeks after they've put their American-sized sofa in the right place and hung a picture of the Lord Jesus Christ in the American-sized lounge. She could book a table at the restaurant in the same hotel as last time and tell them all to come over for dinner on her dollar since Mrs Powder-Blue Hairband Garfield might not be able to locate her powder-blue saucepan in her fucking powder-blue kitchen. All of this Paulette could do if Paulette was someone else and could bear to turn up where she's not wanted.

She picks the receiver up to ring Garfield back and give him a piece of her mind but she puts it back in its holder, harder this time, and it makes a good noise. She picks it up again and puts it down harder still but she doesn't care about it going down in the right place, she just mashes the receiver against the dial a couple of times until she hears a clink.

Clink, clink, clink. She smashes the phone against itself for a good long time and Paulette not even breaking into a sweat, just cracking the plastic and watching the circular dial fly across the room like a missile and the body of the phone splitting right down the middle and some nice colourful wires poke out of the receiver at one end. *Bam!* The phone is dead.

On her way to work through town, Paulette buys a new phone in satin white with a harp-style ring. She makes sure it's working by Sunday and waits for Bird. Soon as he comes on the phone, she asks to speak to Garfield and puts some new dates to him. Well now, he says, spring will be chaotic because the girls are taking exams and his hardworking, fertile and pale blue wife has a new job in real estate, and she needs to concentrate on making a good impression. And Curtis is coming up to an important time in his school year. Oh yes, it's all different, bigger, better and richer in America, Paulette. And then Curtis goes to camp in early June for a month and when he's back they're all going to Montserrat to visit his family. As for the summer, can't she remember the heat from last year? Well, summer is worse. Oh no, not a good idea to come in the summer, so that's out of the question. But come autumn-time, maybe when it's cooler. Yes, autumn-time.

Still, Bird rings every Sunday with his news and she makes sure she is stone-cold sober for seven whole minutes.

36

October. Paulette's birthday. Forty-eight years old and she's been dressed ready to go out since six o'clock when he said he would come. But it's ten o'clock now so even though she knows he's ringing, she cannot answer the phone.

This one is called Ray but the name doesn't matter because there has been Ken and Bubba and Emerson so far. What Paulette didn't realize is that provided you smile at a man when he looks at you and give them a little encouragement, provided you don't ask too many questions and don't push their hands away on the first date, it's not hard to get some company. It could be a man you meet at the bus stop like Bubba on his way to work at the sorting office, happy to get out of the madhouse of his wife and three children. It could be a man like Emerson, the porter from the hospital who never even told her what his home circumstances were, and Paulette didn't ask.

But this one is Ray from the kitchens at the Grand Hotel where she gets her bus to work and it's him ringing Paulette's phone with the new harp ring.

Each affair has the same life span, two months more or less. The first few weeks are full and delicious. That's when the man's hand on your back feels like electricity. You could eat each other up, gobble, gobble, until the juice runs down your neck and still you want more. Then comes the next phase where the man that took you out dancing and took you out to a nice country pub now wants to stay indoors because what if they get seen and someone tells his wife? By indoors, he means upstairs in bed. Then the man stops giving you little compliments and doesn't notice your good cooking, but still, the lovemaking is all right and at least you've got someone spending time with you.

But then, one day, the man starts moaning about the same wife, about his work or about money or his children, bringing his warm stinking shit into Paulette's house and putting it on the table like it's a bunch of roses. Oh no, no, no! That's not the deal. The deal is drinks, sex, dinner and laughs. So, Paulette has to remind the man exactly what his function is in her life, that he has a job and he must stick to his role. He must add value, not subtract it. That's when the man starts to make excuses about not turning up when he should or not turning up at all, like tonight, and ringing to say he won't be coming.

So, let him ring, yes. Let him ring the harp thirteen times. She could turn the volume down or turn it off altogether, but she needs to hear it all, every note, so she knows it's over. Then silence.

Paulette goes upstairs and gets undressed. She strips the bed of all the lingering smell of him and loads the washing machine. She finds the few things he left, deodorant, a T-shirt, socks, and puts them in the bin. She moves her bed six inches to the right, back where it should be, nearer the window. Only one person will be getting out of it, only one person needs the room. Now she can open the wardrobe door wide and find her blouse in the morning.

She goes to the front door to lock it and sees on the mat an envelope with the writing she recognizes.

To Paulette, Happy Birthday. With love, Nellie.

37

The very next week, when Sister McKenzie calls Paulette into the office at the end of her shift, Paulette knows exactly what it's about. It's not like Marcia didn't warn her about her timekeeping and Tanya didn't tell her she was losing friends on the ward because she was unreliable. It's not like some mornings Paulette can't smell her own breath with the stink of stale rum and has to suck mints all day. And her uniform doesn't fit properly any more because of the weight she's lost but it's nothing some good cooking and a solid sleep can't fix.

Okay, she missed a few days here and there and once or twice she's overslept but considering Paulette's given the best part of twenty years to the job, working weekends and bank holidays, some leeway is due, and Sister McKenzie has always been fair.

She knocks the door of the office and sits down opposite Sister McKenzie, who holds a finger up because she's counting something.

'One second, Paulette,' she says.

The room is mostly furniture, filing cabinets, chairs with posters on the wall and a standing fan and a desk lamp and a coat rack full of too many coats and a computer on the desk and a printer underneath like a footrest, two boxes of surgical gloves, a box of masks and two clipboards and above the desk on a cork noticeboard more 'Thank You' cards than the rest of the ward put together.

'Sorry,' she says again. 'I won't be a minute.'

Paulette sighs and Sister McKenzie looks up. She stops what she's doing and she sits back in her chair, knits her fingers together and raises her eyebrows.

'I'm listening,' she says.

'I didn't say anything,' Paulette answers.

Sister McKenzie points to a tin of chocolates open on her desk. 'Have one of those, can you, so there's less for me.'

Paulette shakes her head.

'As you wish,' says Sister McKenzie. 'So, I say I'm listening, and you say you're not saying anything, but you are. You're saying you don't want to work here any more and I'm saying why don't you leave and you're saying you're good at your job and I'm saying why are you pissing us all off then and you're saying I didn't realize I was and I'm saying yes you most definitely are and you're about to get fired into the bargain, my girl. Would you say that's how the conversation's going?'

Paulette stares at her.

'Or this could be the point in our conversation where you apologize for Mr Burnside this morning.'

'Mr Burnside?'

'Mr Burnside.'

Paulette closes her eyes. Mr Burnside, first bed as you walk into the ward. Private room. 'What about him?'

'What were you supposed to be doing at eight thirty this morning?'

'I was giving out breakfasts and I—'

'Did Mr Burnside get a breakfast?'

'Yes, I gave him—' She stops.

'You see,' says Sister McKenzie, 'the toast and jam and tea with sugar that was made for old Harry Grant, who actually got discharged and went home to his wife this afternoon, somehow made its way to Derek Burnside, who came in here two days ago with diabetic neuropathy and failing kidneys. And if he hadn't told us he'd been given enough sugar to kill him, but just eaten it like he wanted to, he would also be leaving us this morning but going to the morgue. What have you got to say about that?'

Paulette says nothing.

'What were you thinking? One moment's inattention, Paulette, that's all it takes. One mistake.'

Paulette draws her breath in and Sister McKenzie takes Paulette's hand.

'Or we have a different conversation. I've just totted up your holiday allowance. You have two weeks and five days left. In this conversation, you tell me you're taking nineteen days leave and in that time you'll sort your life out and the old Paulette will come back to work on the first of November and we'll pretend this never happened.'

Sister McKenzie has her head on one side.

'Hmmm?' she says. 'Because you used to be my best nurse and now you're the worst. You're drinking too much and you smell like a brewer's yard. You're slack and you're dangerous and I don't want you on my ward. Or anyone else's ward. So, since you're not speaking, I'll just tell you that from tomorrow you're off shift, you're on leave, and if you don't come in as someone I recognize on November the first then I'll sack you.'

She turns back to the papers on her desk.

'Oh, and we never had this conversation. Off you go.'

Paulette doesn't remember getting from Princess Alexandria Hospital to her house but somehow she's there in her kitchen standing by the sink. She fills the kettle for a cup of coffee and puts a mug on the sideboard. She feels the tears coming from five miles away but they're not ready yet.

She takes the coffee upstairs and puts it on her bedside table next to a dirty glass and an old magazine.

She drops her dress and gets under the blankets. She tips in a little tot of brandy because the rum has run out. She puts *Woman's Weekly* on her lap and reads the front. 'Boost your IQ' it says, '20 Steps to A Stress Free Home!'

The tears come while she's reading. She wipes them away because it's hard to read about how to decorate a yellow bedroom and get the most out of your slow cooker with salt water in your eyes.

38

Paulette wakes up to Maggie whistling in the garden. It's been a long, long time since they've said more than hello. If Paulette is at home, she's in bed. And if the door knocks, she doesn't answer, she's got nothing to say to Maggie but harshness. Kitty's left home to go and live with her ambitious boyfriend and Gemma's in Ireland. Maggie's found herself a new man now, so she's got clothes to hang out on the line and someone to make dinner for. Sometimes she sees Maggie look up at Paulette's bedroom window but Paulette steps back and pulls the curtains closed.

It's eleven o'clock in the morning so Kang's will be open. She pulls on the only pair of trousers that stay on her waist and a jumper that used to belong to Bird. She ties her hair back and picks up her purse. Takes a carrier bag out of the kitchen drawer and walks across the park.

There are still some flowers this late in the year. Dark orange and purple and some little pale green blooms nodding in the wind. Not a bad day for some fresh air and there's no rush to get anywhere. She has nineteen days to herself so she can take five minutes to sit down. Must be ten wooden benches spaced around the big square lawn in the middle of the park with little flower beds at three-foot intervals. Plenty of money has been spent on keeping it looking smart all these years and she hasn't really noticed before. Over there is a gardener and over there is a man sitting on a mower and someone else picking up litter. All them jobs just so on an autumn day a woman with nowhere else to be can sit and admire the Lord's creation.

She can just see the sign for Kang's beyond the railings. It's calling to her. She puts her face up to the sky because even though the sun is far away, it's still got a little heat left in it, winter's not here yet, Paulette. She closes her eyes and takes a deep breath and suddenly it goes dark. When she opens her eyes, he's standing there looking down at her.

'Good morning,' he says.

Shirt & Tie, freshly shaved. He's smiling but a smile is an unfamiliar thing on his face and she doesn't like it. She doesn't like that he can smile and she can't, that he can look better than the last time she saw him and she looks worse. She doesn't like his new coat and the fresh comb tracks in his silver hair. And she doesn't like him looking down at her.

'Are you all right, Paulette?' he says. 'Is there anything I can do?'

Paulette stands up. Nothing. That's what she says. Nothing. She walks away slowly so he can see she doesn't need his concern and crosses the road to Kang's. Mr Kang takes the bottle off the shelf as soon as he sees her.

'It's cold,' he says as she puts it carefully in her carrier bag. 'You need to wear a coat next time.'

Three days on the trot, she gets up late, has a little drink with her coffee in the kitchen and walks to the park. She finds her bench and sits down. Sun clinging on by its fingertips, a few rays doing their best against the fresh wind. Every day, she thinks the same thing. What's happening to her? What has happened to the building bricks of her life? When last did she open all the windows and let the breeze whip through her house and take the staleness out? When last did she clean the oven with baking soda and fresh lemon or turn the mattress? She tries to get a foothold on the precipice but slips back every time and it's two hours before she walks home, her legs stiff from sitting, chilled to the bone.

Doesn't take a fool to know she's getting sick. She can't drink anything and she can't get out of bed. She's got no fever and no aches, but she can't get up, can't get dressed and can't seem to care. She sleeps all day. She wakes in the middle of the night to the sound of distant sirens and fighting cats and knows as sure as a seven-day week that she must not give in to the claws pulling at her soul. Yet she does nothing but doze and turn like a mummy in the sheets then wakes in terror and sleeps again. It goes on until she can't tell if it's morning or evening, if she's alive or dead. She faces the wall and cries, making noise like a baby, sounds she didn't know a grown-up woman could make. But she must not give in.

Then, one day, she hears something downstairs.

Metal on metal. A frying pan on the stove or a metal lid against a pot. She throws off the blankets and tries to stand but her legs buckle. She grabs the handle of her bedroom door and creeps out on to the landing, leaning against the wall, gripping the banister. She stands still as a statue on the landing. She tiptoes to the window to see if Maggie is in the garden so she can call for help. No.

She stays there for a few more seconds. Fish is what she can smell. Robbers don't make dinner.

She creeps a little forward and peeks down the stairs. She takes each step quiet, heel to toe, and sidles into the kitchen and sees him there. Long hair now, curling behind his ears, and a back so broad she wouldn't know him from behind. He turns and sees her.

'It's late,' he says. When she looks further in, she sees the table laid for two, wine glasses, napkins, everything.

She folds her arms over her chest.

'Look there, see your cardigan, Paulette.'

She picks it up and slips her arms in as he pours orange juice into the wine glasses like it's champagne.

'Taste,' he says.

She takes a little sip and nods. He pours another two inches out and curls the carton right at the last moment so no drips spill. He's wearing a white shirt and black trousers. There's a crisp white cotton apron around his waist, tied behind with a bow. His face has no expression whatsoever, so Paulette says nothing.

On two of her good plates, he puts a golden Johnny Cake with saltfish, fried plantain chips and a salad. As a last flourish, he sprinkles her food with parsley, bright green, chopped fine. The food is set out neat, like a picture.

'Sit down,' he says, and he sits opposite, beckoning with his knife for her to start. 'While it's hot,' he says.

She puts the napkin on her lap and cuts a piece of plantain, which is fried to perfection, not greasy at all. The salad is made of pineapple, onion and mint, a combination so foreign it shouldn't work but it's sweet and fresh. And the saltfish? Lord God, if she didn't know better, she would think she cooked it herself. She says nothing.

'People are worried about you,' he says.

'Who is people?'

'Maggie. I saw her in the supermarket. And Frank said you'd lost weight. He said he sees you in the park looking rough.'

Paulette looks him full in the face. 'I should have taken my key off you when I had the chance,' she says.

'But you didn't.' He answers quick and tops up her glass.

Paulette is not really hungry but she's not so sick that she can't see the fork shaking in Nellie's hand. She can also see a frosting of sweat on his forehead and under his arms and she realizes how long he must have been in the house while she was sleeping. How quiet he must have been to not wake her until he had to, knocking the pan lid on the saucepan. She has to hold back a smile.

'Did you use fresh thyme,' she says, 'or dried?'

He puts his head one side. 'Paulette, you are talking to the new sous chef at the Paradise Grill in the Midland Hotel.'

'The Caribbean restaurant?'

'Started in June. On a trial. I had to prove I could do it.'

'What did you make?'

'Same thing you're eating right now.'

'No wonder they gave you the job.'

His voice changes then. He puts his knife and fork down and knits his long fingers together, something he got from his grandfather.

'When I went to the interview, I told them about you. I told them a black woman brought me up. She taught me everything I know. Not just about food. I told them I needed the job so I could show you that you didn't waste your time and you didn't make a mistake with me.'

Paulette purses her lips together, says nothing because she can't.

'And they told me to tell you that you did good.'

She breaks the crust on her Johnny Cake and takes a bite.

'So did you,' she says.

39

Nellie tells her everything. He says Frank is going to a new group at the community centre for some kind of talking therapy called CBT. Paulette really and truly hopes someone firm is in charge of that group because when Frank is ready to let loose no one else gets a word in edgewise. And, on top of that, he's got his own counsellor who Frank says challenges his assumptions and takes no prisoners, whatever that means. And because he's got new tablets that ease his mind, him and Nellie have found their way to peace. And now Nellie's got bona fide employment, Frank has stopped with the university business and is talking about taking some of the savings to get Nellie a car. So, it's calm as it can be with the two of them so different in every way.

After working a nine-hour shift, Nellie comes to see Paulette every day for seven days straight. He opens the front door with his key and calls out, 'It's Nellie.'

He brings her food from work, fancy versions of good old-fashioned dishes they call 'Soul Food'. He shows her a copy of the menu and describes what he can make and how much he has learned, knife skills, sauces and delicate pastry. They invent little flourishes he could add to impress his boss, things the white customers will think are tropical and exotic. Mango in the coleslaw, curls of lemon peel on steamed hake with deep-fried okra, a fresh grate of coconut on the rice and peas. Her and Nellie know different.

'You don't really need them things, Nellie, but this is high-quality cuisine we're talking about,' she says as she eats and he cleans up the kitchen, fussing around her, filling her glass and wiping down the surfaces. Nellie makes notes, puts sugar in her tea and makes the house come alive again.

On the eighth day, he sits down opposite her and asks her when she's going back to work.

'Wednesday,' she says.

'Right,' he says with his arms folded. 'You've got two days to fix up.'

She went to smile but he was serious.

'You need to do something with your hair for a start. And wash your uniform. At least now you don't look like a skeleton. You look like the Sweet Pea I always knew.'

Paulette nods, her heart blooming under her jumper. She reaches her hand across the table, palm open, and he puts his on top.

'Can you eat a banana fritter?' he says.

Paulette knocks Sister McKenzie's door and waits.

'Come in!'

She sits down and waits for Sister McKenzie to speak.

'Who am I talking to?' she says.

'Paulette Burton,' she says. 'The old one.'

Sister McKenzie nods. 'Good,' she says. 'You've been missed. And you are very much needed here, Paulette. This is where you belong. And we're chronically short-handed on Fleming Ward so you can start there. Quick! Quick!'

Paulette stands up. 'Just one thing, Sister,' she says. 'What if I wanted to become a nurse?'

'Yes.'

'I mean, what would I have to—'

'I said yes,' says Sister McKenzie. 'Yes, it's a good idea. And it's an overdue idea, I might add, one you should have had a fair few years ago. At least it's evidence that you're thinking straight again. Good. I'm pleased.'

Sister McKenzie sits back in her chair and frowns.

'And don't get thinking I want to lose a good auxiliary because I don't. It's not about having the brains to be an excellent nurse, because brains are easy to come by. You, my girl,' she says, tapping a biro against her chest, 'you've got the right stuff in here. Heart. And that's rare. Come and see me at the end of your shift. I'll tell you what you need to do.' She turns back to her desk and passes something over her shoulder. 'Oh yes, and this came for you.'

It's an envelope that says *Nurse Paulette*.

It's two hours before Paulette can open the letter. She slips back into the groove of her job like she never went a thousand miles and a broken heart away. The coming back was quick and easy and, apart from a little tiredness in her legs, she's good as new. Thank you, Nellie. Everyone says hello and asks if she's been on holiday. 'Yes,' she says. At breaktime, she stands in the staff kitchen waiting for the kettle to boil sucking a boiled sweet from one of a dozen tins all over the ward. A nurse. She can be a proper nurse. She won't tell anyone right away, not before she's spoken to Sister McKenzie again and found out all the details. It will mean studying and night school and exams but Paulette's never been afraid of hard work. And at the end of it all, Paulette will get a good pay rise and wear a proper blue nurse's uniform with a white belt and white hat. Who knows how far she can go? She places her hand on her chest. Heart.

She remembers the white envelope. It's a 'Thank You' card and inside is a photograph of two little babies. She turns the photo over and it says, *Robert and Adam.* Then she reads the card itself.

Dear Paulette,

    It took me ages to track you down because all I could remember was that you were black and that you were on duty the day I gave birth to my boys. Anyway, someone told me your name, so I just had to write to show you how they are. You probably won't remember the day they were born but I remember what you said to me when I was so worried about whether Robert would survive. You said I had to be strong for him and that he'd be fine and I don't know why but I believed you. And so did Robert and you're right, he is a fighter, he's had a few close shaves but he's still here and doing brilliantly. Thank you for your kindness, and for knowing what I needed to hear that day.

    Love Lizzie x

40

Paulette has bought a pair of black trousers with a high waist. She's bought a red silk blouse and, for the first time ever, a bright red lipstick to match. She's already got a gold chain and a pair of patent shoes so no need to go mad even if the invitation to Christmas dinner did come on a proper card with silver edging, written with an ink pen and addressed in her full name. The man likes to do things right.

The whole house reeks of winter punch, warm and strong with nutmeg, vanilla essence and allspice. She made it yesterday, but some smells bury deep into bricks and bones and Paulette knows that one day, when she is gone, someone could come into her house and say, 'A St Kitts woman lived here.'

She's decanted the punch into two screw-top bottles and put them in the fridge. She leaves the heating on because she'll only be a few hours. These days, she's got things to do when she comes in from work. Make the dinner, tidy up, clear the table and then sit down with her books and her notepad. She's doing the first part of her nursing diploma covering all the basics with assignments to hand in and little tests every couple of weeks. Nothing Paulette can't handle. And at work, Sister McKenzie's giving her different tasks and letting her swap into the other wards when they're short-staffed so she can get more experience. There's no time for Paulette to dwell on the past or what could have been because what's coming is good and that's all that matters.

After dinner, she'll pop in on Maggie for a last drink. It was Paulette that made the first move after she went back to work. She knocked Maggie's door and, before she could open her mouth, Maggie was grabbing her up and sitting her down and saying sorry and telling Paulette how worried she had been about her and how much she was missed and how good neighbours are better than gold and like gold sometimes they need polish or some kind of Irish saying that Paulette didn't quite catch but she meant she was in the wrong and Paulette could see how she was hurting. They drank coffee and Maggie had five cigarettes because some things don't change even when the rest of the world tilts on a different axis.

She won't stay long at Maggie's because she'll have a house full of visitors, and anyway, this is her one single day off from studying and she wants to stretch out on her own sofa and watch a good film. At least on Christmas Day the telly is reliable.

And then, later on, Bird will ring to say 'Merry Christmas', which will be the best part of the day. He will tell her all his news and there'll be noise in the background and he'll be eager to be off doing young man things but his voice will be a tonic if only for fifteen minutes. She's not saying nothing about becoming a nurse. No, no. Wait until she gets the full certificate, until she's passed every single exam and got her uniform, and then she'll take a photo of herself in her blue dress and send it off. Curtis will tell Garfield and his wife and they'll all know that Paulette is a somebody and she's made herself a future.

She punches the cushions on the settee until they look full and then reads the cards on the mantelpiece because she's a bit too early, and anyway, she likes to read them through now and again.

Curtis, Garfield and Angela and the girls, Maggie and Kitty and Gemma, Marcia and family, Jennifer and Tanya, everyone at work, Rev. Harris, Jane and Peter from number 32, Paul in Manchester and his new wife whose name Paulette can't read. And Nellie and Frank.

The afternoon air is tight with frost and Paulette's breath swirls white in the streetlight as she turns into the grove. She stamps on the front doorstep, knocks the door and waits. She can smell food. Now, Nellie cooking is one thing. Shirt & Tie is a whole other circumstance. Paulette has to hope that Nellie is in charge of keeping the turkey moist so she can eat the overboiled vegetables with a gravy disguise. To be on the safe side, Paulette has brought extras – a rich fruit cake without burnt cherries, the chilled punch, a bag of nuts, her good appetite, two Christmas presents and a large bottle of brandy.

When Shirt & Tie opens up, he offers his hand as if to say this is a formal occasion, and it is, because the last time Paulette saw him she ignored him and the time before that she ran him from her front door with hard words and anger.

But today, all their trespasses have been forgiven and cancelled one another out.

She shakes his hand. 'Merry Christmas, Frank,' she says and he nods. Shirt & Tie has a brand-new shirt and tie for the occasion, a crisp white shirt, still with folds from the packet, and a green tie with flecks of gold in a Windsor knot. He's nervous, anyone can see that, so she passes him the carrier bag with all the things she's made and closes the door behind her.

'Put that in the kitchen, Frank,' she says to give him something to do. 'And the punch goes in the fridge.'

He walks away and Paulette goes into the front room. Hardly looks like the same place with a decorated Christmas tree and spray-on angels at the window. Gas fire on full and the telly showing little choir boys in red and white, side-partings and scrubbed faces. You can just about hear them praising the little town of Bethlehem in five-part harmony.

The kitchen table has been brought into the middle of the front room with a tablecloth and three crackers, and Paulette places the gifts she's brought under the tree. A book about railways for Frank and a voucher for Nellie so he can buy what he wants from the new fashion shop in town.

Shirt & Tie comes back and asks her to follow him into the kitchen. He hands her a small box tied with a ribbon and clears his throat. He stands under the harsh bright light in front of her and blinks like he's trying to remember what to say. Nellie is nowhere to be seen. Frank must have told him to stay out of the way.

After a little cough into his fist, he starts.

'I'm afraid it's not much but I'd like you to accept this gift with my thanks and my appreciation for what you have done for us, for Cornelius and me, over the years.'

Paulette holds the box tight but she can see that the man's not finished. He coughs again.

'And also I would like to acknowledge your forgiveness which I know has been difficult and which I also know is undeserved. And furthermore,' he says, slower still with a little break in his voice from the effort and the meaning he's putting in it, 'I would like to tender my apology for the future that I took from you and for anything beyond that which I have done to contribute to your pain.'

The man steadies himself against the cooker. Paulette can tell he rehearsed it for a long time, probably with his counsellor. Make it short and sweet, the man must have said. And speak clearly. Well done, Frank. Paulette swallows and takes a deep breath.

'Thank you,' she says. She opens the black velvet box and inside is a gold St Christopher.

'It's from both of us,' he says. He picks up two small glasses of sherry and passes one to her.

'Merry Christmas, Paulette.'

'Merry Christmas, Frank.'

Immediately, she hears Nellie thundering down the stairs two at a time. He smiles as he moves aside so Paulette can get to the mirror in the hallway. She takes out the necklace. Shirt & Tie probably doesn't realize St Kitts is really called

St Christopher so the necklace has a special meaning, but there again, Frank is a one-off and knowing him, he went to the library and did a full week of research before he decided what to buy.

She fastens it around her neck and lays it on her chest, smiling at her reflection and the full circle of life. There she was, little Sweet Pea, sitting in the sun on her grandmother's lap, the sea shushing in the distance, and here she is now, wearing St Kitts around her neck, a gift from a strange man in a strange land but with the same sense of peace, the same sense of completeness. Near enough. And when the time is right, she'll speak to Bird again about coming back home with her, to show him where his people came from, where his mother grew up, the little house, the old church, the little river. All right, he says he's busy now but people change and one day he'll be curious so Paulette will just water the seed every so often and wait for it to grow.

She sees Nellie watching her in the mirror, watching like he can read her mind. He kisses her on the cheek.

'Suits you, Pea,' he says.

In the end, it's all right. Better than all right. Paulette and Nellie make enough conversation so Shirt & Tie doesn't have to say too much. His new medication has slowed him down but still he eats his food with perfect manners, resting his cutlery between each mouthful, drinking his wine white-man style, using the green paper napkin like it was made of silk. Nellie is full of stories about the customers in the restaurant and how much he makes in tips. He's caught a bit of confidence and patois and a way of speaking that makes Paulette laugh. He's running jokes and styling stories about his day so that he's pure entertainment, just like the little boy he used to be.

And sometimes, when people see a white boy in a Caribbean kitchen, frying and seasoning, Nellie says he stands up extra tall and tells them everything he's learned and who from and how he's going to be a great chef one day, have his own restaurant and decide on the decor and the menu. Frank nods along, tells him to walk before he can run, but there's pride in there too and an easiness with the boy that's new and not before time.

The punch comes out at the end of the afternoon, slips down nice and easy, sweet and creamy, and while they're watching an action film about escaping from a prison camp, Paulette tells Nellie how to make it.

'And use the rind of the lime – some people use lemon, but I prefer lime. And buy a good vanilla essence, none of that watery stuff you get in the little bottle. You know the one I mean.'

He nods.

'Get a pen and write it down, Nellie,' she says when the credits roll.

'No need,' he says. 'Did I tell you I've got my driving test in February? And when I pass, Frank says he'll get me a car.'

'Since when did you call your grandfather "Frank"? You're not too big to forget your manners, you know, Nellie.'

They both turn and look at Shirt & Tie asleep in his chair, a newspaper on his chest and his feet stretched out, crossed at the ankle, his long white fingers curled around the punch glass, drained to the bottom. Nellie gets up, slips the glass from his hand and covers him over with a blanket.

'He would never let me,' he says.

Paulette starts clearing the dishes, silently scraping all the food from one plate to the next so she doesn't wake the old man. There'll be saucepans and roasting dishes in the kitchen and some things that will need to soak. Better to start early before they get too dry. And the extra food will need putting in the fridge. She wonders if Frank even has Tupperware. She should have brought some from home.

Nellie stands up and takes the plates from her hand. 'I'll do that,' he says. 'You take it easy, Paulette. It's my turn now.'

Paulette looks at him, his eyes sharp, his hands strong from work, his hair long and curling behind his ears, right at the hinge of boy to man.

'Nellie, you'd better start saving,' she says as he gathers up the dishes. 'You and me are going to the West Indies next year. If you're serious about being a chef, you need to know the taste of good herbs and spices. Fresh things, straight from the earth. We'll go to the best restaurants on the island, even the tourist ones, and you can come back with some ideas to take to work. It's not a holiday, you know. You'll be learning all the time. But it's up to you.'

The plates clatter to the table and he flings his arms round her neck and doesn't speak for a whole minute.

'Thank you,' he whispers. Ten clear seconds of love and the best of everything between them.

'Come, Cornelius,' she says, tapping his arm. 'We've got work to do.'

Acknowledgements

From minor characters in another work, Paulette and Cornelius grew and grew until this story became theirs and I had to give them centre stage. It took some time to see them clearly and I want to acknowledge the help I had from the wonderful Mary-Ann Harrington, whose ability to excavate the unwritten and the unsaid is a true and rare gift. This book wouldn't be possible without her.

To Karen Whitlock and everyone at Tinder Press and Hachette who have worked so hard to bring this book into the world.

For expert advice on the viability of pregnancy in women with severe brain injury, my thanks to the brilliant Professor Susan Bewley, Professor Mary Munro, Brian Cleary, Professor Gerry Lee and Professor Maeve Eogan. Your help and generosity are very much appreciated. Similarly, I would like to thank everyone who so kindly gave of their time, personal stories and expertise on epilepsy, neurosurgery and care homes, particularly George Malcolm, Saskia Baron, Carol Palmer, Gillian, Louise Fein, Annie Goodyear, Stephen Unwin, Jan Burns, Sue Reed, Joely Dutton, Anna Korving, Emma Norris, Chris Hutchinson and the many other people who wrote to me out of interest and kindness which is what this book is all about. If I have forgotten anyone's name, please forgive the oversight.

Acknowledgements

For input on sentencing and the law, the ever-wonderful HHJ Rhona Campbell came to the rescue: thanks, Rhona.

I did a lot of research which does not appear in the book and my thanks go to Michael O'Reilly and to his late wife Noreen for taking the time to help me understand forest management.

Other people that I pestered for help are Miles Hunter, Josh Davis, Paul McVeigh, Andrew Wille and Adam Sharp aka Mr Structure.

To Catherine Morley and everyone at the University of Leicester where I am Jean Humphreys Writer in Residence, my gratitude for being given space, time and support to write this book, thank you so much.

Heather Belmonte, constant, reliable, efficient and caring. The best personal assistant and friend I could have had over this last year. Long may we continue.

To Peter Straus, my agent, my sincere gratitude for being there and for your help and advice throughout and to everyone at Rogers, Coleridge & White, my thanks. Thank you also to everyone at JULA.

My friends, all of you who listen to me moan and rant, laugh and cry, worry and celebrate, you are so very much appreciated and never taken for granted. I am so very lucky to have you in my life – Cat, Lezanne, Beth, Steph, Sylvia, Sue, Adam, Nina, Helen.

To 'right-handed' Steve Evans, cheers. Everything is very al dente – the laughs, the hugs, the sunshine and the tennis. T&Cs apply.

Acknowledgements

My sister Tracey O'Loughlin has been the source of culinary expertise from day one and any recipes in this book that have made your mouth water come from her kitchen. Dean O'Loughlin, Kim Squirrell and Karen Wrai Karn, my first and best readers, thank you for your time and counsel, true and straight as an arrow. Love to Conrad O'Loughlin, our big brother.

Bethany and Luke, my wonderful children, this is for you – as always – with my everlasting love. The Circle of Ng is strong.